THE DOOR
IN THE WALL

BOOKS BY OLIVER LA FARGE

THE DOOR
IN THE WALL

Stories by

OLIVER LA FARGE

With a Foreword by William Maxwell

HOUGHTON MIFFLIN COMPANY BOSTON

The Riverside Press Cambridge

Fourth Printing   W

FOREWORD

Y ou can behave very much as you would anywhere else — with certain limitations. It goes without saying that you don't ask questions about tribal customs and ceremonies. And since they don't know you, I think it is probably a good idea not to ask questions at all. Keep your eyes open, and see what there is to see. And don't try to charm them. It throws them off balance if you rush in and try to make friends with them immediately. In this respect they are like children. So you wait. You don't do anything until they have had a chance to sense who you are, the aura around you . . ."

I can hear his voice telling me this. We are in a small open car driving through the heat and the glare of the desert country, between Otawi, New Mexico, and Santa Clara. And I have asked a favor of him: I want to spend a night in an Indian reservation. I have known him for years, but not well. And the favor is not a light one.

Like everything else in that landscape, the Santa Clara pueblo was visible from a distance. The green was cottonwood trees, and cottonwood trees meant water. We arrived in the late afternoon, drove up a narrow washboard road, turned a corner and then another corner, stopped to speak to a young Indian who was leading a white horse, and stopped

again in front of an adobe house. Oliver turned the motor off,
I picked up the sleeping bag he had loaned me, and we went
inside. In the sudden and very welcome coolness and darkness
I was introduced to his adoptive uncle, Vidal Gutierrez, and
his wife. They were middle-aged, and, as people go, they were
not intimidating. Oliver stayed for perhaps half an hour, talking with them, and then said goodbye and that he would pick
me up the next day around noon. Thinking I ought not to
waste my opportunities for observation, I went for a walk
down by the river and got eaten alive by mosquitoes, to the
considerable merriment of some men who were cutting hay.
Supper was as elaborate as a meal in a Wisconsin farmhouse,
with lots of little dishes, and as far as I could make out, everything was made of cornmeal cooked in different ways —
twenty-seven kinds of hot and cold, wet and dry cornmeal
mush. At dark the family went to bed in another room, and I
brushed my teeth and got into a sleeping bag on the living
room floor, and, since sleep refused to have anything to do
with me, listened. Voices. Encounters. Laughter. A barking
dog, or was it a coyote? Night sounds. The last human
sound — and it went on for a long time — was of some adoles-
cents sitting in a row on a wooden bench in front of the
Gutierrez' house. I have the impression they were talking
about life. Then there was a night bird, and after that total
silence. At four o'clock in the morning, an old woman came
out into the plaza and began chopping firewood. Then voices.
Encounters. Laughter. Day sounds. This was twenty-three
years ago, but I doubt if last night and the night before and the
night before that at Santa Clara were any different. After
breakfast we sat and talked until Oliver came to get me. Mr.
and Mrs. Gutierrez were the most intelligently inquisitive

people I have ever met. They left no stone unturned, and when I was thanking them for their hospitality, I thought I detected in their eyes a forgivable complacency; about one white man, at least, they had found out everything there was to know. I knew no more about them than I did when I arrived.

Because I had spent the night in a place where Oliver's heart was, driving back across the desert was not the same. We talked out of the whole of our experience instead of the customary thin slice. From that day on, this happened invariably, every time we met. He became, without any formal swearing in, my adoptive older brother. At intervals a long envelope with a Santa Fe postmark would arrive on my desk at *The New Yorker*, and in it there would be a manuscript, and when I had finished reading it I would know somewhat more about Indians, and about anthropology, and about human beings in general, than I knew before. In time I came to believe completely in Talvert University. As for Wally Caswell and Dr. Lancaster and Elvira Stafford, and poor old and forgetful Dr. Sibley, I would know them anywhere. At the same time I know that there is no such place and no such people, that it was all created out of Oliver's mind. Autobiography was a form he could manage brilliantly, but he had a reason for avoiding it when he wrote about Indians. What he wrote about them must be true and accurate, but there must never be an identifiable Indian or a recognizable Indian village. Something vitally important was at stake — his other, active relationship to them, as their defender against the usually lethargic and sometimes monstrous behavior of the United States Government. The cause was always forlorn and frequently hopeless, but that didn't prevent him from taking it on. And in the time that was left to him, he wrote.

The sound of his voice, the aura around him, is in these twelve stories.

WILLIAM MAXWELL

CONTENTS

THE DOOR
IN THE WALL

THE CREATION
OF JOHN MANDERVILLE

I<small>T WAS</small> a real irony, Applegate thought, that the ultimate returns from his whimsey should have been brought to him by the butler, all unknowing, on a silver salver. The whimsey was his creation of a new John Manderville, and Applegate had had no conception, at the start, of where it would lead. He had lent himself to it, he supposed, simply because he was rather out of a job.

Turning fifty, John Applegate did not have to work at anything. He had plenty of money, his scholarly reading had become desultory for lack of a goal, and he was tired of leisure. He lived in South Marnick, which was too far out of New York, and too rural, the houses standing in too wide grounds, to be called a suburb. His neighbors considered themselves cosmopolitan, and they were in fact on the bright side. They had money, and ability, and not a few of them had traceable ancestries. Among them, Applegate was accepted, and respected for his scholarship and his travels. Because he was known to be a scholar, people made allowances for his tendency to sit silent when conversation was liveliest and for the rarity of his clever remarks. His acceptance was further insured by the fact that after he married and gave up the professional practice of anthropology, he had shown a streak of business ability. He had not merely lived gracefully on his wife's money; he had increased it, and ended by sitting on the boards of several companies.

His wife, Priscilla, was handsome, and young for her age, and she spared no pains to stay so. She was intelligent and an excellent hostess. She was pleased with her husband, and glad that his interests differed from those of the businessmen who surrounded them. They had a son, who had recently married, and an attractive daughter.

Applegate had become accustomed to the way his life had changed since the days when he was a young instructor on his way toward a Ph.D., yet he could still marvel at it. In his youth, as Priscilla sometimes said, when he wasn't helping moldy professors teach grubby students, he was squatting in some septic Indian village talking to unwashed old men, and eating the most appalling food — stew, mostly, made of old mutton or goat — in order to save money. Her description was somewhat exaggerated, but no more than that. Applegate *had* worked among the Hopi Indians of Arizona, who are not famous for their cleanliness. He did eat the native foods, supplemented with only minor items bought at trading posts, and, furthermore, he had lived in native houses and slept on the floors. That was all good research technique, of course, but it also helped him to save something out of his meager stipend, and when he returned to civilization, he needed it. He rarely spoke of the Hopis — the South Marnick people did not find them interesting, and, after all, since that period of his life he had visited the Ubangis and the Jíbaro head-shrinkers — but once when Priscilla was teasing him about them he did remark that if you have barely enough water for drinking purposes you don't waste much of it on washing, and that a goat that has been eating juniper has a fine flavor. Then, seeing a look of disgust on someone's face, he stopped talking.

Not long after Manderville entered his life — or, more exactly, reentered it — Applegate had a conversation with Bill Whittaker, who was his and Priscilla's most intimate friend. Whittaker recalled it later and told people about it. He and Applegate both had to spend the night in town, and they had dinner together at one of their clubs. The South Marnick crowd went pretty heavy on the cocktails anyway. The two men did the same that night, and perhaps a little extra, for being stag together. And after dinner they had a few highballs. As Bill said later, *In vino veritas*. Applegate praised his wife almost to the point of being boring about her. "Pris opened up my imagination," he said. "When we were married, all I could think of was living a little more comfortably and going on with the same routine — Ph.D., getting to be a professor or a curator someday, all that, and the slow, grimy field work you've heard Pris kid about. My whole career, at that point, depended on sitting on the ground cultivating an old gink who didn't speak English, through his nephew."

Applegate stopped to relight his cigar; then he laughed. "The old boy's name was Youkehumai, and the nephew's, God help me, was — still is — Wallace Kinanumptiwa." In telling about this conversation afterward, Bill did not remember the names; he simply said they were ludicrous. "Then I married," Applegate went on, "and shortly after that I gave up being a practicing anthropologist, and saw something of the world instead. I've had some really swell

expeditions — safaris and things. I've brought home all sorts
of stuff. I'm a benefactor. And I'm on the boards of institutions I'd hoped might hire me someday. I owe it all to
Pris."

A bit after that, Bill said, the conversation became vague.
Applegate got to rambling on about the Hopis, and said something about how their spirit was life, and about their concept
of time, until Bill said, "Let up. I can't follow you, and I bet
you can't follow yourself."

"I'm sorry," Applegate said. His next words Bill remembered exactly. "I was getting around to a point, old man,
which is that Pris kept me from sort of turning into a Hopi.
Those people are sitting on hundreds of millions of dollars'
worth of oil, and they won't sell it because they're afraid
that would change their way of life, which is the only way
they know. Me, I would have failed to take advantage of
Pris's money, and probably lost Pris in the end, because I felt
that I was committed to the kind of life an anthropologist has
to lead, and couldn't imagine any other. Only, Pris had good
sense. And patience, of course. You've no idea how patient
she was with me. She convinced me that it is shortsighted to
spend your life digging around in the ruins of the past, without even knowing the present. And, of course, someone had
to take over the management of all that money, which turned
out to be fully as absorbing as the rituals of the Hopis. I don't
know how Pris knew I had a knack for that kind of thing, but
she did. A wonderful woman, my boy."

Bill asked why the Indians wouldn't sell their oil, and Applegate said it was partly that they knew what oil had done to
some of the Oklahoma Indians and were afraid of what would
happen to their young people, and partly a religious matter,

having to do with the integrity of their land, that was too involved to explain. Then he changed the subject.

That evening, John Applegate was stimulated not only by the drinks but by the developments then occurring in the Manderville affair. That had started when Talvert, his old university, to which in recent years he and Priscilla had made some handsome gifts, forwarded him a letter from a priest in a place called Ocotán, in southern Mexico. The priest wrote to say that a North American named John Manderville, who had for many years lived in that population in a state of disgrace from a vice of alcohol, had ultimately passed on, having repented and been received into the Christian Church. In his dying hours, he had spoken many times of his antique teacher at the University Talvert, John Applegate, and had asked that his scientific works be sent to him. The priest would forward the same, the value of which he could not judge, as they were all in English, if Señor Applegate would accept the charge.

After a moment's thought, John remembered Manderville — a tall, skinny youth, a junior, he believed, at the time that he, Applegate, left the university. Manderville had been an intense student, a solitary, friendless. The department had been small in those days, before the social sciences became popular, and the anthropology majors and graduate students had been like members of a club, but when they were out on the portico of the museum having a smoke (the building was a strictly "No Smoking" fire trap inside), Manderville didn't know how to join the others. Applegate had thought him something of a screwball, and judged that he would do well in anthropology, a science in which odd numbers have always flourished.

But why the deathbed remembrance of him? Routinely, as part of his duties, he had had the young man to his quarters a few times to discuss his studies, and they had had some rather good talks. That year, Applegate recalled with some amusement, he had acquired a dozen bottles of inferior Burgundy, of which he had been immensely proud because it was imported — a rare thing for a man of his means to have during prohibition. Feeling sorry for Manderville, he had offered him some. The man must indeed have been badly off if this mild friendliness could leave so deep an impression on him. As Applegate thought about it, it came back to him that the poor fellow had accepted the wine eagerly, and drunk it too fast, and that he had been slightly put out because he felt obliged to pour him a second and a third glass. Also, it was after a glass or two that Manderville had opened up and become interesting. So the seeds of his vice were in him then. He had shown signs of brilliance, too; there might be something of value in the work he had left behind. Applegate wrote to the priest, telling him to send on the papers.

They came. There were several pages of notes on the natives of the region in which Manderville had lived, more than half of it illegible or incoherent, and most of what could be made out covering matters that others had already reported. Then, there was a draft of a paper on the influence of spontaneous groups within a formal organization, which was brilliant. It was not publishable as it stood, however; the presentation was erratic, the author knew far too little of the relevant literature, and the theoretical side of the paper, which was what made it important, needed to be supported by more observed data, preferably from a people more tightly organized than the Tzeltals of the Ocotán region were. In short,

Applegate thought, it needed data from a tribe such as the Hopis.

That thought caused him to get up and take from the drawer where they had lain untouched for so long the field notes of his early years — the fruit of three seasons of ever closer friendship with old Youkehumai and Wallace Kinanumptiwa. Applegate was seized by a most diverting idea. He would complete Manderville's thesis; he would crown the unfortunate man's career.

It was easy enough to find out that Manderville had graduated *magna cum laude*, had earned no higher degree, and was listed in the alumni directory as "lost." He had published three short articles in minor periodicals, all descriptive ethnography and none more recent than ten years ago. The man must have just sloped off to Mexico after he graduated, with some idea of doing research on his own, and slowly deteriorated.

Applegate himself had published hardly half a dozen papers. His anthropological reading had become sporadic. On the expeditions that Priscilla's money had financed, he had left the heavy research and, afterward, the long, dull grind of major publication to the earnest young men he took with him. Now he was in for some real work. As he considered it, his plan grew more elaborate. He would re-create John Manderville — an interesting coincidence that they had the same first name. He would give him some more publications, leading up to the big one. There had been, he decided, two John Mandervilles. There had been the peculiar character who reached too eagerly for a drink and who finally went to pieces, and there had been the gifted scholar who, put at ease by a little wine, talked very well indeed and showed great promise. The latter he would restore, or, in no small measure, create.

Applegate was a member of the Players Club, and frequently stopped in there when he was in town. It was an easy matter to step around the corner to the post office on Twenty-third Street, where he rented a box in Manderville's name.

He began working as he had not done in years, and was annoyed when a directors' meeting or other business interrupted him. As Applegate went along, the new John Manderville became more and more real. As he approached middle age, he had filled out, becoming fairly solid, like Applegate himself, but sparse living and constant field work had kept him from developing a pot. He was a rather shy man, ill at ease in smart society, happier in the company of other scholars, and, as is so often the case, entirely sure of himself and relaxed in the unaggressive company of Indians. Since he had no advanced degrees, he could have but little academic rank. Anyway, he was more a research man than a teacher. He probably had a position, part curatorship of a small museum or academy of sciences or philosophical society — perhaps a state historical society — and his salary was just about enough to live on. Applegate became fond of the man, and half envied his quiet, studious career. Manderville did not have to brace himself with cocktails evening after evening in order to deal with the bright company of South Marnick. Applegate dismissed the thought that the real Manderville might have become a drunkard under any circumstances.

In Manderville's name he wrote and placed three articles based on his Hopi notes, two in the *Southwestern Anthropologist* and one in the *American Anthropological Review,* which was nice going. The articles resulted in five letters of

inquiry from fellow-scientists, one of whom claimed to remember meeting him at the last Powamu ceremony at
Mishongnovi. Then Applegate sent the article on spontaneous groups, now highly polished and backed with ample observations, to the *Review*, confident that it would be taken as
the lead paper, which it was. It occurred to him that, whatever the original Manderville's unrealized potential might
have been, he, Applegate, would have been a pretty good scientist had he continued on his original course.

It was then time for the letter he wrote every year to Wallace Kinanumptiwa — a brief line of greeting, a gesture of
sentiment toward a lost friendship. Stimulated by his other
activities, he did something he had been putting off year after
year — he used various connections to obtain from the Bronx
Zoo a quantity of feathers of parrots and other tropical
birds. Such feathers are more precious to the Hopis than
jewels, since some of their rituals cannot be performed without them. Also, since the importation of feathers of tropical
birds into the United States is forbidden, the tribe suffers from
a chronic, critical shortage of them. He mailed the feathers to
Wallace, along with his letter. It did not surprise him that the
Hopi was slow in thanking him. The Hopis live not in our
continuously elapsing time but in an element within which
they seem to move about and, as Whorf has shown, which
can also be accumulated. They have less cause to hurry, their
time does not get lost so easily, and they can more fully savor
a pleasant occurrence. The feathers were a gift of importance,
they had undoubtedly caused great pleasure, and it would be
natural for Wallace to wait, to mature and complete his appreciation, before he expressed himself.

Applegate found himself at loose ends. He could not do much more with his field notes unless he rounded them out with more data. Manderville, he feared, had had his fling, and Applegate, too. Being now well up on all recent Hopi material, he did turn out a minor paper called "Neglected Leads in Hopi Ethnography." He did not think any of the big periodicals would take it, so, at random, he sent it to the *Margass Review*, published by the Margass Institute of Man, a small endowed museum and research institution situated in the southwestern part of the Middle West. He was not surprised that the paper was accepted, but he was both startled and amused when the director of the Institute wrote to say that it had been given funds for field work in the Southwest proper, and to offer Manderville a position. The director addressed him as "Dr. Manderville." His creation, Applegate thought, was assuming remarkable life just when it could no longer continue. First a scientist claimed to have met him shortly after the real Manderville had drunk himself to death in the Mexican jungle; now he could have a job. The job was an assistant curatorship, involving some museum work in addition to his field and desk research. It was also hoped that he would teach a seminar or two at the neighboring state college, for which he would receive an additional honorarium. Applegate decided against getting out of it by pretending that Manderville was already employed; that web could become tangled. Instead, he had Manderville take refuge behind his ignorance of museum techniques and his lack of degrees, pointing out that the latter not only disqualified him for a curatorship but would also make him unacceptable to the college.

For the next three weeks, Applegate would be confined to

South Marnick by a variety of social and business matters. He considered terminating his creation by simply giving up the post-office box and leaving no further address, but the few letters that had come there were the only ones he had opened eagerly in years. He postponed, and took the risk of turning in a temporary-change-of-address order in care of himself.

About a fortnight after that, the butler brought him, upon a silver salver, what struck him as the ultimate returns from his whimsey. The mail reached his house in the afternoon, and he had given orders that when he was working in his study, he should not be interrupted by it but should have it at five, to scan before the cocktail hour. That day the butler brought him the usual assortment—nothing urgent, nothing interesting, except for two that could be called "Manderville items," although one was addressed to him under his own name. That one was postmarked "Second Mesa" and addressed in pencil, and contained Wallace's annual reply. The other was from the Margass Institute, for Manderville.

They were having people in. He heard guests arriving, so he stacked the letters on his desk and went out to play host. If three martinis did not make him feel gay, they made him bolder. He slipped out of the living room for a hasty first reading of the two letters. He took up the Margass one first. The director of the Institute wrote that he had never held too much with the requirement of degrees, that the stipend offered was, after all, only thirty-six hundred dollars a year, and that the author of "Interaction of Spontaneous Groups with the Formal Organizations of a Structured Society" *and* of "Neglected Leads" was perfectly qualified for the position.

The college would be glad to have him, and museum techniques can be acquired.

Wallace thanked him for the feathers and mentioned some ceremonies in which they had already been used. He said he had another grandchild, a girl. Then he wrote, "It been too long since we see you. I am sponsoring Niman this year. You always like to come to that. You better come out for it if you can't come sooner." Applegate stood for a moment, holding the letter, thinking of the Niman, which was to him the most beautiful and the strongest of the Hopi ceremonies. Then he shook his head and dropped the letter on his desk.

Applegate returned to the living room. The talk sounded loud and jumbled. His wife's voice — bell-like, well modulated, but carrying — was clearly distinguishable. Everyone said that she had a beautiful voice. The only titles worth considering any more, she was saying, were the British. Applegate poured himself another martini. He could not remember when he had not been high about this hour. What would he do if he were suddenly transposed to the Hopi villages with a ceremony going on? Dramatically, but with conviction, he told himself that he was forever cut off from that primitive world. His daughter sat between two young men, both of whom were strutting for her. His daughter, he was quite sure, was unchaste. He made an ugly comparison concerning her relationship to the two. His eye lit on his son's wife. He did not like her. She pretended to be an intellectual, but in fact she was a bore. It would be a long time before she produced a child. By moving about, glass in hand, standing near but not joining this group or that, Applegate could appear sociable yet keep out of the talk for fair periods of time. He followed this procedure now. Vaguely he thought about how to answer the Margass letter. He considered killing Manderville off and doing an obituary for the *Review*, relished the thought briefly, and then discarded it. Manderville was too much fun to kill quite yet.

Three days later, Applegate had a luncheon at the Waldorf with the trustees of a civic organization to which he and Priscilla had decided to make a gift. The chauffeur drove him to New York and deposited him at the hotel. He checked his hat and coat. (It was a warm day and he had taken the coat only in case of rain.) Then he disappeared.

The police searched diligently, and Priscilla put the best private-detective agency there was on the job, but no trace of John Applegate was ever found. He had simply disappeared, and no disappearance this side of the crew of the *Mary Celeste* could have been more unreasonable. Gossip to the effect that there had been some failure in his marriage was spiked by Bill Whittaker's tale of Applegate's admiration of Priscilla and his gratitude to her, which left the mystery deeper than ever. The newspapers made a thing of it, and since new false leads kept turning up, there were brief stories about it from time to time for months, and writeups with references to Judge Crater.

Wallace Kinanumptiwa had been a bright but rather solemn young man. In the agelessness of his early fifties — which for a Hopi is just about full maturity — he also had the humor and the sensitive, penetrating understanding of people, of which humor is an essential, that had characterized his uncle, to whose priestly position he had acceded. He and John Manderville, of the Margass Institute, sat together on sheepskins on the floor of the room in Wallace Kinanumptiwa's house that Manderville had rented. They were tired and at ease. The Niman ceremony had been beautiful. In it had been clearly apparent what it is the Hopis hold to be of more worth than a fortune in oil. Now the sacred period was over, and the two friends could be at ease together.

Before them on the floor were cups, a pot of weak coffee, a native basket holding fragments of the blue corn bread called piki, and a bowl of stew made with goat meat. As the goat's diet had included juniper and sage, its meat was as savory as it was tough. The onions and the canned green chili in the stew had been bought by the scientist. Neither he nor Wallace had washed his hands before eating, but since they dipped the stew up with spoons, they did not think that important. It was a dry time of year and water was scarce.

John wore a small beard and mustache, both grizzled, which gave him distinction of an academic sort. Sparse living and two months in the field accounted for his flat stomach; he was not as spare and hard as his friend, but he was in good shape for a white man of his age. The room in which they were eating was the one he had rented as a young man. It was well-kept and austerely bare. The floor was of hard-dried mud, on which the evening sun made a red-gold flood inside the doorway. The walls had been plastered with the same mud, and whitewashed, not very recently. From the ceiling, which was made of small sticks resting on round beams, several prayer feathers hung. There was a fireplace in one corner, near which Applegate's bedding was neatly folded and piled. A few garments hung on one wall; a box and a duffelbag suggested other possessions. Against another wall were one chair and a table; on the table half a dozen reference books, writing equipment, and notebooks.

They finished eating, belched comfortably, and lit cigarettes from John's pack. Wallace's wife came in to collect the dishes. She had once been slim, quite lovely, and shy; now she was broad, motherly, and self-assured. She did not regret the changes time had brought. She was next in line to be clan mother of an important clan. She had four daughters, all of whom had children, she had several good sons, her brothers occupied the positions for which their lineage made them eligible, and she was genuinely fond of her husband. She and Wallace were people to whom one could entrust with entire safety the secret that until recently one had been someone else.

The two men thanked her for the meal. She responded, and then she said, "I got to put my old man to work for a while," and spoke to Wallace in Hopi.

He stood up. "I got to go haul wood or I'll be in trouble."

Alone, John tried to concentrate on a thought that had come to him while watching the katcinas during the ceremony — why it was that masks that made no attempt to look like faces suggested the divine better than the finest portraiture — but he could not. His mind wandered. He should have been utterly happy, he thought, and until recently he had been, but now he was not. For several weeks, his happiness, his peace, had been leaking away; at times he had felt he did not know himself. His unease was becoming acute. What should have been an absorbing line of thought only led him back to what had come over him in the middle of the Niman, with the lines of singing katchinas splendid in the plaza. He had been suddenly attacked by one of those fears that, psychology says, arise merely from one's opposition to the thing feared, like the feeling that one might jump from a height. He imagined himself — or, rather, Applegate of South Marnick — unable longer to forgo his martinis, and the ruin that his drinking, or even a smell on his breath, would cause to his relations with the Hopis, who despise drinking in any case, and during a time of ritual and holy thinking consider it plain blasphemy. Shaking himself out of that, he had thought that, as Manderville, he had been in a bad situation among the Tzeltals, since the natives of southern Mexico drink, and frequently get good and drunk, during their religious observances. He had had a sudden recollection of the sweetish fire of *aguardiente* and its strength in the stomach, and he had somehow conjured up a vision of a drunken ceremony here in the Hopi plaza until he saw, with a sense of fright, that there was a thin, dark curtain between him and the katcinas, and he was seized by the idea that the powers present in those masks knew what was in his mind. In his room, after he got away from those phantasms, he was obsessed by the simple thought of a drink.

The subject had come back more and more frequently — at first, as now, at the cocktail hour, then at almost any time, including on waking. It was only fifty miles of decent road to Winslow, and at a bar there, the evening before he drove onto the reservation, having received a distressing martini, he had switched and enjoyed a couple of excellent whiskey sours. He did not desire whiskey sours now; he imagined the good bite and taste of a neat whiskey after so long a drought. He thought of having one, and knew perfectly well that it would not be just one. Neither his funds nor his work would permit his remaining any length of time in town. Vodka makes but little smell on the breath, and with chlorophyll tablets . . .

His mind ran like a mouse about the bare room, cunningly selecting hiding places.

With eagerness and distress he knew he was about to tell Wallace's wife a story and drive to Winslow. It was inevitable; it was his pattern. There had been at least a partial preparation for it in more than twenty years of Applegate's pattern. He had a sudden, vivid image, part visual, part emotional, of his study, the adjacent plenitude of cocktails, the life without demands or dangers, and the butler bringing the letters on a salver. He could never return to that; it was done. His commitment was inexorable. The thought of irreversible fate filled him with cold fear; then he embraced it, seeming at that moment to slip from one aspect of himself, one personality, into another, and as he did so he relaxed and his expression changed. In the end, if need be, he could go to Mexico; in fact, Mexico and much less constraining conditions of life might be preferable. Given the reputation he now had, which this season's work would increase, he could create a decent enough situation for himself down there, his wants being so simple — one might almost say single. He rose slowly to his feet. With the mixture of amusement and appreciation a man of brilliance feels toward a good but lesser man who has built not only better than he knew but far better than he intended, he thought what an amazing job Applegate had done of re-creating him.

INDEPENDENT RESEARCH

H E WOKE in the full heat, feeling *Oh Lord!* as he stared up into the shadows of the high-pitched roof. Then he remembered, today the mail comes. A pulse of excitement rose, calming his jangled interior, and he swung from hammock to earth in one motion. The too sudden change of position sent pain shooting through his head. Drunk last night. Ugh. He poured cool water from the earthenware jug into the basin, dowsed his head, drank from the jug.

He brushed his teeth, thinking that he'd have to send out for a new supply of brushes and paste soon, then remembering, if the letter comes, if Sheffield . . . Hope and excitement stirred in him. He stripped off his pyjamas, washed himself with a free sloshing of water, and dressed in white shirt, khaki trousers and sandals.

Hearing him, Paquita came in from the other room. She wore nothing above the waist. Her figure was still good, but maternity had spoiled her breasts.

"Art thou ready to breakfast?" she asked.

"Yes. Coffee and oranges, no more."

He considered shaving, but his hand was too unsteady. The coffee and fresh fruit helped him. He stared across the room at his desk, where a bottle and glass stood by the lamp. That wouldn't do. It was the way the fever weakened one, partly, this business of feeling poorly a lot of the time, and bored. But it would not do. By God, I've got to clear out of here, he thought.

In his lowered physical condition, self-confidence took flight. He saw himself stuck forever in Chancuén, bound forever to Paquita, to poverty, heat, malaria, taking more and more to drink. A kind of inland beachcomber. One knew the sort of thing — old Stornheim . . . Hell! He finished his second bowl of coffee, lit a cigarette and rose. Not me. I have work to do, that keeps one sane. He put on his hat and went out.

The straggling village was shady with trees, save for the little plaza which civic pride kept bare and glaring. He followed a habitual path, under mangoes, banana and coffee groves, down to the river. Standing on the bank, he stared at the clear water, the tangled jungle wall opposite. Out of the green mass a pair of brilliant parrots darted, crossing diagonally towards him. There was peace here, the illusory best of the tropics. He turned back. The few Indians he passed spoke to him respectfully, and he answered them in their native tongue. It looked bad, not having shaved.

Six weeks; yes, the letter should come today. Two weeks to get to Talvert, a week for Sheffield to talk it over with his committee, two weeks for the answer to get here, a week for accidents and delays. Right.

In front of his own house he stopped and looked about him. He felt a sense of possession towards this village, the palm-thatched houses, the people, the fields and jungle around it and the blue line of the mountains to southward. He'd been up there. He'd encompassed all this, the job was all but done. Folk-lore, religion, daily life, language, crops . . . "Comparative Ethnology of the Highland and Lowland Rashti," a monumental work. All this country he held within his head and his writings. Wait till Sheffield sees it.

He turned and looked at his own house, thinking that he'd be sorry to say goodbye to it, and delighted to leave it. Palm-thatched, it was a sizable building of wide, upright boards, whitewashed. The south side, facing the street at the corner of the plaza, had two doors, leading to his room and the kitchen. At the corner a wide opening with a counter, and shelves behind it, was the store. When he bought the place from old Stornheim, he'd intended to let the store go, but he saw the job would last longer than he thought, and Paquita wanted to run it, so he'd invested all of thirty dollars capital . . . He looked at the stock with some amusement; candles, two bolts of bright cloth, a couple of machetes, some needles, nails, vermouth, malaga, kerosene, native salt, tobacco, thread, onions, perhaps two dozen kinds of goods. If he left her the store and house, and twenty-five dollars cash, she'd feel herself well treated.

He wondered what had come of Stornheim. The German had had the wholesale agency for Benedetti when the chicle-gatherers were working out from here. When their camps left this section, he was ready to sell out, knowing that without that little extra balance of money, the power to employ, to be generous, a white man's position here was intolerable. With it, he was a sort of king. The scientist strolled back into the house, thinking of his predecessor, a hardheaded man, elderly, completely disillusioned, completely sunk in the tropics. Tipsy every afternoon, drunk every night, and each six months or so another girl from the village employed to —

as he said — help in the kitchen. The young, golden-skinned girls with yellow flowers in their hair, part of nature's system to ruin a northern man.

In the north wall of his room was a big window, closed by two shutters with small, diamond-shaped panes in them. The diamonds annoyed him — Teutonic taste. He had thought of replacing them, but about the only way to get new glass up from Puerto León unbroken, would be to go there himself. Looking on this as a merely temporary home, he'd given up the idea.

He settled at his desk. The layout was interesting. Everything was in the most meticulous order. On the wall just within reach of his arm was a sheet headed "unfinished business," carrying a list of passages to be completed or corrected, data still unsecured. A few items had been checked off. In front of him stood a dozen scientific books, mainly on Mayan ethnology — Sapper's *Nördliche Mittel-Amerika,* Seler, Brinton, Landa's *Relación,* Starr, Vernier and MacDougal's *Highland Survey* and so forth. Slips of paper, numbered, marked passages which would be needed. His field notebooks were handy on a shelf, the one now in use lay at his left hand, also marked for reference. Two boxes held his manuscript, *The Highland and Lowland Rashti* by Thomas Cowning, the magnum opus. There was a box labeled "Miscellaneous," and another labeled "Correspondence." Writing and drawing materials were in order; the whole layout called to work. He took out, as he had often recently, the copy of his letter to Sheffield.

It was a good letter, it restored confidence. At the end he had remarked that the fever was getting him down, and he had had a bout or two with dysentery, but saying so did no harm. The rest was what mattered — that having lost his position at Talvert in so inauspicious a manner, he had found it hard to get another. So he had taken his savings and settled at Chancuén; operating from there as a base he had, he believed, made and written the definitive study of the Rashti tribes. The work was ready for the printer save for a few details, and he had run out of funds. He asked for five hundred dollars to enable him to clear up some small matters for which travel was needed, and return to the States, where he would hand over the finished report to the Talvert Department of Anthropology. If the work satisfied them — and he was sure it would — he asked for a research fellowship, which would enable him to continue on the same lines. He suggested a program of investigation of the neighboring Chacol tribes, which ought to prove interesting.

He nodded and sighed as he set down the letter. Sheffield was kind — that wasn't the point. The Director cared deeply for science. He had done a unique job, he would stand on that. It would cost them five thousand to duplicate it.

He glanced at his list of unfinished business, then rose and pushed the shutters open. By the shadows, it must be about eleven o'clock. He opened Field Notebook V, and reached for the manuscript. When he picked up the pencil, he found his hand shaky. He shook his head. That had been bad last night. Such a performance frightened him. He looked up, to the left, at the shelf of bottles of *aguardiente* in which had been steeped orange peel and a little honey, "Curaçao of Chancuén." If he didn't take a little, he'd lose a day. He poured a jigger of the strong stuff and drank it down with a slight effort. *Ha-agh.*

Today the mail comes. Six weeks. He shook his shoulders

and went at the work. His pencil moved slowly, elaborately neat. He took infinite pains over a paragraph, selecting each word, then stopped for a cigarette.

He needed a cross-reference to his section on the Blood Sacrifice, and turned to it, then fell to reading the pages, feeling his skill and mastery as he did so. This had been a job! It ought to stand as a classic. And until he went up into the mountains, five years ago, no one even dreamed that such a ceremony existed. Reaching the desired reference, he noted it and let the pages drop. Slowly the sheet before him was filled. He sat back, staring out the window. Nearly noon. The mail was due now. He'd like to cross off another item on the list, but he felt too disturbed to keep plugging. He put each thing away in order, ready for continuation, fussed a little with the layout of his writing materials, then rose and paced the room.

The hurried explosions of an exhaust bounded and echoed from the forest on either side of the river, and tore through the quiet of Chancuén. He started, stiffened, wheeled and watched from his window. Through the trees he caught a glimpse of the launch and its green and white government flag. With uproar the great world touched this isolation. He heard the motor stop, and a voice hailing. The launch was coming up to the landing. While he took a drink, lit a cigarette, and picked up his hat, there was quiet. Then the motor started again, a splutter, hesitation, the steady roar. What little the world had for Chancuén had been tossed ashore, the launch headed hastily downstream to tie up for lunch and siesta at Malec, where there was a cantina.

He walked slowly across the plaza, feeling almost numb. The pain of hope, fear of rejection, the worse fear that there would be nothing. José, trotting past under a bundle of goods from the store, greeted him cheerfully. Half a dozen natives lounged by the post-office door, at one end of the white, solid *cabildo*.

Don Jorge, the mestizo post-master, said, "*¿Qué tal, don Tomás?*"

"*Pues bien. ¿Y usted?*"

"*Bien, gracias.*"

"Any mail for me?"

"A package, that your man took."

"But — letters?"

Don Jorge pointed to the four on his table. "Only these. None for you, unhappily. You expected —?"

"I thought possible —"

"Next week, perhaps."

"Probably. It doesn't matter."

He kept a calm front and light tone of voice. One must. He strolled back. Alone, in front of his door, he paused a moment, stared at the ground, and cursed swiftly.

Paquita was setting the table. "The goods came," she said.

"All correct?"

"Yes."

He gave himself a drink, and having downed it, stood looking blankly at his desk. Suspense. Another week. Well, he could use it crossing off more of those unfinished items. I've been dilatory. O.K. He took his place at the table.

His first-born toddled in. As he sometimes did, he observed the brown child from the point of view of home. A sleeveless shirt, not reaching to the navel, was its only garment. Hands, feet, knees and backside were heavily dusty. He'd fathered this, it would be known always as Tomás Caunín, and the village and the child itself would perpetuate through all its life the tale of its origin. The thought of girls at home, the university town . . .

Paquita talked of small things as she served him. He ate, looking at her from time to time, half listening. Just before the rains break the scientists pull out. From Veracruz to Venezuela, on foot, horseback, in canoes and boats, by narrow-gauge and by most amazing motor roads they converge on the ports and the steamers. In good health, or with remarkable diseases and remarkable sores, with little bottles containing the insects that caused them, with notebooks and specimen cases, with hard-won success and assurance of returning at the head of a better equipped expedition, or conscious of failure, or knowing that the appropriation has run out and good work must be left agonizingly unfinished, they head back for home. Then the rains come down, and a place like Chancuén is a morass, the river perilous, the jungle impossible. Mule-trains for the chicle camp at Cerro Redondo regularly bog down in the plaza.

A man financing himself can't afford to go home. The rainy months are allotted to intensive work in the home village, collation of data, the beginning of the great book. Paper is damp and tears easily, the lines of ink drawings blur, progress is hampered by infuriating, irrelevant delays. For six months the constant activity, travel, and normal fatigue have kept life swiftly moving, but now monotony, standstill sets in. Juan Tzac made the proposal himself, and his daughter, a divinely pretty little savage, was willing. Why not?

Her world was here. She had no understanding of why or at what he worked, save that from the mestizos she knew that there was distinction in being a *científico*. She had no curiosity about it, no imagination or thought of his outside, vast world. Only once, when shy strangeness had first been replaced by intimacy, she asked him about the blonde women of the North. She was unchanged, an illiterate Indian, but she had become used to him. She knew and encompassed him. There was an alarming essential wifeliness, and a vague superiority of entire understanding. She bored him, she was more than useful, he was fond of her. Sometimes he wished he were in a position to take for a while another little newblown golden figure — Antonio Cum's girl — and drove out the thought, shocked at its implication of weakening fiber.

Above all, I've got to get out of here, he thought.

Today he trebly needed his siesta. He allowed himself another drink, to insure sleep. He woke late, feeling much better, able to shave. There was work to do. He had meant to ride over to Esteban Culal, the medicine man, and spend the evening filling in some gaps in his data, but he decided on deskwork instead. He put in a piddling and unproductive afternoon, yet supper took him by surprise. He believed that a man should change into a linen suit every night, an essential discipline and matter of self-respect, but this night he forewent it. He felt too tired and dull.

Three afternoons later he was surprised at his desk by the sound of another machine on the river, a higher, shriller crepitation. Watching, he saw a catamaran pass, made of two dug-out canoes lashed together, driven by an outboard motor. Its master was hidden under a palm-leaf shelter. This type of outfit was favored by oil geologists, undoubtedly it carried a compatriot, or an Englishman or German. As he listened, the motor stopped. The man was landing here. He finished hastily the sentence he was writing, straightened his desk, rose, picked up his hat, then turned back to look at himself in the mirror. The room was in order, save that the blanket had fallen out of the hammock. He refolded it and put it back.

As he stepped out, he saw the man coming across the plaza with the Secretario Municipal. The Secretario pointed and turned back. He's looking for me, he thought. Is he from Talvert? His heart pounded.

The visitor was about twenty-six, of good height and strong, brown-haired and blue-eyed, with a two-days' stubble of gold on his chin. He wore a pith helmet, white shirt, khaki breeches and engineering boots. A jaguar-skin pouch surely was for his notebook. He had a camera slung from his shoulder, on his belt an automatic pistol. The whole type woke in the observer a wistful longing, the sense of his own fraternity, the wish to prove that he still belonged.

Pausing at the door, the stranger asked, "Dr. Cowning?"

"At your service." The sound of English, the sound of one's own name correctly pronounced!

"I'm Edgar Hutton, of Talvert University."

They shook hands. Hutton saw a tall, skinny man with a slight paunch. The brown hair, receding slightly, emphasized a high, full forehead. There was an effect of the upper part of the head being too much for the chin. Cowning wore a white shirt of native make, slacks once khaki, washed to a cream color, and native sandals. His blue eyes were bloodshot, his hand slightly shaky, he showed the effects of malaria. Clothes and man were scrupulously clean, and he was fresh-shaven. Hutton noted that gladly; his mission could be an awkward one, he was eager for good signs.

"I'm delighted to meet you, Dr. Hutton. It's lucky you

came today, I just happened to put off till tomorrow a visit to a local medicine man called Culal. Won't you come in?"

Inside, Hutton said, "Dr. Sheffield wrote me, about your letter, you know, and I came up. I'm running a dig at Chactún."

Cowning nodded. He felt excited. "Fine. I have some legends about Chactún, by the way, which might interest you. Have you a hammock with you? I'll send down to the landing for your things."

"If it's not too much trouble."

"None at all. Have a chair."

He went into the other room. Hutton heard the man's voice, speaking what sounded like fluent Rashti. A woman answered, and then spoke to someone else. He had caught a glimpse of a child about a year old. Well, that was Cowning's business. If a man lived in a place like this for five years, any man — Question was, had he any stuff on the ball? Which of Sheffield's alternatives would fit? He examined the desk. Neat, ready for action, work in process. It was almost a stage set; this man must be passionately methodical.

Cowning returned. "Your duffle will be right up. It's about supper time. Have a drink?"

"Thanks, yes."

Cowning took down a bottle and two jiggers. "Curaçao of Chancuén," he said. "Here you are. Here's how."

"How. Could be worse."

"Yes. So Sheffield sent you? How are things at Talvert?"

He asked about this man and that, then lost interest. The thought of Talvert was tied in with too much unpleasantness, the awareness of his failure in many minds. He glanced out the window.

"Supper'll be ready in a minute. Help yourself to the wash-stand. You don't mind if I change? It's all right slopping around like this during the day, but I make it a rule to put on a suit for dinner."

Hutton looked at him with approval and some surprise. "Not a bit. Fly to it. I'm traveling sort of light —"

"Naturally. That would be asking too much."

Cowning pulled aside the matting which hung over a tier of corner shelves. His hand hesitated over the pile of suits, his heart sank. The top suit was little more than lace, the next more than half eaten, another hopelessly mildewed, a greenish growth . . . He realized Hutton was watching him. Surely it hadn't been so long — a little slack recently — I always —

"Seems as if everything wearable was in the wash. The laundry service is a little irregular here." He tried to sound amused.

Hutton nodded. "Things turn out like that in the tropics."

"They do that. Another drop before dinner?"

"No, thanks."

"I shall if you don't mind."

"Sure."

He was upset. Not only the impression that had been made on Hutton, but what it revealed of how time slipped by. I've got to get out of here. The drink and a wash refreshed him.

Paquita brought in supper. Hutton hardly glanced at her, beyond answering her "*buenas tardes*," taking in quickly the elements of a typical situation.

"The idea is," he explained, "Sheffield wants me to look over your report."

"Of course. Quite right."

"Then I think I'll be able to make you an offer for the Division."

"Fine. We'll tackle it after supper. Do you eat chile?"

"Sure thing."

"Help yourself. As I wrote Sheffield, there are a few items that need checking, a few gaps. Most of it's ready for the printer."

When they were fed, Cowning asked, "A drop of liquor while you read?"

"I've got some brandy; would you care for that?"

"Brandy!" Cowning lingered on the word. "I've had no such luxury for a year or more. Fine. I'll get tumblers."

Hutton sat at the desk, Cowning to one side. He was nervous, did not wish to seem over-eager, puffed at his cigarette and drank his brandy and water in big gulps.

"I'll leaf through, first," the younger man said, "get an idea of your headings and contents."

"Right."

He read the whole of the Introduction, an exposition of method and a really brilliant, compact thesis on the application of functionalism. This man had a mind.

"You ought to run that as a separate article, doctor."

"Think so?" Cowning glowed.

"I do."

The headings were interesting, their order logical, but even more interesting was the physical appearance of the manuscript. At the beginning, the writing was neat, clear, cursive and simple, titles and subtitles in plain block letters. In the latter half, the script became more and more elaborately perfect, the headings keeping pace, until the writer seemed to have hung and dallied over every letter, capitals were laborious, the product giving an effect, not merely of neatness, but of a method of procrastination. The early drawings were well done, the later ones, again, overworked, with a good many erasures and a rather unsteady line.

"Looks interesting," he said. "Mind if I glance at your field notes?"

"Not at all. They're the key, of course."

He took the books numbered I and VII. The writing in I was about the same as that of the beginning of the report, the drawings, in pencil, were adequate. The notes seemed well made, complete. In VII the writing was alternately clear and sprawling, almost illegible, the sketches crude and hasty, the notes incomplete, trusting altogether too much to memory. The two contradictory phenomena complemented each other. Knowing the difficulties of desk work under field conditions, he still felt that the whole thing, notes and report, hardly covered five years' time.

"It's all interesting, doctor," he said.

"I think so." Cowning hesitated. "Do you mind if I sponge a spot more of your brandy? It's such a rarity."

"Fly to it."

"Have some yourself."

Hutton's glass was still half full. "No thanks. *Todavía*."

Cowning poured himself a liberal measure. The other glanced at his wrist-watch — 7:15. They'd dined early. He reached for the report again.

"I wish you'd look over Section IV," Cowning said. "You can hardly read it all tonight. I'd like your opinion on that."

"Certainly." He ruffled sheets, found the section. "The Blood Sacrifice, eh?"

"Yes. It's quite a remarkable ceremony, confined to the Highlands. I was lucky."

"Have you seen MacDougal's report on it?"

"MacDougal?"

"Yes. I suppose you haven't. It came out only this year, in the Institute Memoirs."

"No." Cowning felt lost. This couldn't be. It was his. "He didn't mention it in the *Survey*."

"He didn't know about it then." Hutton glanced briefly at his host. "What village did you work in, mainly, up above?"

"Yibán. But I sampled most of the others."

"MacDougal was at San José the last two seasons. I guess you missed each other."

"Recently, what with the fever, you know, and being short of cash, I've been up there relatively little."

Hutton looked at him again. The uncertainty which began over that business of the clothes, had grown markedly. There was almost a frightened look. This Sacrifice business meant a lot to him. He began to feel sorry for the man.

"Have some more brandy," he said. "Help yourself. I get it right along. Go ahead."

"Thanks, I will." Cowning poured. "There are some details missing there. My plan is to go out through the Highlands, spend a couple of weeks there with my informants, cleaning up."

He knew MacDougal, a thorough man, rather dull, and impatient of human frailties. How had he got back up there?

Hutton found the account interesting in many ways. All through it was a failure, an effect of incompleteness and glossing over gaps in material and treatment. It wouldn't stand with MacDougal's job, yet there were points of importance that the other scientist had missed, an astonishing understanding of the native temperament, individual and in the mass, and again and again flashes of the same brilliance of reasoning he had seen in the Introduction. That about a possible Nahua derivation of ceremonial words, tying with Toltec archaeology, was a lulu.

It was after half-past nine when he laid the papers down. Cowning had refilled his glass a couple of times. What a capacity — a daily routine, most likely.

"May I see your field notes on this?"

"Of course. This one."

"Thanks."

He glanced through it, thinking. From various remarks, from the implied and explicit evidence of the documents, you could reconstruct — The first dry season here, he went to the mountains, did some good work, discovered this. The next season he went back, enriched from what he'd learned down here, and put in a couple more good months. He came down knowing he hadn't finished, but he didn't go back, he persuaded himself there were only details lacking, and wrote this account. Hutton suppressed a sigh and helped himself to a weak brandy-and-water.

"What about it?" Cowning forced a light tone. "Did Bill scoop me?"

"I'm afraid he did, but you've got a lot he missed. Mind if I look at some of the rest?"

"Go ahead."

Hutton read over the list of unfinished business. It had been on the wall for some time. There were twenty-two items, of which five had been checked off. Some of the others were grotesquely important.

Cowning reached for the brandy, saw how low the bottle was, and poured himself a dose of aguardiente instead. Over a new cigarette he studied his guest. Humiliating to be investigated by a man who might have been one of his students. An intelligent young man who knew how to punch the clock and keep his job. Competent, and a decent fellow. Neither he nor any of the smug, endowed bastards could realize what he'd been through, the difficulties overcome. How could he live with them again at Talvert? Better here, if they'd let him have the publications, to keep abreast of the work and not be scooped by men like Bill MacDougal.

By the stars it was close on eleven. Hutton laid the papers down.

"In my letter, I spoke of a research fellowship," Cowning said. "I want to go on with my work, keeping this headquarters. I don't particularly want to take residence at Talvert, though I plan to visit the States." It sounded all right, yet he felt a wavering sense of shame at his own words.

Hutton nodded. "I'm quite sure that something satisfactory can be arranged." He yawned. "It's after eleven, and I've had a long day. Will you excuse me if I turn in, doctor?"

To himself he thought, it's alternative C, then. He has a contribution to make, of sorts. He had always known Sheffield was kind and wise, but this was almost clairvoyant. It was good to work under such a man.

Cowning's heart picked up at "something satisfactory." It had been a shock to know that the Sacrifice was already reported. Like the rotted clothes, his ignorance of Bill MacDougal's presence up there pushed him towards realizations

about the passage of waste, cumulative days, a picture of himself that he did not desire. But of course the work was good.
He became brightly talkative, caught himself slurring a word,
and checked, ashamed. Hutton turned in. He blew out the
light, took a nightcap silently, and relaxed in his hammock.

He was awakened at an ungodly hour by the sound of
splashing water and whistling. Blinking, shaking his head, he
saw his visitor at the washstand. I must correct my hours, he
thought, and got slowly from the hammock. He felt dizzy,
almost sick, and still rather tight. The water and toothbrush
helped. He wasn't sorry Hutton was going, he wanted to be
alone.

Paquita was up, and showed no surprise at the early rising.
Hutton ate two eggs and some fried bananas; Cowning stuck
to coffee and fruit.

The younger man looked him over, feeling pity and some
contempt, and thinking how sad it was that the forehead and
the fine brain behind it dwindled to so inadequate a chin.

"Here's the situation, Dr. Cowning. The research fellow-
ships are filled. You know University procedure. Perhaps
later . . ."

Cowning nodded.

"Sheffield authorized me to take up your offer on the report if I thought it justifiable, and I do. Regardless of Mac-
Dougal and some other publications, you've got some swell
stuff. Of course, it isn't quite finished. We've got a new per-
iodical, with good backing, *Talvert Contributions to Anthropology*, a quarterly. If you don't mind being edited, we'll run
selections from your material in that."

"Certainly."

"We'll give you an appointment as Correspondent. As you

send in further material, amplifying the report or entirely
new, we'll pay you about two dollars per page printed. It's
not much, I know. This will give you some capital in hand,
leave you free to work as you please, and later, on the
strength of your showing, we can reopen the question of a
research fellowship."

"I prefer that," Cowning said. "I want the independence,
and to continue this intensive method."

Hutton nodded. "About the manuscript, I want you to let
me take it. I'm heading for Puerto León now. My instructions
are to wire Sheffield from there, and he'll send the money and
appointment direct to you, without delay. Of course if you're
strapped —"

"No, no. I can hold out."

"All right. We'll have it typed and send you back a working copy."

While Cowning listened, he thought what the money and
freedom meant to him — research, security. With twenty-
five a month — A quick thought of Antonio Cum's daughter,
something the Indian had hinted, was pushed back out of his
mind hastily. There was no point in returning to Talvert, to
the cold, and the smug, rigid people.

"I need to receive publications," he said.

"We'll put you on our list, and you can order through us."

"I really need the *American Anthropologist*, and I'd like
some kind of current events magazine."

"Fine. We'll have them sent. Is it a go?"

"It is."

They shook hands. Not a bad bargain either way, Hutton
thought. How the man seized on an arrangement which
pledged him to nothing.

"I'll pack up, if you don't mind."

Cowning's heart was torn as the manuscript was wrapped in waterproof cloth and packed. Some parts of it would appear in print, his name in a scientific paper again. Their remaining talk was jerky and awkward. When the catamaran turned and raced downstream, he waved and hastened back to his house.

It was barely seven o'clock. He felt terrible, but knew he couldn't get back to sleep. Oh well, today's special; he took two drinks in succession. Tomorrow he'd go see Culal, and cross off that item. Throwing himself back in his hammock, he lit a cigarette, thinking. His position shaped itself, he fitted the pattern together.

Publications arriving, the *Anthropologist* and this new Talvert quarterly, a magazine, various books. A formal position, his own stuff in print. These were the materials of respect and self-respect. He would be up with the times. When white men came through now, there would be the solid evidence . . .

Five hundred was a lot of money here, and beyond that one could live indefinitely on sending in folk tales alone. He'd bet Paquita knew dozens. Then in time, by force of publication, he'd be reestablished, and get a regular position, a salary. This was a temporary stage. He had a goal to work for.

He rose and stared at the mountains, recapturing the feeling of four years ago, of preceding seasons, the long rides, the coolness, the sense of capacity and effort. He'd head up there pretty soon. After the money came. Meantime, clean up small stuff here. Today's a private Fourth of July. He took another drink and went into the kitchen.

He stared at Paquita. There was a balance to be reestablished, an attitude to be corrected. That man was sent by the big University in the North, he told her, because of the importance of his work. In a fortnight he would touch five hundred dollars — fifteen hundred *estrellas*. She was impressed, crying *"¡Ay, Dios!"* He told her that he was officially named *Corresponsal de la Universidad Talvert*. They were anxious to buy more of his work. Looking at her, the thought of Cum's daughter passed through his mind again. He pressed home the importance of his news, triumphant. Today, he said, he would celebrate.

With another drink in him, he sat down to rearrange his desk. The missing boxes had made a gap. He stopped in midcourse, thinking, feeling upset in the stomach, feeling distrustful of himself, futile. In the back of his mind he knew that the term "Correspondent" was so all-inclusive as to be meaningless. He knew that the arrangement completely protected Talvert. So many institutions maintain local correspondents who send in small, local stuff, folklore and so on, the total mass of which is eventually useful to some scientist, and which in itself is utterly petty. He saw himself in a hard light, moving through all his lifetime in Chancuén.

"Hell," he said. "Nuts."

He swung in his chair, facing the mountains again through the open doorway. Three years of idle intentions, days slipping by, while an accredited scientist came and went up there, thorough, dry, industrious. Postponements . . . His interior felt weighted down, his breath caught. The man's homely face with the big-lensed glasses seemed to look at him from behind the blue ridges, pointing out — pointing out — facts.

Raising his fists, he cried, "God damn you, Bill MacDougal!" In a voice which rose high and cracked.

THE SENIOR ASSISTANT

O<small>N WEDNESDAY MORNING</small> of the third week at Popil, in the Petén country of Guatemala, Dr. Lancaster, director of the expedition and chairman of the Division of American Archeology at Talvert University, asked his senior assistant, Wallace Caswell, to run a line due east from the middle of the east edge of Mound D-II and see what he found. They had then been at work on the ruin only ten days, the preceding time having gone to building a camp with such amenities as guest quarters and a refrigerator that ran on kerosene. The instructions to start working eastward meant a sharp departure from the plan up to that point, which had been based upon what little the director and Wally had seen of the ruin's layout when they scouted it the year before, but then one of the charms of archeology in the great rain forest that overlays most of the Maya Old Empire in Middle America is the expectability of the unexpected. Poking about with the tip of his machete in that deceptively aimless-seeming way he had, Dr. Lancaster had determined that in addition to the wide flight of steps that led from Plaza II up the west side of Mound D-II, there was another on the east. The mound, a long terrace four meters high, faced both ways, and since an east-west arrangement of various structures bisected Plaza

II, beginning with the high mound A-II, on which stood the remains of an imposing temple, he thought it likely that something worth special attention lay to the east. The Mayas were given to laying out their great centers so as to create lines of sight and axes tied either to the cardinal directions or to such points as the ascensions of Venus or the sunrise at the equinoxes.

Wally Caswell was a tall, bony, blond young man who lacked only completion and defense of his dissertation to receive his Ph.D. This was his third field season. He called Joe Landon, a younger graduate student, to come up and help him with his tape, and proceeded to locate the center of the terrace's east edge with an exactitude that Joe considered incongruous for the start of a pace-and-compass survey. Joe was a greenhorn; he found Wally a trifle above himself, inclined to be bossy and overserious. Wally was irritated, without good reason, by the number of junior graduates they had with them this year. He marked his point of departure by piling up four stones, which, he noticed, were fragments of nicely cut blocks.

With his machete, Wally verified the existence of the second flight of steps — typical Maya construction, with high risers and narrow treads. It occurred to him suddenly that as it was generally agreed that the ancient Mayas practiced ceremonial drunkenness, these stairways must have caused some terrific falls. He climbed down the slope. His expression had been solemn, rather discontented; now it was brightened with humor.

He carried a number of items in an *ixtle*-fiber pouch, including a small drawing board on which he had stretched a piece of metric graph paper. When he had reached the ground below the terrace, he took this out and wrote on the edge of the paper, "W-E Center Section of Pl. IV." Thus he assigned the number IV to the presumptive plaza on which he stood, writing it with a touch of defiance, since the director might have other ideas about the proper sequence. He added, "Scale: 2 mm.=1 pace," and "Pace approx. 84 cm." He marked "W" on the left-hand margin, "E" on the right. From somewhat below the middle of the left edge, he drew a slanting line, dropping through eight of the graph lines and coming forward three, to show his estimate of the mound's slope. With his Brunton compass he sighted on the first tree that stood due east of him; then he headed toward it. As he went, he cut the brush that was directly in his way; when he reached the tree, he blazed it. Then he turned back and counted paces from the tree to the foot of the terrace. He drew a corresponding line on the paper, marked the tree by a circle three millimeters in diameter, stepped around it, sighted on the next tree in line, and went forward.

He felt, and looked, happier than he had been in days. He was conscious of the quiet of the bush, which at night became so loud with insects. The sound of chopping and of voices from where the crews were at work was already faint, muffled by the vegetation. He enjoyed the soft, green light — rather like the light inside an aquarium — in this forest, which seldom allowed a glimpse of the sky or the penetration of a shaft of sunlight. Being alone like this, cutting his way, was *right*. He expected to find nothing that was not entirely ordinary, but he would find it by himself, and that pleased him more than he would have admitted. It fitted the picture — the picture that you made in your mind from listening to the Maya men talk when you were still an undergraduate and what field work you did was in your back yard or in the safe and sanitary Southwest, and that proved true when you, too, rode into the high bush. He knew perfectly well that the conjunction at Popil of a sizable unworked ruin, an exceptional supply of clean water, and, only a few miles away, an airfield on the Guatemala-Flores route, reachable by jeep track, made possible not only the present deluxe camp but also the important project of complete, long-term excavation for which it was set up. His own position in that project could favorably shape his career. Still, irrationally, romantically, he resented the comfort, the size of the staff, the presence in camp of a woman — the director's wife — and the arrangements for receiving visitors. The Maya field, to his mind, was an exclusive, he-men's club for a select group who could fight their way through tangled forests and bottomless mud, live on inadequate supplies of foul water, and, in the teeth of the most rugged conditions, carry out work that combined fine technical skill and deep scholarship. On expeditions alone with Dr. Lancaster, as he saw how precisely the older man fitted these requirements, his admiration for him had been elevated to an excessively high point. For some months past he had been experiencing disillusionment and reaction. He had thought the man was, one might say, the high priest of the goddess he himself served as acolyte, but that pure shrine could not be entered by anybody who indulged in ambitious toadying. This disillusionment and the disagreeable emotions it gave rise to underlay and largely caused all his other gripes and resentments. Now, as he worked alone, he forgot his irritations, relaxing into the simple, mechanical demands of what he was doing and into the peace of the forest.

At thirty-seven paces plus four trees he came to a rise. He uncovered steps again. This mound was a little higher than D-II — about six meters. Probably it was another of the terrace type, although its length could not be determined until someone cut a trail north and south along it. Wally could not see more than a few paces to either hand. He marked it on his section and labelled it A-IV. He was somewhat disappointed. It had been reasonable enough to expect that, on the line he was following, he might come upon an altar or a stela, carved and inscribed, as he crossed Plaza IV, or that here A-II would be balanced by a similar high mound and major temple, in which one might hope to find inscriptions. Of course, anything at all might be a few steps ahead.

At the top of the mound, he blazed a tree widely and took another bearing. Six paces — his left foot found no bottom. He half fell, his left shin hitting against something that hurt even through the leather of his boot, caught his balance, and yanked his foot out. That bang on his shin was peculiar. The hole was large (he was not small-footed); if it was a lair, it would be of a large animal, but there was no pile of thrown-out dirt, no wear of frequent passage at the lip. He poked with his machete. It sounded against stone. He squatted and dug. Under a few inches of humus, he partly uncovered a cut slab. He started to enlarge the hole. Dirt fell in, sounding against the bottom not far below. He stayed his hand, alarmed. That had been bad technique; he would hate to have Dr. Lancaster know of that. He marked the hole on his profile, then cleared brush around it. Three meters farther east there was an irregular depression. Things were getting complicated. He turned back and headed for Plaza II, knowing happily that he had a likely find. As he walked, he used his machete to open up the trail a little more.

Lancaster was pleased. "A chamber? Any size, do you think?"

"I don't know, sir. I dropped a little dirt in, and it sounded as if it fell — oh — a couple of meters." Wally was not guileful, and this curious, truthful lie surprised and delighted him. "Then, three meters due east, there is a depression, an irregular dip."

"Probably a cave-in. There may have been an entrance from that end — we'll see. You go get what we'll need to start with — don't forget candles and a lamp. I'll round up Juan Pedro; we'd better have him along. Oh — and bring some rope."

Fifteen minutes later, the three set out for Plaza IV — the number had been accepted without comment. Lancaster was somewhat shorter than Wally, his hair gray, his partial baldness concealed by his hat. He was not at all soft, but he had a nice little pot. Juan Pedro Cutzcab was small, older than the director by five years, and built like a track athlete. He had been Lancaster's foreman on many expeditions. He did not look anywhere near his age, he was mahogany dark, and his teeth were shockingly bad. The three of them were hung about with an assortment of tools, from a camera to a geologist's pick.

Within half an hour, having enlarged the hole and removed the slab against which Wally barked his shin, they were ready to enter the chamber. Evidently a similar slab had fallen in, probably broken by roots. In that country you will see heavy stone-and-mortar walls torn apart by the delicate roots of grass, while trees and vines carry on a slow, mad rampage of destruction.

Delicately, with shared excitement, the archeologists lowered a fat camp candle. Its flame burned clear, showing that the air was safe, and by its light they saw that the chamber was of some size. They let down a knotted rope, its upper end made fast to a tree.

Dr. Lancaster said, "Really, Wallace, turning up a tomb like this with Mrs. Westermark due in this afternoon is most timely." He added, as if the words were intended to ward off what they said, "Of course, there may be nothing in it."

Up to then, Wally had been feeling as closely united with the director as on their earlier field trips, but the mention of Mrs. Westermark broke the union. Here it was — the grubbing for money, the inflated importance of any old bat who might be shaken loose from some cash, the self-abasement, the unworthiness. Thus aroused, Wally noted with distaste the director's premature use of the word "tomb." Early in their association, he had noted that the scholar used the old, incorrect, conclusion-drawing terms, like "pyramid" (there being no true pyramid in the Maya area) and "palace," and had put it down to an amiable archaism, the result of early association with the naïve yet great founders of Maya studies, who established beyond possibility of change such names as Temple of the Sun, Temple of the Warriors, and Pyramid of the Moon. Of late he had concluded, sourly, that the director used them because of their popular appeal.

Dr. Lancaster said, "It's your find, Wallace. Wouldn't you like to be first in?" In his voice now Wally detected the memory of early finds of his own and the sensation, never entirely dulled, of being the first to set foot in a city, in a temple, in a room. He answered, "Yes, sir, I guess I would."

"Shine the lamp down there first, and look out for snakes."

Wally moved the electric light over as much of the floor as he could see. "Nothing stirring, but I think I see a pot."

"Good!" And then, anxiously, "Watch where you set your feet!"

"Yes, sir." Wally went down the rope. It occurred to him that his surge of feeling of a moment ago had been excessively harsh, but he resisted softening. Dr. Lancaster passed down the lamp, candles, and tools.

Unscientifically, the chamber could be described as fourteen feet long by a shade under eight wide. The stone roof was corbel-vaulted, the center line crowned by long, thin slabs such as the one on which Wally had barked his shin. It was just under five feet above the floor at the spring of the vaulting, a little over seven feet down the middle. The east end had partly caved in. Later, they determined that this, and the depression above, had been caused by the uprooting of a moderate-sized tree when an old mahogany crashed, carrying the young tree with it. The wall at that end was largely collapsed, the neat, cut-stone symmetry broken, the floor littered with stones and earth. Most of the floor was masked by a thin layer of dust, but here and under the hole near the west end that had betrayed the chamber there was dried mud.

The director joined him and took the lamp, casting its beam around the floor. "Pottery," he said. "And there — jade." He let the light rest on one red-and-orange bowl. "Look at that — diagnostic." He picked out several more. "Tzakol, all of them. This is earlier than I'd thought."

This was what Wally remembered from the other expeditions — the scholarship instantly available, the tone of excitement that made the man suddenly young, and the blend of sharing and unobtrusive teaching.

Revolving slowly in one spot, like a lighthouse lamp, the director shone the beam on the west end and drew a breath. "Good Lord!"

Wally stared. Then, with an inspiration of memory, he said, "Like Comalcalco."

"Yes."

The west wall was covered with very smooth cinnabarred plaster, on which two priestly figures, three-quarters life-size, were executed in bas-relief. Between them and on either side of them were single lines of hieroglyphs, also modelled in relief. The director turned to the east. "Probably both ends were like that. We may be in for a nasty job of salvage and reconstruction over there." He said it with the relish of a master craftsman facing a challenge to his skill.

Making sure there were no objects in the way that he might step on, he walked up to the wall to look at the inscriptions, Wally following him. The left-hand column was made up of text glyphs — those glyphs that no one has yet deciphered and that, it is hoped, contain statements going beyond the purely calendrical and astronomical calculations that can now be read. At the center row, made up of half a dozen ovals — or, rather, rectangles with strongly rounded corners — a hand-breadth high and raised from the wall about half an inch, he held the light steady and said, "Look!" He pointed with his left hand.

Rather as though he were reciting in class, Wally read the top two glyphs aloud: "1 Ahau 8 Kayab."

"Followed by extraneous remarks," said Lancaster. He

studied the remaining glyphs. "Nothing else helpful. Still, if it's a period end . . . If it goes with the other evidence, we can assume it is, and have a fair date."

The Mayan day and month designations rotate upon each other within a solar year, and any given combination, such as 1 Ahau falling upon day eight of Kayab, recurs every fifty-two years. For complex but entirely practical, mathematical reasons, however, the "long count," with which the Mayas measured historical time and astronomical intervals, uses a unit that only approximates a year. Although these units were quite artificial, they made a big fuss over the endings of major groups of them, especially of twenty pseudo-years, the period they called *katun*, the last day of which was always Ahau. The multiple combination of Ahau with a particular number occurring on the same day of the same month can occur at a *katun*-end only once in about a thousand years. Hence, both men were thinking, if Linton's ever-useful tables showed that the combination 1 Ahau 8 Kayab came at the end of a *katun* at a time that fitted the evidence of the pottery, style of masonry, and such other evidences of approximate age as might come to hand, then it would be a safe assumption that the date in the inscription was no mere coincidence, and the inscription could be placed exactly in the "long count" of Maya chronology. Where that would put it in our chronology would remain part of a gorgeous debate that has been going on now for almost exactly seventy years (Gregorian).

Lancaster looked at his watch and sighed. "I wish I could settle right down in here with you, but I'd better climb out and circulate. Get your candles lit before this battery runs out. I guess the first thing is a floor plan, and locate and number the loot so we can take it out. Do you need anything? Need any help?"

"Not for that part."

"I'll tell Juan Pedro to make a ladder and have a proper trail cleared." He looked around again. "We'll have to sift for bony fragments, although I don't think there's much chance. Well — give me a leg up."

He climbed the rope remarkably well for a man in his fifties. Briefly, Wally's thoughts followed him with contemptuous pity. He had hated to leave the chamber, but he had to, because everything had to be just so before Mrs. Moneybags turned up this afternoon. Vaulting ambition that o'erleaps itself. Money-raisers get division and department chairmanships and deanships — if that's what you're after. It was a shame. Kneeling, Wally lit and set out several of the fat candles and switched off the lamp. The softer light filled the whole chamber. He drew in a breath, then sat back, letting what he saw soak in.

What struck him first was the quality of freshness. The neatly cut and laid-up limestone of the side walls and roof was creamy, reflecting the light gently; the mortar between the blocks was exact; except for the two points of damage, the work could have been finished last week. These surfaces seemed to have been made for candlelight. The old people had candles and used them ritually; in this place, imagination could create a scene. Then, there was the silence. Consciously he softened his breathing and stayed the hand that had reached for a smoke. An ancient silence — silence and light. "Thou —" How did it go? "Bride?" No, "foster child." "Thou foster child of silence and slow time." He studied the two figures on the shiny, rich, deep-red wall, modelled with strength, simplicity, and delicacy. Tzakol . . . He stared at the bowl the director had so promptly identified. Tzakol, all right, which meant before the full Classical Period — a good fifteen hundred years ago by any reckoning. That was lots of slow time. His cigarette pack was unopened. He took it out, tore off paper and let it drop, and lit up. Then, bothered by littering this floor, for all its dust, he put his hand down to retrieve the scrap. His finger touched something smooth and hard. Brushing delicately, he uncovered a jade bead, half an inch long, smooth, fresh, and shiny. Again he felt the stored, retained time. Contemplative, he was reluctant to move about. Taking a soft brush from his pouch, he dusted at other lumps contiguous to the first bead, and uncovered the parts of a necklace lying much the way it would lie if it had been laid down and the string had crumbled away. Or had it been looped around a neck and rested on a chest that had crumbled away — with no little help from the ants? This probably had been a tomb. Tomb or not, there was nothing spooky about it; its quality, he decided, was, above all, *peace*. You could sit here and contemplate forever. With a jerk of will, he set himself to work.

The first thing was rough photography with his small camera. Later, Werner would come to do a real job with all his equipment; for now, the main thing was to show the objects on the floor — especially the arrangement of the necklace — since they would have to be taken up, and to get some passable shots of the bas-relief and the chamber in general. There was no reason to believe that anything would collapse overnight, but sudden, strange disasters did sometimes happen.

After that came a floor plan. Absorption and sense of communication with the walled-in past became more complete with occupation. He was unpleasantly startled when the rope was pulled up and a ladder of wood bound with lianas let down in its place. At other moments, he was faintly aware of voices up above and the sound of cutting, but it did not break through his mental enclosure. Making a plan was a simple matter, and it brought him for the first time close to the east end.

The debris formed an irregular pile across the end of the floor. It consisted mostly of cut stones piled higgledy-piggledy, covered in some places with varying amounts of dirt, in others bare. The pile sloped upward shallowly into the rubble-and-dirt fill of the mound itself, from which its rearmost and highest part was derived. The raw, exposed fill made a shallow cave with crevices in it in which could be seen signs of the passage of water and from which spread little deltas of mud over the fallen matter. The cave-in and the hole in the roof, both of them, must have happened within the year, Wally figured. First he thought what a shame not to have found this room before the damage; then he realized that if it were undamaged, its finding would have waited until, if ever, a trench was run through the mound. As far as he could see, there was no stratification in the fill. The Mayas often enlarged mounds at intervals, leaving older floors and walls buried inside — almost as though they knew that someday archeologists would work their remains and they wanted to be helpful. The interior of the mound would be gone into carefully later. His present business was to get the artifacts in the tomb ready for removal. Even so, he took time to brush and scrape delicately, lying on his belly,

at the cut slabs at the outer edge of the pile. On the near side
of one he found a layer of plaster, the same smooth, rich red
as the west wall. There it was, the big job, as Dr. Lancaster
had forecast — to see how much of that surface could be
rescued. Of course, the boss himself would have to be in
charge but Wally hoped he could have a major part in it. It
was *his* tomb. The thought carried in his mind not the slightest connotation of his own interment. He was unaware of his
acceptance of the word "tomb." He turned from the debris
to the open floor, feeling the strongest of all archeology's
lures — the undying wonder about what the next operation
may uncover, the answer that may be hidden under the next
spoonful of dirt, behind the wall, in the fragments, to be painfully assembled, of a jar, a carved stone, a multi-millennial
flint tool, or a plaster surface. The wonder is there from minute to minute and from year to year, and the fact that the
answers found are few and usually both minor and abstruse
makes no difference. Wally had felt it as he stepped out from
Mound D-II; it was strong now in different terms, more precise and more exciting.

His floor plan was drawn on paper ruled in centimeter
squares. As he worked along the floor, he marked each object
before entering a corresponding mark on his plan — a simple
serial number followed by an identifying "C1-A-IV," for
Chamber 1 in A-IV. Jade will not take ink, so he wrote each
bead's number on adhesive tape and stuck it on. Then he
marked on the grid of his plan the exact location of each
item outside the debris area, including the pieces of the roof
slab that had fallen in. As he worked, the back of his mind
was busy with the question of the collapsed wall. Apart
from that tricky, difficult, perhaps totally unrewarding

problem, there was nothing he couldn't take charge of himself. His sense of peace was enlarged by the anticipation of many days' work in his tomb quite alone. A man's voice calling "Hey, Wally!" was a crashing intrusion. He was ashamed of the harshness of his answering "Yes!"

It was Landon. "The boss said he was sure you'd forget about eating. May I come down and look?"

"Come along."

The younger man was pleasingly impressed. They climbed out and walked along what was now a well-cleared trail. Joe said, "You've got the better mousetrap, and here's the path all ready for the V.I.P.s to beat to your door."

Wally suppressed an angry answer. "Yeah, I suppose so," he said. After a couple of steps, he said, "Every time I really get down to work, I'll have to knock off and start kowtowing. There's a rich old battle-axe coming in this afternoon, and I understand some hot shots from Oxford will be with us next week. What we need is about twenty miles of good, muddy mule trail."

Landon laughed. It didn't bother *him*, Wally decided. The thing was, people like him had not worked in the intensity and closeness of one-man and two-man seminars with Dr. Lancaster — above all, had not been partners with him on the little expeditions — so they did not realize, had not the means of knowing, what greatness had gone astray.

After lunch, the director dutifully climbed into the jeep to go and meet the plane. Mrs. Lancaster was plainly happy and excited about having a visitor. She liked herself best in the role of hostess to the influential and important, Wally thought, remembering the difference between her manner toward him and other students, when he had been a guest at her house, and her manner toward older visitors, of position. He even suspected that she might be responsible for the director's deviation from the true path.

The artifacts were removed from the tomb and carried to camp. They made a nice display on a table in the building re-soundingly known as the "laboratory" — a simple, screened shack with a number of long tables and some shelves carrying materials for cleaning, repairing, and packing. Regardless of scruples about playing up to money, Wally took pains with their arrangement, setting the jade alongside the shards of one of the few broken pots, which were painted a gay red and yellow. Then he stretched semi-transparent drawing paper, of the kind architects use, over a cross-ruled sheet on a large drawing board, and put a dozen sharp pencils and several bandanna handkerchiefs in his pouch. One of the handker-chiefs he would tie around his head so as just to cover his eye-brows; the others were to insure that his hand would not grease the paper. You get so that you hardly notice the heat — indeed, in the tomb it was pleasant — but in the humid air you sweat, and drops falling from your forehead can ruin paper, as can the moisture of your hand. Thus equipped, and with a jar of water for refreshment, he went back to the job, after telling Werner firmly that his photography would have to wait.

Drawing and photography complement each other: neither alone is sufficient. The most meticulous copyist emphasizes what interests him, or fails to show what, for whatever reason, he fails to see. His drawing will bring out why he sees a skeletal jaw on a face attached to the glyph for "day." The photograph will show a scholar, ten years later and two thousand miles away, that what the artist took for an accidental damage to the eye is the remnant of an item of design. Both the skeletal jaw and the unnatural eye importantly affect the value of that half-glyph, and, in turn, may alter the reading of the whole inscription. Wally was of an age to have ample belief in himself. It was quite clear to him that the measured drawing was the superior, the ultimate reproduction. He also knew that it was an act of love, and a communication with the long-dead artists whose work he confronted. It is not enough to make an exact measurement and take that over onto your crosslines; you have to feel the quality of the line, the still living *intent*, or your work will not fulfill its purpose. Pure efficiency would have seemed to call for setting Juan Pedro to sifting the thin layer of dust, since that job should be done before there was too much trampling, but Wally wanted solitude. The work was demanding. On the wall in front of him the greater part of each figure was shown in a few flat planes bounded by bevelled edges that had the definite quality of strong lines drawn with a brush, but the faces and hands were modelled in fine detail, still without losing the effect of the bold outlines.

He studied, made over-all measurements, marked a layout, stopped to smoke a cigarette slowly while he contemplated. When the cigarette was done, he realized that he had been studying the whole work, and had not really examined the row of glyphs with which he would start, by way of getting his hand in. He took ten minutes looking at those, having at the back of his mind the determination that his eye, backed by a brain. should miss nothing that the mindless camera might find. Then he began drawing. In due course, he had the characters down to his satisfaction, and moved to the first figure. In motion — dancing? Quite probably. Priest or chief — hereditary, or how were they chosen? Probably by some form of inheritance. Call them priests, bearing in mind that it had been a theocracy. Did the same man (such as the original of this one, if this was portraiture) rule, dance, sacrifice, and pore over the ancient books — the mathematics, astronomy, and history? At commencements, professors who had English or Continental degrees wore some pretty fancy, even gaudy, robes, but you never thought of a learned man, a scholar, wearing a headdress like that. For an instant the thought of Dr. Lancaster intruded itself humorously and unpleasantly. He drove it out. The thing was to get the main lines of the figure first, and when you guided yourself by the dots on the paper, taken from the measurements, you lost the run of it. He concentrated absolutely, his lips slightly parted, his tongue lying between his teeth on the right of his jaw, his expression lost and serene despite a slight knitting of his brow.

"Hello, down there!" It was worse than this morning. It was acutely painful, shattering, and it made him start so that he fudged a line. Dr. Lancaster's voice spoke again. "Can you receive visitors?" All so cozy and hearty and — dear Jesus!

He pulled himself together. He glanced at his watch — four-thirty. He could have been pleased that he had not been interrupted earlier, but he preferred to note angrily that by the time this visit was over it would be too late to get back again into his drawing. Well, he thought, manners, dammit, and called "Come on down." He placed his drawing with its face to the wall.

Lancaster descended first, then through the opening came jodhpur boots and trousers — the latter of white material showing grass stains, the legs leading Wally's eye to a broad rear, which was, he soon saw, the pyramid upon which the upper portion of Mrs. Westermark was built. She was in her late fifties, he decided. She wore a pith helmet, which seemed too good to be true. She was short, rather square, and in her face there was a good deal of authority. Mrs. Lancaster came last. Her khaki shirt and slacks seemed serviceable and right. Lancaster gave her a hand as she came down, but did not fuss as he had over Mrs. Westermark. Wally stood to one side, came forward to be introduced and receive the rich woman's condescension, then retreated again.

The director said, turning to him, "By the way, I checked, and 1 Ahau 8 Kayab ends *katun* 10 — couldn't be neater."

Mrs. Westermark said, "What does that mean?" and Dr. Lancaster turned back to her, explaining. He knew how to simplify and to adapt his information to his audience. Wally felt a distasteful admiration as he pointed out the day and month glyphs, was mildly humorous about the faces that expressed their numbers, then, without actually getting into the arithmetic of it, explained about the rotation of those dates upon the wheel of the *katuns*. This day and month date ended the tenth *katun* — the midpoint — of the ninth cycle. According to the latest thinking, that would be in the third century of our era. Wally noted with wonder the things that his teacher omitted, feeling a pedant's urge to interrupt and fill in the lacunae, although actually he wanted no part of the spotlight. The talk went on to the figures themselves and the possible significance of the tomb. In regard to that, the director let his imagination go pretty freely.

Mrs. Westermark looked all around her, then back at the figures. "Then you can't read those other hieroglyphs?"

"No so far."

"So you really don't know who these people — kings or whatever — were?"

"Umm — no, we don't."

"Or whom this tomb was built for, those offerings made?"

"No."

Like most students at his stage, Wally was proudly conscious of how much had been made known to him, hence of how much had been found out in the face of such extraordinary difficulties, by such amazing deductions, interpretations, and syntheses. He found the woman's questions belittling, so considered them stupid.

Mrs. Westermark surveyed the tomb again. With solemnity, and with obvious satisfaction, she pronounced, " 'Look on my works, ye Mighty, and despair!' " Wally found it expedient to face toward the broken wall.

The party remained about ten minutes more. Dr. Lancaster explained, with the same simplicity, the work to be done on the east end. This led Mrs. Westermark to ask several questions that made considerable sense. There was something, Wally remembered, about money she had put up for fitting together some Graeco-Roman frescoes — something like that. Apparently she was not entirely stupid. Finally they left, Mrs. Lancaster reminding him not to be late for dinner. The afternoon was about done; he could as well have left with them, save that he preferred to be out of their company. It was no use picking up the drawing again at this point. He took it easy, smoked, poked in the dust, and reluctantly left his tomb in time to reach camp before nightfall.

A shower, a change (the old camps had never been like

this), a cold cocktail relaxed his rigidities. Mrs. Westermark said that she would like to watch the work in the tomb for a time in the morning. She promised she would just sit quietly. The director looked dubiously at his assistant. Wally thought rapidly; he'd be damned if he'd work on the drawing with her breathing on his neck. "We ought to get the dust sifted before there's more walking on it," he said. "If I can have Juan Pedro and a bucket man, I'd like to get at that. It won't be very interesting, I'm afraid, but Mrs. Westermark's welcome to watch."

It was agreed that Mrs. Westermark would turn up after she had gone with Dr. Lancaster to look at a small temple with an unusually well-preserved roof comb that had been cleared of grass and brush that afternoon. She inquired about sending out telegrams, and learned that that could be done from the airfield. She said that if her business would let her, she might want to stay on and watch the work on the east wall. She had spent a couple of days at Arachnid, in western Turkey, when they were uncovering and piecing together a fresco, and had found it most interesting. Wally looked upon her mightiness and despaired. She was a woman of power and authority, mistress and manipulator of a great fortune, and if she chose to lodge herself in his tomb, there was no way to get her out of it. Then he saw that Dr. Lancaster was pleased, and saw that reflected and doubled in his wife's expression. She looked rather like a fisherman in the act of netting a splendid trout, and he was shaken by disgust, shame, and anger that left him stricken into total silence for the rest of the meal and the evening. He was tired, but that night he had trouble getting to sleep, and he rose in the morning feeling gritty and unhappy.

* * *

Juan Pedro came down the ladder and looked about him with professional interest. He gave the figures on the wall only passing attention, remarking that they were "fine demons," and was clearly quite unaware of the strong resemblance between the larger figure's profile and his own. His concern was with the floor and the fallen wall, where there was work to be done and where he might make a find, such as a piece of carved jade or an unbroken pot, for which a small prize would be forthcoming. He had, Wally believed, virtually no curiosity, most certainly no sense of kinship with the builders of the ruined cities he helped uncover. As foreman, and as recruiter of the other workmen, which undoubtedly meant kickbacks of one kind and another, he made a better income than most Indians of the Petén country, and in that lay his interest. When he had surveyed the chamber, and not until then, he set aside his long, wicked-looking machete, leaning it against the wall toward the east end. Like most natives of the region, he was never out of reach of that tool — or weapon — day or night.

In the dust they marked off lines forming half-meter squares, and then they ran the dusty and dried mud in the square at the foot of the ladder through the sieve. Finding it sterile, they scooped it into the bucket and signalled to the man above to take it away. Under the dust was a plaster floor. They had cleared half a dozen squares by the time Mrs. Westermark and Dr. Lancaster arrived, the latter carrying a camp chair, which he set up near the ladder, for the guest. He explained to her that, while the sifters were looking for anything they might find, they were watching especially for traces of human bone, which would confirm that this was a place of burial, and for fragments of carbon. Laboratory tests of the amount of radioactivity remaining in samples of carbon could give an important confirmation of dating by other methods.

Wally pointed to a square near the debris of the east wall, and told Juan Pedro they would work there next. He had a childish desire to keep as far away from the woman as possible. The Indian picked up two lighted candles and carried them toward that end. He was aware that this formidable old lady was a person of importance, and he had a good deal of the showoff in his nature. He held the candles toward the rubble face and studied the litter. The three North Americans, their eyes having followed the moving lights, watched him. He squatted slowly, with a great, false effect of not knowing that he was observed, set down the candle in his right hand, raised the other higher, then drew out of his sash a small diamond-shaped mason's trowel.

"*Espérense,*" he said, "*creo que tenemos una olla bonita aquí atrás.*"

Lancaster interpreted, "He thinks he has a jar back there."

From where he stood, Wally could see the light strike what seemed to be a portion of a sphere, rather shiny crimson and black. Mrs. Westermark stepped forward to see better. Juan Pedro reached out with the trowel, delicately pushing aside dirt until the point scraped the object. Wally saw it change shape, the curve of the sphere grow larger — but stupidly, astonished, and not reading any meaning into what he saw. Then the coral snake reared its deadly head, Mrs. Westermark screamed, the Indian jumped up and back, tripped, fell into the woman, and both of them tumbled comically and grotesquely onto the floor. At the time, Wally did not think the sight particularly funny, though he was aware of its incongruousness, and whatever his feelings of the moment actually were, they became more confused when, to his horror, he heard himself let out a short, harsh laugh. He wasn't laughing at her, but from a shocked feeling that his secret wish was being magically fulfilled. Then, to make things even worse, he saw Mrs. Westermark glaring at him, and knew that she had heard. Not apparently hurried, Dr. Lancaster took up the machete by the wall and with a nice flick decapitated the snake. Then he and Wally bent together to help the visitor up, both of them clumsy with haste and embarrassment.

Juan Pedro got up slowly, retrieved his blade, and climbed out, without a word. The director appeared not to know whether it was worse to speak or not to speak. He hovered by his guest, opening and closing his mouth, his irresolution in unpleasant contrast to his recent, sure action.

Mrs. Westermark took a deep breath. "I think I'd like to go back to camp," she said stiffly.

Dr. Lancaster said, "Yes, of course." As she walked to the ladder, he turned to Wally. "You'll have to come out of here, too, until we take care of Juan Pedro. I'll explain later. You can pass the time with your pots."

Wally had an impulse to argue, but this was no moment for it. With some pity he watched the director help Mrs. Westermark up the ladder, then go up himself. He followed slowly. He dawdled on the trail, and on reaching camp went directly to the laboratory. Werner was photographing the pottery, so Wally took it easy, and stood watching him. To his surprise, hardly ten minutes after he had entered the building Dr. Lancaster came in. "The lady will rest in her quarters until it's time to be driven to the airfield," he explained. "Paul will take her. Wait just a moment." He went to the shelves, fumbled along them briefly, and came up with a thin bundle wrapped in bark. He stopped to speak to the photographer pleasantly, pointed out an aspect of a vase that he wanted shown, then joined his assistant. "Let's go."

As they went out he said, "Juan Pedro has to do a little praying — make medicine, you might say — and for everybody's morale it's desirable for us to be in on it." He opened the little bundle to show half a dozen slender, amost black candles. "Beeswax," he said, "the original Maya article. I saw these in the market at Santiago when we came through, and I bought them on general principles. You never know."

"But I've seen him kill snakes before, and it never bothered him."

"It's not that, it's *susto* — fright. Did you notice how carefully he moved? His soul has been shaken loose; he could lose it altogether. I think it's a very old belief. Anyhow, it's an interesting bit of ritual."

They had gone past the workmen's quarters to a fairly open space beside a very large tree. Here a stick cross had been set up in a pile of small stones, in front of which the Indian squatted, nursing a fire.

"With the temples of his ancestors all round him," Lancaster said in a low voice, gesturing toward the cross. He handed over the candles, and he and Wally hunkered down.

Juan Pedro lit and set out several candles. Then he put some lumps of the native incense called *pom* on the coals. He prayed rapidly in Maya, a language of which Wally had an archeologist's smattering — a few words and phrases picked up in the course of field work, and terms, such as *katun*, the names of the days, and the names of old gods, many of which were unknown to modern Indians. He thought he caught both his own name and Dr. Lancaster's — "Don Carlos." Quite clearly, Juan Pedro gestured east, south, west, and north, and, as he did so, it made Wally's hair prickle to hear, unquestionably, references to the Chaks who rule the directions. Along with these reminiscences of a once great antiquity there came a long listing of names of saints, and a good deal that was simply rapid, urgent, heartfelt, unintelligible praying. Incense, candles, even a cross, Wally knew, were used by the Mayas when the Spanish first came to the New World. He thought of the priestly figures on the wall of his tomb, of the ruins of temples so far uncovered, the whole great complex of buildings and mounds, not only here but all through the area, the inscriptions, the carven stelae. This ritual was pathetic, and at the same time it had a tattered, blurred antiquity about it. Also, it was not without power. Juan Pedro produced three eggs, passed one over himself, one over each of his companions, maintaining his spate of prayer as he did so. He passed the eggs several times through the last of the incense smoke; then he crossed himself and got up, smiling.

"There we are," he said, in Spanish. He looked up at the high overarching of green leaves and gold lines of light, and nodded. "I must go and take care of these eggs. I'll be at the tomb after lunch." He turned and went off.

Lancaster said, "That business with the eggs is European, I believe. The rest was run-down Maya." He, too, looked up, then he looked at his watch. "I don't see how he does it. Literally, he can't read time, but he can tell you what time it is whenever you want, day or night. We have an hour till lunch. Let's go on back to your job."

Wally felt relaxed and untalkative, as though that poor little ceremony had had some authority, or he had caught something from the ministrant's belief and satisfaction. They walked along, exchanging only a few brief remarks relating to the structures they passed.

Their manner mocking the old superstition, they searched the tomb by no means casually for sign of the snake's mate, but there was none. Wally took the body, climbed up, and threw it well into the bush.

"So very Egyptian," Lancaster remarked when he came down again. "Curse of King Tut, and all that — the serpent in the tomb."

Wally smiled. "Yes."

"Let's look at this mess." The director nodded at the fallen wall.

They set candles and knelt together. Wally showed him the stone with the red plaster finish he had spotted.

"There you are — that settles it." The director shone the bright light of the electric lamp about, picking up other fragments of the purplish red. "I'll have to ask you to hold off this until I can work on it with you."

Wally had to say, "Of course. I've never tackled anything like this."

Both of them spoke in the hushed voices that the place demanded.

"What's your program for now?" Lancaster asked.

Wally considered. "Finish sifting the dirt before we have any more visitors . . ." In spite of himself, a little sharpness showed in his voice. He added, improvising, "Or before Werner tramps around with all his gear. Then I think we should get the photography done, and then I'll get back on the drawings."

Lancaster nodded. "You have rather had thundering herds in here, haven't you?" He looked slowly around. "And it's not the place for it, is it? Well, those Oxonians will be coming through early next week. I don't expect they'll stay more than a night, since they're on their way to Penn's big glamour job at Tikal. There are no other interruptions on the schedule for quite a while. After they go, I imagine we'll be able to start on this, and that will fit your timetable. You can have Werner whenever you give the word. While he's fussing about, you could do your cross and long sections." He had been speaking slowly, thinking aloud, with waits between sentences. He rose to his feet with a little sigh. "See you at lunch."

Again he hadn't wanted to go, Wally thought, and he had known why he, Wally, would linger, even though he could not get any work done in the little time before noon. Then he realized, as he lit a cigarette, that Dr. Lancaster's presence had not disturbed the quality of the tomb. When you direct a project this size, you have to keep popping out and directing it, he supposed, and if you are good enough, you know about little things like Juan Pedro and *susto*, and take time for them, too. Belatedly, with a touch of humiliation, he recalled several mentions of that belief in his reading. The candle nearest him guttered. It was low. He blew it out, then another that was also nearly gone. In the decreased light his tomb was mysterious, and the end of his cigarette showed red. He stared at the coal. The serpent in the tomb. Once again, indulging in superstition, he half accused himself of having conjured up that creature, it had so well served his purpose. He seemed mean to himself now. Mrs. Westermark's thousands would continue to go to the work in the Near East — What was his name? Korinsky; not even in Anthropology. Although he closed his ears to such things, he had to be at least faintly aware of the many projects that were put forward within that Department, all competing, and then, in their turn, the Fine Arts boys came before the dispensers of funds with their showy Classical-Near East Archeology — talk of glamour! Uneasily, he pushed aside the thought that seeking funds might be an inescapable part of a selfless dedication to science, and shielded himself with the counter-thought — carefully left unreasoned, as might a bridegreoom overhearing talk of someone's divorce — that this would never be for him.

He changed position with a harshness of motion. He sat in half dark, looking at the relatively well-lighted west wall. He took another puff at his cigarette, contemplating the two figures. Always afterward he would associate them, and his aesthetic feeling about them, with his moment of first realizing what an incredibly game old sport Dr. Lancaster was.

NO ROSETTA STONE

The rooms on the upper floor of the hotel opened on a handsome gallery, from which a staircase led down to the patio between the dining room door and the deep archway of the main entrance. The boy, Jimmy Chambers, came out of his room and proceeded to the stairs at the rate of one who has lots of time on his hands. He was eleven years old, and a relatively small amount of empty time could become a serious problem. Actually, he was not greatly worried. The town, he had found, had a great variety of resources for a boy who spoke fair Spanish and carefully observed the Latin-American courtesies and formalities. He was dressed for riding, wearing high, elastic-sided shoes and tight-fitting, blue trousers in the local style, because in order to get out of going with them to make a formal, farewell call on the bishop, he had told them he was going for a last ride. He knew perfectly well that he would not ride, because in the U-shaped dip between the peaks of San Angel and sad Santa Clara he could see the sun gleam on an arc of silver cloud, which meant it would be raining before the afternoon ended. Don Julio, from whom he hired riding horses, had taught him that sign, and it always worked, but they didn't know it.

In reality he was sorry that he was not calling on the

bishop. He and the bishop had hit it off nicely, and the old man would have served him a glass of wine the same as the others and addressed him as if he were an adult. He would have gone, only this morning they brought up the name thing again, and he was angry. Just not going with them was an inadequate way of expressing his anger, although both of them were always anxious for him to do things together with them and sorry when he did not. It was as if success in building a joint relationship with him was necessary to the welfare of their marriage, which gave him at times a sense of power that was not entirely enjoyable. All the same, at this moment he was unsatisfied and wished there were some more emphatic way he could strike at them, something, if possible, that would appeal to Dad.

The matter of names was more complex even than Jimmy realized. To begin with, he had no term for them, the two of them, the pair, except the simple pronoun. She was his mother, but what was the professor? Not his stepfather, since his father was still living. He rejected the term stepfather absolutely, although here in Atetenango, rather than the final impossibility of having people think the professor was his father, he accepted gingerly the term *padrastro* and the assumption that Dad was dead, which was a form of treason. The man was, then, his mother's husband, nothing more, and anything he did in the capacity of a father was out of order or else solely as his mother's delegate. There was no term for them, then. They could not possibly be "my parents"; anything on the order of "my family" was untrue, false to his father. They were simply "they."

The couple would have been wise to have let the boy go on calling the man "Professor," without comment. It was by that name he had known and liked him before the divorce and the marriage, the title fitted with the boy's enjoyment of his talk about Maya archeology and exploring in the high forests. Jimmy's father was an old Latin America hand, with a bit of buccaneering about the ways in which he had made his money, and it gave the professor status to have travelled the narrow trails, hunted for his meat, dealt with the people. That, and his father's unexpectedly easy agreement, had been what made it possible to bring Jimmy to Atetanango on the professor's quest in a cooperative, even an eager frame of mind. Then, when they had settled themselves, four weeks ago, they had to turn around and try to make him call the professor something more intimate, such as "Pa" or "Pop," or even, incredibly, "Dad." Thinking of it now, he felt himself grow hot again and there was the sensation of something moving in his stomach. Finally, in desperation, he had offered to call the guy "Uncle," and that had stopped the business. "Uncle" — "Uncle Ham" for heaven's sake, because you couldn't be forever reciting "Hamilton." What a name! So right then he quit working with them in the bishop's library, although until then he'd been as excited as Mother or the professor himself over the possibility of finding a Maya Rosetta Stone.

Little by little the name business calmed down, and Jimmy went back to calling the man "Professor" a good deal of the time, and thought that the professor preferred it. These last few days, when it was clear that the great idea was a bust, that whatever of Bishop Durán's collection of "heathen books" may once have remained in the library had been lost for keeps when the anti-clericals sacked the place in the revolution of '38 and they had come too late, he had been feeling really friendly towards his mother's husband. It had been such a good idea, so carefully worked out, the possibilities had been so stupendous, and the professor was taking his disappointment so gamely. Then this morning Mother had to start the name business all over again, and that tore it. She was beautiful, she was his mother, she had always been swell and he loved her, and he did wish she wouldn't be so *wrong* sometimes.

Under the deep archway, where the great doors were folded back like the gates of an ancient castle, Alberto, the *mozo*, lounged with his grey serape wrapped around his throat. He wished the boy good afternoon, calling him Santiago, and the boy responded in proper form.

"So tomorrow is travel," he said. "You go for keeps?"

"Yes, unfortunately." He did not think it was at all unfortunate, but that was the right thing to say.

"From here to the capital by car, and then in an aeroplane — *ziss* —" Alberto made a sweeping motion of his hand, "New Orleans, and *ziss*, New York. Your mere home is not far from New York?" He knew the answer, but he made it a query.

"Not far from there."

"I should like to see those big cities."

"I wish you could come with us, your house is there. But those cities are not so much better than Atetenango. They are noisier, they are crowded, that is all."

"Still, I should like to see all that life, that movement."

"There are no views such as you have here; one cannot look up and see mountains."

Alberto nodded gravely. "Yes, our landscape is fine; our situation is beautiful."

The deprecation of the North American cities, the politeness, the final, infallible reference to the local scenery, were things his father had taught him. The professor spoke Spanish, a trifle haltingly and with a flat accent. He knew the standard forms, but his use of them was different. Jimmy stepped onto the sidewalk in close touch with his father. Irritation and resistance changed to a sense of being sturdily and successfully loyal. It was astonishing, he thought, how Dad — call anyone else Dad! — had called the turn, and wonderful how he had stayed with him through these five weeks.

His mother had put it up to Dad; then he himself had talked it over with his father on the following Sunday. It had been a little awkward, because he couldn't explain without telling about the wonderful detective sort of job the professor had done, only Dad made it easy for him. The point was that some of the old Maya manuscripts collected by Bishop Durán around 1600 were probably still in the bishop's library at Atetenango and that the original bishop had had a translation of at least one of them written in like a trot — in short, a Rosetta Stone for the Maya writing. He went on and explained that some of the hieroglyphs, the ones that had to do with the calendar and mathematics, had been deciphered, but the real meat of all the writing was still unknown.

His dad looked at him smilingly and said, "And you'd like to be in on the discovery, and you'd like to visit Central America, only you're afraid I won't like having my summer with you cut in half."

"I don't want to have my time with you cut down, either."

Dad tapped him lightly on the shoulder. "Good boy. I'll have you stay on with me through September to make up. Of course you want to go, and the chance is too good for you to miss. It just hasn't worked out for me to take you to South America; my trips have come at the wrong times these last few years, but I shall when I can." He leaned forward slightly in his armchair and looked at the boy with humor and conspiracy. "Of course your mother hopes that this will bring you and Ham closer. You mustn't blame her; it's only natural. You'd be in a mess if you didn't get on with the guy, but don't let the glamour overwhelm you."

Shortly he was testing Jimmy's Spanish, of which the boy had had three years, and coaching him in the fine art of making friends in Latin America.

Jimmy went around two sides of the plaza with no special interest. The Indians squatting at one corner with blocks of salt for sale no longer intrigued him. At three in the afternoon there was little other life about. In front of the barracks he passed Major Rojas and felt a slight sense of triumph at getting out "*Su servidor, mi comandante*" before the officer could speak, so that he had to answer "*Igualmente.*" He knew the major only through these casual encounters, but since the man made a point of greeting him with some elaboration, it had become a game to be first and to be elaborate. Jimmy thought that next time he would say "*A sus órdenes,*" or "*Quedo á sus órdenes*" if he could think of it.

The encounter put him in communication with his father once more. "Don't let the glamour overwhelm you." Uncle Ham was all right, he supposed, but he had no glamour. Dad was the one who was loaded with that, in the adventures of his past, his smile, his profile, his — his *unreformed* quality. Tomorrow they started home, and Jimmy could see no way now in which, as he had hoped, somehow he could score off them, or off the professor, do heaven knew what that would be evidence to Dad that his trust had not been misplaced, that would make Dad laugh and pat his shoulder and look pleased. For weeks he had nursed the thought that if he went to the bishop and in apparent innocence let it be known that his father was still alive, that indeed both his mother and her husband had been divorced, the bishop would have put them out of the library instanter. He knew he could not possibly do it, but the idea of it had excited him and sharpened his sense of power. Now that weapon was gone and the chance that anything clear-cut, describable later to Dad, would turn up was nil.

There was no one at the tables in front of the little café. As they stepped out on the gallery on their way to the bishop's, Uncle Ham (using that name for him in his thoughts was a form of invective) had gazed at the sky in his ignorance and said, "It looks like a clear afternoon. Let's all meet at the Flor de las Sierras at five and listen to the band."

This was the rainy season, July, for heaven's sake, and even if the book said that Atetenango was at an altitude of 4,200 feet in an arid section of the northern *tierra templada* and that therefore the rains in June, July and August were extremely light, he ought to know that a clear sky in the early afternoon meant nothing. In the gap between the peaks — the gap of Canilal, Don Julio called it — the cloud now rose high, gleaming on top, dark below. At five it would be raining, and there would be no concert.

He turned left at the corner and entered the Turk's store partway down the block. The proprietor's name was Kasanjian and Jimmy supposed he was Armenian, but everyone called him "the Turk." His youngest daughter, the last remaining unmarried, was behind the counter. She sold Jimmy some peppermint drops and said she had heard that tomorrow he was leaving for good. She was supposed to be beautiful, but the boy thought her eyes too cowlike. He had heard long, humorous histories of the vast pains the Turk had gone to to get his two older daughters suitably married, and of what was being negotiated for this one. As he went out the door he felt sorry for the girl. People should marry for love. Also, they should stay married. His face darkened. His father was as much to blame as his mother, they were both to blame. It wasn't the divorce he minded so much; as a matter of fact, life became more agreeable after those two got out of each other's hair; what he didn't like was her marrying again.

Suddenly he heard her again as she spoke this morning and the final, awful, ". . . you call your father 'Daddy' so why not let Uncle Ham be your 'Dad'?" For heaven's sake, he'd started calling his father "Dad" about a year ago, because "Daddy" sounded babyish. He wasn't going to have any second father put over on him, he wasn't going to be a traitor. He hated thinking about these things, it upset him and made him feel ugly and uncomfortable.

As he came under the shade of the market roof he realized that in fact everything was working out just right. The professor had failed, and so what would have been terrific and made him famous turned into nothing at all. Like when you blow up a paper bag and get all set for a big pop, and it turns out there's a leak in it. Then, with a sense of discovery, he realized that his father would be pleased that it had worked out this way, that he had never wanted it to succeed, although for his — Jimmy's — sake he had said nothing.

He stopped thinking about his problems as he came to the

row of food stalls, small ovens and charcoal braziers, benches, and simple tables. Most of them were run by old women, cheerful and enchantingly various. He stopped at Margarita's and gave her the peppermints he had bought. He accepted coffee and one of the hard-shelled, round, small, delicious alligator pears of the country. The other foods on display were bright and smelled temptingly, but he dared not try them. Not only they, but Dad, had warned him emphatically against casual eating, and there were plenty of hovering flies. He said yes, that tomorrow was travel and that he was going for keeps. At least he did not know how soon he would return. The market women said they would miss him and begged him not to forget them entirely. They were affectionate and sad and humorous all at the same time and they made him feel relaxed and warm. As he heard himself answer them, he knew that he was using words and idioms he had never learned at school, and at times was getting off sentences with that authentic sound as of tearing cloth. His father would be proud of him.

He roamed the market for a time. The place had a special appeal for him. He saw in it something ancient and romantic, related to things he had read, although he could not have told in what way. He inspected live chickens, turkeys and pigs. He came out on the Avenida Guzmán on the side farthest from the plaza. The sky was entirely overcast and rain was plainly imminent. So that was that for sitting at the Flor de las Sierras. He turned down the avenue, then to the left on a small street two blocks farther along, to say goodbye to La Octavia and her mother. He came to a store the front of which was little more than a medium-sized doorway, containing a slim selection of goods of which empty bottles and hammocks were important features, the bottles each with a cork tied to its neck by a piece of string. There was a shelf holding a small assortment of liquors, and at the back a doorway without a door. The opening led to a wonderfully primitive kitchen-living room. The store was not licensed as a *cantina* or restaurant, but intimate friends of the owners might sit back there for a drink of liquor or wine, or an excellent gourd of foaming chocolate and plate of shortbread.

The old lady, Octavia's mother, slim, neat, and wrinkled, sat in the store. After the usual greetings he told her, "I have come to say goodbye, for tomorrow is travel, and then, I do not want to leave Atetenango without one more drink of your fine chocolate."

"We heard you were going. The professor has finished his work?" She spoke of the "professor" because she had seen that *padrastro* troubled the boy, and attributed that trouble to a delicate sorrow, which pleased Jimmy and made him faintly uncomfortable. Then, as rain began to fall outside, she remarked that there would be no more customers and went to close the door. "Go to the kitchen," she said. "Octavia is there, and the captain." She turned and called through the inner doorway, "Octavia! Santiago is here to say goodbye. We must give him a *merienda*."

The captain was Flores, a somewhat rough-hewn cavalry officer, dark, with a fairly heavy mustache. He and Jimmy had hit it off the first time they met, although the reverse might have been expected.

Octavia called to Jimmy to come in. He stepped down — the store had a wooden floor, the big room had none — and was not in the least surprised to find the young woman sitting on the captain's knee. She was plump, good-looking, cheerfully unneat, and Jimmy was quite sure his mother would disapprove of her thoroughly. According to the market women, Captain Flores was married.

Octavia smiled and said, "Good afternoon, Santiago. Come in and sit down. We must celebrate you before we let you go."

He said, "Good afternoon and thanks," and to the captain, "*Caballero, á sus órdenes.*" His manner towards the officer was solemn.

Flores answered with equal gravity, "*A sus órdenes, joven.*" On the table beside him stood a bottle of a pale green liquor, a jug of water, a tumbler, a small shotglass and an ashtray.

Jimmy sat down, thinking, as he had many times before, Dad will get a poke when I tell him about this. The whole basis of his relationship was this straight-faced exchange of politenesses in an absurd situation, which he had initiated when they first met. It was all his father's dish and not at all his mother's.

The old lady came in saying, "Santiago wants chocolate, he says, but he must have more than that. Where is the bottle of good wine, the one we had for the *cofradía* on the Day of the Cross?"

Octavia stood up. "I'll get it. You make the chocolate."

They mixed their patties of cacao, cinnamon, and sugar fresh every morning, which was one reason why their chocolate was so good. The old lady fanned the coals in the stone and earth stove with a basketry fan, set water to boiling, dropped a patty into a tall, narrow gourd, poured on water, and swizzled vigorously with a carved stick. Octavia brought him half a dozen little cakes of shortbread on a dish and a small glass of Malaga. This was less elegant than the bishop's service, Jimmy thought, but it was really more fun. Octavia's mother brought him the chocolate. He moved his hand towards his pocket but she stopped him with an emphatic gesture. "No. You are leaving; this is for friendship."

The captain lifted his shotglass and said, "*Salud*."

The boy raised the wine and answered. They both sipped. The old lady, settling herself on a bench, asked again, "The professor has completed his task?" and added, "Was anything historical left in the library after the anti-clericals wrecked it?"

Because the professor had said that he did not want the real nature of his search commonly known, lest, if they found what they hoped for, public interest prevent getting permission to take it from the country even on a loan basis, Jimmy had said that the professor was engaged in "historical investigations," which was indefinite and sounded well. He had also let it be known that he assisted in the investigations.

He said, "He has examined everything, but there is not much left. I don't think he found anything really historical."

Octavia was standing beside the officer. Shortly she would sit on his knee again and probably he would give her a sip of his liquor. Dad *will* get a poke out of this, he thought. He drank some chocolate. Everything was all right, really; he had plenty to tell his father, all the evidences that he, too, would make a real Latin America hand, and both of the professor's projects, finding the Rosetta Stone and capturing him, were failures.

He realized that Octavia was talking and he had missed the

beginning of what she said. ". . . sold them by the kilo for fuel. Many people bought them with the idea of saving them for the Church, but afterwards it turned out that if you admitted you had bought any the police were likely to jail you as a sympathizer with the revolution, so people burned them after all. People like us have no place to keep books, anyway."

Captain Flores said, "What about that picture book you had? You remember, it looked a little like comic strips and there was a sort of writing. It could have been a work of the ancient Mayas. Is there anything left of it? Perhaps the young man would be interested in it."

She said, "I don't know. The neighbor's children were playing with it."

The old lady said, "I took it from them. It is a thing of the heathen times I am sure and those pictures looked like devils to me. I did not know what bad luck it could bring them. I put it in the storeroom, in that old chest with the crosses carved on it. For me, I think we should burn it entirely, now, unless indeed a scholar like Santiago here wants to take it away. Go get it and show it to him."

Jimmy could feel his heart beat. It could happen. There were only three Maya codices known to exist; the find of even part of another would be tremendous. If it turned out to be one of old Bishop Durán's trots, that would be even greater. He was flattered by the way they all assumed that he was learned enough to judge the thing, remembering how the captain had said once that he was *un joven muy científico*. For four weeks he had kept aloof from their researches, but he well remembered everything the professor had told him, and he felt a swelling pride in the time he had spent trying to

understand Morley's *Introduction to Maya Hieroglyphs* and
his success in memorizing the signs for the days and the
months.

Octavia was rummaging in the last of the chain of four
rooms that made up the house, beyond the bedroom. Jimmy
and the captain toasted each other again. The back door was
open. It dripped with rain, but behind the rain was a lighten-
ing. Probably it would clear for one of those amazing, gold
sunsets and turn cold.

"Do you think there will be a band concert today?" he
asked. "It's Wednesday."

"Not with that infantry band," Flores answered. "They're
the delicate kind. Now if my regiment's band were here
. . ." he went on into entertaining improbabilities concerning his regiment's music. The sweet wine and the chocolate
went well together and both joined with the anise-flavored
sweetness of the *pan dulce* in a taste combination that might
be barbaric but that he would remember all his life as one
of the essences of Central America.

Octavia came back. She handed Jimmy a sort of document, of heavy, clay-coated paper folded screen-fashion to
make somewhat over a dozen pages on each side, about ten
inches high by four across. By the look of one of the end
sheets, another portion had been torn from it at some time.
The whole thing was in bad shape. The torn fold must have
lain in God knew what, it had been soaked into ruin. He ate
a piece of shortbread, finished his chocolate with a last swig,
and made something of an act of settling himself to examine
the thing. Octavia sat on Captain Flores's knee; he urged her
to take a sip of his liquor, she demurred, she accepted, her
mother smiled, then all of them watched the learned boy.

Well, he thought, this looks like it. At least, here was the jaguar god and here was the one with the fancy nose, and here was a column of days beginning with Three Ahau. You could see why the captain thought it looked like comic strips. Above the pictures were what the professor called text glyphs, the ones that presumably explained what it was all about and that no one could read. He opened at random near the middle, and found two pages of what seemed to be pure text, without pictures, day signs, or the lines and dots with which the Mayas wrote their numbers. Most important of all, between the columns of hieroglyphs were lines of small, crabbed writing in Latin characters. Under the day sign he had recognized was written "3 ajau" clearly enough, but most of the writing totally defeated him. He thought it was not in Spanish but in Latin.

This could be the key, the thing that would break all the writings, the host of carven inscriptions, wide open. Perhaps this would be known as the Chambers Codex since he, Jimmy Chambers, had found it. In imagination he tasted a heady, exotic fame. That most of the glyphs were utterly strange to him meant nothing, but as he turned one of the solid text pages sideways and tried again to make something of the script, it was his inability to do anything with the minuscule, antique hand that checked his excitement, then brought it tumbling down. Well enough that he, the boy, had been the lucky one who stumbled across this priceless document, but that was all he could be. Luck, and nothing more than luck. The professor, Uncle Ham, his mother's husband, his *padrastro*, Dr. Hamilton Aury would be the one who deciphered, published, harvested the glory. Probably he would agree to calling it Chambers Codex, or however you would put that in Latin, like the Codex Peresianus; that was the sort of guy he was, and his mother would gently point out that it was kind of him. It would be kind of him in a sense, for it was the professor who followed up all the odd little leads, the narratives of travels of high-ranking monks, found and gave a new interpretation to the passage in Count von Stengel's book about his travels in Central America in 1866, who had done all the long, slow detecting and deducing that had led him to the belief that, of all the towns and cities in the Maya Area from Honduras to Tabasco, and of all the cities in Spain itself, it was here, in Atetenango, that a codex and translation such as this might be found. The credit would still be the professor's; and sitting here, knowing the man, Jimmy could clearly visualize his joy. So everything wasn't coming out right after all.

Slowly, lingeringly, he swallowed the last of his Malaga. He laid the codex on the table beside him. He spoke slowly, thinking over his words. "This is an ancient writing of the Mayas, all right, but it is of no use for a historian. No one can read it. You should take it to the museum in the capital, to the archeologists there. I'm sure they would want it. I suppose it was kept in the library here as a curiosity."

"You take it to the authorities," said the old lady firmly, "and they ask a thousand questions and the police come in."

Captain Flores said, "Libraries keep everything. I know, I have been in several on occasions. The people who run them have a mania of books. They keep everything. I say nothing good of those anti-clericals. Had I been a man when they revolted, I should have fought them, but it is a good thing sometimes, I think, to have these old storehouses cleaned out. Like when I inspected an old arsenal at Puerto Valdez one time. Nobody had ever emptied it. There were still a number of Spanish flintlocks in the back, and even some guns with bell mouths. I had them melted down."

Jimmy nodded. The wine made a little glow in his stomach, but he was full of silence and he wanted to get away from there.

The old lady said firmly, "We should burn that book. It is heathen and it holds God knows what wickednesses. We must burn it entirely."

Octavia said "Yes." She rose, took a single step towards the boy, picked up the codex, and flipped it onto the hot coals of the stove. Their eyes followed it, so that they did not see the boy raise his hand and open his mouth in protest. Whatever he had intended, it had not been this, but he was still wordless, unable to think of a way out of his own net. Octavia fanned vigorously, the heavy paper smoked and twisted, then flame broke out. There was nothing to be done. She sat down again on the captain's knee, then altered her position to refill his little glass. He held it to her lips and she sipped from it.

The boy saw, through the back door, that the rain had stopped and sunlight came at a flat angle. It must be close to five. He should go and he wanted to, for a soaring sense of power was replacing his first distress over what had been done. Wishing that every detail should be pleasing to his father, he followed all the rules for saying goodbye, accepting *abrazos* from both the women and returning them, and hurrying nothing. It was not hard; he was excited and impatient, but he was fond of these people. He clasped the captain's hand warmly.

The air in the street was already cool. There was a chance

they'd be at the Flor de la Sierra, still hoping for a concert, so he headed that way, and in due course saw them. They had overcoats on. Their sitting thus, waiting for something they ought to know would not happen, seemed fitting, a summary of their destiny. He felt stronger than ever, so much stronger than either of them, or both of them. Then, to his astonishment, there was a blast of sound from the barracks gate and the infantry band came marching out, heading for the bandstand. People were moving onto the plaza and beginning to stroll.

They received him cheerfully, as they should not have, said that the bishop had asked after him, and hoped he had had a pleasant afternoon in spite of the rain. His mother said, "If you want to stay and listen to the band, you'd better go get your coat. It's turning chilly. Since this is our last night, we'll make it a celebration, even if there's nothing much to celebrate."

The professor said, "The bishop's wine has got to your mother, I think. Me, too. We're not in training for sipping so early in the day. Get your coat, and then come and have a glass of sherry."

The two people facing him were simply not the two with whom in his mind he had battled through the afternoon. This was his mother, the reality, whom he loved, and this was the professor, a good guy, taking defeat gamely. He knew the fun to be had with them when they were in their present mood. Feeling drawn to them both and all unsettled, he said, "I'll go get my coat."

He walked along rapidly, then almost at the door of the hotel stopped still, one foot ahead of the other, one hand slightly raised. He stayed frozen like that a moment, then brought his second foot up in line and lowered his hand. He could never tell his father what had happened; what he had caused to happen went far beyond anything his father would approve. He would never be able to tell anyone, and he would not be able to forget it. He was going to keep on carrying this around inside himself. He began to move very slowly, wondering how on earth he could go back and sit with them and face their affection.

JOURNEY IN REMEMBERING

THE LEGEND of Dr. Sibley — Professor Emeritus Sibley — had been impressed upon Elvira Stafford almost as soon as she had arrived at Talvert University to take over the new Chair of Nuclear American Studies. (Nuclear America, it must be explained, has nothing to do with fission or fusion, but denotes the region from Peru to Central Mexico within which the beginnings of aboriginal New World civilization occurred.) Elvira's impression was that Dr. Sibley must be very ancient indeed; that if he did not quite go back to the Toltecs or even the late Archaic, he must have joined the faculty at least about the time that it was debating whether Darwin's theory of evolution should be taught. All she had wanted was to have the cardboard box of peculiar, bright-colored potsherds, apparently from Nicaragua, taken to the old man's house, in the hope that he could tell something about them. Central America was not his field, but the cryptic card lying on top of the collection carried his initials. Bringing him to the Museum of Man, wheelchair and all, seemed an excess of effort for an uncertain return.

She did not express this thought bluntly, for the others concerned — Dr. Lancaster, chairman of the Division of American Archeology and officially her direct superior; Dr.

Bogue, director of the museum; and young Wally Caswell, who had unearthed the box in the course of straightening out the stuff in one of the old Middle American storages spaces — had sat under Dr. Sibley. They were all Talvert men, as were most of the anthropological faculty, and she was the first woman member of it — a new member entering something of a club, and doing so with a lot of rank for a newcomer, for a woman, for a scholar of her age. Lancaster and Bogue had sought her out, had been frankly glad to get her, but it would take time, she knew, before she would be truly accepted.

She said, "Isn't that an awful lot of trouble, bringing him over here?"

Arthur Bogue, removing his hand from the phone he had just set back in its stand, said, "He said he didn't recall the stuff from my description, but that if he could see it *in situ* it might jog his memory."

He looked faintly guilty. Elvira read him well enough; his old teacher saw an opportunity to revisit his museum, and who was Bogue, with all his honors, to say him nay? Then, to all of them the remark about seeing the material *in situ* was cogent. Charlie Lancaster, Wally, and Elvira Stafford herself were thorough archeologists, and the director, although his particular field was Polynesian ethnology, had wide-ranging interests and had done a fair bit of digging in his time. An archeologist has an ingrained feeling for the small, surrounding clues, the value of context, equal to that of any detective in the world.

She said, "I hope when he gets here he'll remember."

She had not intended to be disagreeable, and as soon as she spoke, wished the words back. Dr. Sibley's memory was famous, and here, it seemed, it had slipped.

Lancaster said, "I suppose it's a small item, but still — it's surprising that he didn't remember it at all." He turned to Caswell. "Wally, you took a seminar with him just before he got sick, didn't you? How was his memory then?"

"Just what I'd always heard." Caswell paused, a smile in his eyes and at the corners of his mouth; then, in a passable imitation of the old professor's voice as it had been before his illness, he said, "You'll find that point considered in Gudmund Hatt's *Moccasins and Their Relation to Arctic Footwear*, I believe Chapter 5, about page 143. Then you should look at Vladimir Ouchenskov's 'The Circumpolar Stone Age,' in *Institut Istorii Material'noy Kul'tury Akademia Nauk*, Volume III. There is a mimeographed translation of it in the boxed-pamphlet stacks, but you'll have to ask Miss Tenterden for it." He paused again, then added, "I tried to memorize that Russian citation, but I think I've left something out. He didn't."

It occurred to Elvira that the old man's lapse of memory might be assumed, to get himself brought to the museum. If so, she rather liked him for it, and she looked forward to seeing this phenomenon in the flesh.

For Dr. Sibley, the journey to the museum was an adventure mixed with humiliation. Age and illness are full of humiliations, and one of them is having solicitous, strong young men hold you up by both elbows when you are fairly sure that, on the level and down the one step from door to ground, up again from the ground to the big sedan that has been provided, you can make it alone. The wheelchair was folded and placed in back with him, the two undergraduates asked him twice if he was all right, which was one time too many, they got in the car, and they headed for the museum.

When Arthur called him up, he had been deep in medita-
tion on a possible correlation between the distribution of doli-
chocephalic people in eastern North America and the inci-
dence of certain single-shouldered stone points. He had
glimpsed a possibility interesting enough (if further consideration and comparison with the data on some recent excavations in coastal Alaska did not blow it up) to cause him to
stop writing and dive into his card files. A question about
Nicoya ware that was not Nicoya ware was jarringly irrelevant, and he really didn't remember. He would, he knew,
given time. Riding along, he smiled with the sense of a small
triumph in having brought about this unexpected visit to the
museum, his museum.

In the last little while since his illness — when you are
over seventy, time flies by with astounding speed, and he
thought of his illness as something that had happened only
the other day rather than more than a year ago — his
thoughts tended to ramble unless they had become centered
and were running well on a single subject. He had learned a
new alarm and a new pleasure in his initial inability to bring a
familiar matter to mind, the prolonged effort required sometimes to recall a key word or fact, followed by a rapidly ac-
celerating falling into place of item after item until he had
them all once more, clear and whole. He supposed he
should start summoning up Middle America now — Meso-
America, the new term — no, that reached only to Honduras;
Middle America . . . But he was diverted from concentration by the pleasure of being out of his house and, at that
point, coasting along between the buildings of the University.
The development of terminology, he thought: Middle Amer-

ica; Sapper, "Das Nördliche Mittel-Amerika;" 18—, 18—, he groped; ah! 1897; and now the more restrictive Meso-America and more inclusive Nuclear . . .

The University chapel was an unfortunate outburst of early-twentieth-century Gothic. When he was a freshman, he had admired it. One's tastes form, develop, change. A new wing was going up on Turner Hall in standard, sound Georgian. They drew up at the Museum of Man. It was honestly, Victorianly ugly, and he loved it.

Then came the business of getting him up the steps — awkward, disagreeable. Nice of Arthur and Charlie to have come out, and it would have been even nicer if they had dismissed the two undergraduates. Noting their easy strength, their pink skins, he assumed that they were athletes, and to such young men old helplessness is pitiable and disgusting. Then he was in the chair again, on the level, and greeting Erik, the janitor, who evidently was to push him.

Immediately inside the entrance were the doors leading to the library — Annie Tenterden's domain — and to the director's office, which had once been his, and beyond that was what he thought of as the "come-on." On one side was the replica of the Assyrian bas-reliefs; on the other, behind glass, a cross-section of earth, expounding the concept of stratification. The strata were something of a fiction — generalized North American; nor would the objects in them ever have been found, one below another, in a single site. At the top, partly buried, partly sticking up through the artificial grass, was a pop bottle. He had wanted to use a beer bottle, but he had set up the exhibit in the early thirties, when old man Stahlmann still ruled the roost, and he had been refused. Just under that, some broken china of an 1890 character, and so on, down to a rusted, broken sword, then a piece of incised Indian pottery leading into the prehistoric. That question of a beer bottle had been only an incident in the battle to get the whole thing set up at all, for Stahlmann disliked popularization, and felt that the arrangement was fraudulent. The stiffest fight had been over carrying the strata through the glacial stages to the beginning of the Mankato, for Stahlmann went right along with Hrdlicka in rejecting the idea that early man would ever be found in America. As they passed the exhibit, the old man looked with satisfaction at the casts of Folsom flints and bones of the extinct *Bison taylorii* near the bottom, and the cast of one side of the skull of Midland Man. One day, he thought, they'll have to do the exhibit over, reducing the scale in order to go down yet further, yet further back in time. *They* would have to — he would not have a hand in it. The thought caused him a rather literary, not unpleasing moment of sadness.

The Midland Skull brought his mind back, as he was wheeled into the elevator, to the clear, well-worn path of his present study and the topic on which he had been meditating since late yesterday. Midland Man was too early to fit his hoped-for correlation, but he — or she, rather — was long-headed. The Russians were doing a lot of work in eastern Siberia now, and they might have highly pertinent material. As he was rolled out of the elevator, he was thinking how stupid it was that simple correspondence with Russian archeologists had become all but impossible.

Thus he was momentarily surprised and confused to find himself in the Middle American Hall. Of course; he was here to see if he could identify some pottery that must have come in long ago and never been properly entered — back before the war, the first one, when there were so few anthropologists, in that rather frantic, wonderful time when they had expanded into what had been the biology museum, when everyone worked at everything and it seemed as if they would never catch up. He had always been aware that there remained odd caches of objects that had never been properly attended to — minor items, here and there, waiting for someone's leisure.

They went through an inconspicuous door into the storage and laboratory area — a long room with many shelves, cupboards, and boxes, a sink, and long tables on which different kinds of objects were set out for sorting, cataloguing, repairing, or photographing. His own center of work on specimens had been on the floor above, with less showy articles, but the character of the place, the effect of confusion in what was, for those who worked there, order and reason, gave him a pang of nostalgia.

He recognized young Caswell, and thought that he must be about due for his Ph.D. The woman, he supposed, was the new professor. Arthur had conferred with him before inviting her to Talvert. Arthur said, "Dr. Stafford," and Sibley took her hand. She was feminine, and not unattractive, he was glad to see; he had feared the striding, mannish type. She had done a very scholarly memoir, whch Arthur had called to his attention.

"I hope you like it here at Talvert," he said. "Are you going on with the distribution of the Uto-Aztecans? Your preliminary study was provocative."

She looked pleased. "I am, but I don't know that I'm

getting anywhere. Most of my correlations don't correlate."

"I know what you mean. The old people are so hanged uncooperative."

Wally brought what looked like the bottom half of a typewriter-paper box. Arthur said, "We thought you might know something about this, Dr. Sib."

Wally set it on Sibley's knees.

In it were nine large, polychrome sherds and a number of small fragments. The backgrounds were a rather cold off-white on which designs had been applied in bright blue, a dull red, black, and several tones of yellow brown. Gay, Sibley thought, but not handsome. On top of the lot lay a dusty five-by-three card; in addition to being darkened by the fine dust, the material itself had begun to discolor.

Dr. Stafford said, "Wally thought it was queer, and so do Charlie and I. It looks like Nicoya ware, but there's something wrong with it. Here's where it was."

She pointed to a shelf in an open cabinet. On it, and on the shelves above and below, were similar pieces, including some pots that had been restored — similar yet not the same, of another quality and, on the whole, much finer, stronger design.

Arthur said, "Those are your initials on the card, aren't they?"

He picked up the card with a hand that, he was pleased to note, trembled only slightly. It read, "Lopesianus, Phase IV, Dono Prestoni, 1915." Then, on another line, over to the left, "See MS." with a following blank space that called for a title, and below that, to the right, "W.F.S." Those were his initials, all right. How young, to note a reference to a manuscript not yet titled, perhaps never written! In confidence and enthusiasm once he had done a few things like that, and sometimes been tripped up by them. The swarming, innumerable projects of youth.

It was his writing, his young adult writing, larger, more open than his later hand, not yet completely defined. The sight of it caused him an experience he had been through before. Ordinarily, he thought of his life, himself in his life, as one continuity only partially distorted these last years by physical weakening. An encounter such as this with a positive evocation of the early Walter Sibley denied that continuity. He had been that young man, but that young man was not now he, knew nothing of him, although his present self, sprung from the other, remembered him totally. The early Sibley rose clear before him, unafraid, somewhat intolerant, happily assaulting the fortresses of discovery. Before that young man his present self was humbled with apology that could never be conveyed, for what he had not achieved, for what he had become, for what he had not become.

He made his thoughts turn to the meaning of the writing before him. Who or what the devil was "Lopesianus," and who was Preston? Nineteen fifteen, when he still played romantically with tags of Latin, a carryover from a yet earlier, inky schoolboy with ambitions to be a medievalist. Froissart — He shook his head with a jerk. He must get back into Middle America; get back into those days. He had developed it first in the hospital; the technique of dredging some one, key thing up clear in memory, around which, he found, other things crystallized, the blurring rolled back, and there came the intense relief of recollection.

Nineteen fifteen — the year of expanding into the other half of the building, everyone doubling in brass, and he, be-

ing at about Wally's stage, had given the course on Mexican archeology. That was a bit removed from Nicaragua,
but it would make a starting point. The key was the flint knife,
the obsidian knife. He had said, teaching that course, "The
key, gentlemen, to the character of the ancient Mexicans."
What was the day name "flint knife"? How could one forget
that, having once known it? Like forgetting the name of —
of — the Aztec they named a beer after — Cuahtemoc —
Cuauhtli, eagle; *Calli*, house; *Olin*, earthquake; *Tochtli*, rabbit;
the drunken rabbits, *Centzon Tochtli* — hold it, don't wander, the day of the knife — *Tecpatl!*

There it was, *Tecpatl*. The flint knife, and the mystic qualities of flint carried over to obsidian. From the sky, the male
element, the obsidian knife, came down and fertilized the female earth. Yes. The flint strikes sparks — He was enjoying
himself, recapturing a sequence of reflections that so long
ago he had found intriguing and promising and then never
completed. The flint is the point of the projectile — the
javelin, the later arrow, which were man's lightning, and the
tongue of the phallic snake darts lightning, as anyone can see.
Lightning brings rain; it strikes the earth; so the snake, *Coatl*,
and the knife, *Tecpatl*, come together, are of the sky, are
male, are fertility, are life; and at the same time, quite obviously, both are death. It went from the flint to obsidian,
and would probably have gone on to metal. But did not the
old European knights think of their swords as feminine? It
would be interesting to look it up. *Epée* is feminine but
glaive is masculine and *Schwert* is neuter. *Gladius*. In the
war, the first one, he seemed to remember that the French referred to the bayonet as *la vierge*. Suddenly, with delight, he

thought of the line, *He hath loosed the fateful lightning of His terrible swift sword*. Perfect!

Charlie was saying something about "troubling you unnecessarily." With a start he recalled the box, heavy enough on his knees. He had let his thoughts wander unconscionably. He had tried all their patiences. Thank goodness they could not know just how far that wandering had gone. Senility. He would remember. In fact, it was now urgently necessary that he remember, but he could see that they were ready for him to go. It was as if something had happened of which he was unaware, but he supposed it was simply his long musing. Best cut it off clean.

He said, "I'm sorry, I still don't seem to connect. Perhaps I'll get it later."

Wally took the box from him. There were politenesses, apologies, embarrassment; more embarrassment, it seemed to him, than the occasion justified. Erik pushed the chair. All the way home he experienced a disagreeable sensation, as though physically the various parts of his body were adrift from one another and his center, his ego, vague and diluted.

He was glad to be settled in his study again. He asked his housekeeper to bring him tea . . . No, nothing to eat, too near lunchtime; just tea. Lopesianus, 1915 — his initials, right enough. Everyone turned his hand to everything in those days, and in the time of expansion there had been a wonderful broadening in having to classify, handle, arrange objects from almost anywhere. He had been lured then by Middle America — the idea of travelling through wildernesses with pack trains, the striking, imagination-stirring ruins waiting above-ground to be stumbled upon, the unbelievably rich loot — and he had made one trip to Honduras.

He half smiled, his eyes looking into space, himself transported back to that time. He felt the freshness of youth again, the physical ease, the mental eagerness, the courage of one as yet unaware of the infinity of knowledge, the thrill of having learned even a little. Horseback in Honduras, learning to use a machete; then he remembered travelling in Ohio in a buggy — a *buggy*, good Lord. By various travels, campfires, haphazard lodgings he came, in the end, back to the museum and the work there in those early days.

That Costa Rican and Nicaraguan stuff — He felt again the sheer aesthetic delight when he had begun taking it out of the storage shelves in the basement and cleaning it. He had not been at all afraid to take on its installation in the new hall, although he had read on the region only enough to cover himself in case there'd be a question in his Ph.D. exams, which there wasn't. That was years before Burrill's big *Pottery of Southern Central America* came out, and he had worked from McCurdy, Squier, Pector, and Sapper, the old originals. It had been as good, as exciting, as an original research project, with Stalhmann and Macmillan coming round to check on him from time to time. He would never forget when Lucas came over from Harvard, the man who really knew, and approved of his work. He could still feel the nervousness while he waited, then the flush of pleasure.

Lucas had been particularly impressed by his having sorted out the López material and set it aside, and had given him the first dope on the man. Burrill published on him in — hmm — Appendix III. Dr. Sibley straightened in his chair and made a series of notes.

* * *

After that shocking exhibition, Elvira tactfully removed herself from the presence of the others without delay. How dreadful for Arthur and Charlie, she thought, settling herself in the armchair in her office. Back in the laboratory, Wally fiddled unhappily with the pieces of an inlaid wooden *atlatl* from Soconusco. The two older men separated without speaking, each going to his own office. Perhaps half an hour later, Lancaster came into Bogue's room.

"I have to unload," he said as he sat down, "and you're the obvious victim."

"I know. My God — the 'Battle Hymn of the Republic'!"

"Of all things. 'He hath loosed the fateful lightning' — O-o-h!" He clutched his head. "And in front of Elvira."

Lancaster said, after a pause, "I understood that he has hardening of the arteries and general debility, but do you suppose he's had a brain hemorrhage? Or would that — " He broke off as the telephone rang.

Bogue picked it up. Shortly afterward he said, "Yes, sir," and then, "Just a minute while I get a pencil." He had pencil and pad immediately before him. He covered the mouthpiece with his hand and said, "It's old Sib." Into the phone he said, "Go ahead, sir." He wrote, said "Yes" at intervals, then, "Appendix III?" A little later he said, "Second drawer from the bottom." He listened again for some time, then said, "I'll tell him. Many thanks. Goodbye." He hung up smiling.

"He says a Maya man like you should have been able to figure it out. Knowing that the *Codex Peresianus* was named for a Pérez, the *Cortesianus* for a Cortez, you should have seen López in *Lopesianus*, and in that case, in the context of

Nicaragua, you should have looked in the index of Burrill's *Pottery of Southern Central America*."

"Good Lord!" said Lancaster, and gave a short laugh. " 'Elementary, my dear Watson.' Eh?"

"Apparently, allowing him time. He says that in Appendix III Burrill deals at some length with the López frauds. Those sherds were brought in by an alumnus named Preston when he was installing the Nicoya collection in '15. They looked funny to Sib, just as they did to the rest of you. Then Lucas from Harvard — Lord, it sounds like ancient history! — identified them. Dr. Sib made something of a study of López and his works; seems he was quite an operator — planted sherds to be dug up so as to authenticate his whole pots — and Sib wrote a paper on him, 'The López Frauds of Nicaragua,' but didn't try to publish it because López was politically powerful and could have made trouble for archeologists. It's in with some other manuscripts — notes and such, by various people — in the second drawer from the bottom of the left-hand column of that bank of wooden files behind Annie's desk."

Lancaster said, "Thank God!" Then his face clouded. "If Annie hasn't thrown it out by now. Of course, the Burrill treatment is probably sufficient."

"Annie Tenterden throw out a scrap of paper that the old boys, the old gods, had written on? Sooner would a Moslem throw out the name of Allah." He picked up the phone. "I'll ring her and make sure."

"Then we'll tell Elvira."

Bogue nodded with slow emphasis. "Then we'll tell Elvira."

THE ANCIENT STRENGTH

THE BIG Pueblo Indian dances — the "line dances," with many dancers in formation, a chorus of men's voices, and a powerful, big drum, or sometimes two — have a quality of surge and ebb that fills the whole village and slowly takes possession of you if you will give it time and yield yourself to it. You don't even have to pay attention all the time, any more than the Indians do. Like them, you meet friends, talk a little, you eat at this house and that, you stand or sit to watch the dance again — nothing too much — and let the ceremony surround you and fill you.

It was while this was happening in the heat and dust at San Leandro, and I was sitting in the shade on the low adobe bench that runs along the foot of the wall of my friend Juan Rael's house, and a corner of my mind was considering the captive eagles on the housetops, and the sense of antiquity colored all my thinking, that I seriously thought for the first time that my mission might really be blocked by the very nature of these Indians, and I had a new understanding of why old Sorenson, who knows the Pueblos better than anyone else now living, had told me that if I wanted to dig in the San Leandro rubbish heap I should be sure I completed negotiations for permission before the people got involved in the big July ceremony, commonly and erroneously called the Eagle Home Dance, the one I was now absorbing.

What I was up to requires some explaining. San Leandro is a Piro-speaking pueblo on the Rio Grande, not far from Santa Fe, New Mexico, that has been right where it is since at least Coronado's time. Some years ago, it filed a claim against the United States under the Indian Claims Act, for which purpose it is represented by a firm of attorneys. The claim is opposed by the Department of Justice. The evidence on both sides in Indian claims cases may involve history, ethnology, and archeology. Both sides commission all sorts of research, some of which has resulted in data of anthropological importance. It was in such a connection that I came in on the San Leandro case. Archeological evidence was needed to support the pueblo's claim, and the lawyers thought that perhaps I would be able to find it. Pueblo-Anasazi archeology is my field — my name, by the way, is Hendricks, and I am an assistant professor in the anthropology department at the University of Northern California. I have worked in Pueblo country for more than a dozen seasons, mostly in the Tewa and Piro sections. I was, I suppose, as well qualified as anyone for what they wanted, and I would be in the neighborhood anyhow, digging in the Rio Azulito site, the ruin of an ancient pueblo ten miles away.

The tribe was asking compensation for the loss of some twenty thousand acres of good grazing land south of its grant. It claimed that it had occupied and used this tract, commonly known as El Cajón, continuously and notoriously since time immemorial and, in historic times, with the knowledge and at least the tacit consent of the Spanish crown, the Mexican Republic, and then the United States. In the turmoil of the Confederate invasion of New Mexico in 1862 and the increased Apache and Navajo raiding that followed, a group of white men had wrongfully and by force seized El Cajón and converted it to their use. The land has a perennial stream on it, fed by three springs, and even today, when conditions are drier than they were a century ago, supports some four hundred head of cattle without overgrazing.

I'm no lawyer, but I agreed with the pueblo's lawyers that it looked as if El Cajón really had belonged to the pueblo by right of aboriginal use and occupancy, in which case the U.S. failed in its duty to protect the Indians and they had compensation coming to them. The lawyers thought it might run to as much as a hundred thousand dollars. Proof that would stand up in court, however, was not as strong as it ought to be. It was possible that I, by archeological means, could provide the additional quantum that would win the case.

A short distance downstream from the largest of the El Cajón springs are the ruins of a settlement of five houses, and near them you can see where some fields were dry-farmed. The San Leandros state that the houses were used as summer lodgings by members of the pueblo who worked that land up to the time of the Civil War, and also served as shelters for shepherds. A field study group from the museum in Santa Fe had worked there one season a few years ago. Their findings confirmed that it was probably an Indian rather than a Spanish-American settlement, that it had been occupied or visited in the mid-nineteenth century, and that sheep had been penned nearby over a long period of time. The crucial period for our case was after 1846, for Uncle Sam could not be held responsible for land lost under Mexican or

Spanish sovereignty. We needed to prove that it was definitely San Leandro Indians, and not people from any one of several neighboring pueblos, who had lived in those houses, and that they were living there up to the period of the Civil War.

Pieces of Indian pottery had been found, but they were Picuris and Tewa wares that were being widely traded in the mid-nineteenth century. Anybody could have had them. There were also some pieces of a curious pottery, marked by delicate floral designs in black on white, that did not connect with anything known but was plainly of Indian manufacture. Chemical analysis showed that the clay was a compound of earths from sources still used by several pueblos, including San Leandro. These shards, the remains of not more than three smallish bowls, could be diagnostic and conclusive.

The lawyers found several old men and women who stated that the shards were indeed from a type of pottery made in San Leandro by their own grandmothers, and that there used to be examples of it around in their time. Unfortunately, Barnes, the director of the museum's dig (and the Department of Justice boys will make the most of his testimony, don't worry), stated that at the time that he unearthed those shards he showed them to San Leandro Indians and drew nothing but blank looks. The point could be made that when Barnes questioned the Indians, neither he nor they had any axe to grind, whereas later the San Leandros had a strong reason to claim the pottery.

The thing was more pro-and-connish than that. I looked Barnes up as soon as I got to Santa Fe. He's a good man, with a sound field technique. His scratching around that little settlement had been a hasty thing, although there was no question about the finding of the shards, and he had had no time to make careful inquiries about them. He had simply shown them to Indians from various pueblos when opportunity offered, then shoved them into a tray, to be dealt with at some future time. He and I had a drink together after his office hours. Over the drink, he remarked that the government's failure to protect the Indians' use of El Cajón was due to the confusion caused by the Confederate, or Texan, invasion. The Department of Justice ought to concede the point, he said, and the pueblo should accept compensation in Confederate money. I passed this suggestion on to one of the lawyers when he was out here. He did not think it funny.

Obviously, what was needed was archeological evidence that the floral pottery was a San Leandro ware of the crucial period. The place to look for that was in the San Leandro trash heap, which brings me to the matter of trash heaps in general and San Leandro's in particular.

Ever since the days of the Anasazi cliff dwellers — nay, before that, back into the Basket Maker II period at least, two thousand years ago — the ancestors of the present Indians were in the habit of throwing their trash out of their settlements, preferably where there was a drop. (I know, the Basket Makers were longheaded and the Pueblos are brachy, but let's not get into labile cephalic indexes, the dolicho remains at Pecos, and all that; it's too complicated.) We do not know when they adopted the present Pueblo custom of an annual village cleaning, but it was probably long ago, and we know that the Indians have been doing it for hundreds of years. San Leandro's trash heap is typical. The village lies on an old alluvial terrace of the Rio Grande that falls off sharply to the east and north. The annual dumping takes place over the terrace's northern edge; through the centuries, this has created a sort of talus slope that should make very juicy digging. There, below the level of bottles and broken phonograph records, and the red-on-black pottery now made at San Leandro, mostly for sale, one might find the floral black-on-white.

One might, if one could get permission to dig there. It was thoughtful of the Old People to dump their rubbish once each year in the same place, for thereby they have provided archeologists with quite beautiful and exact stratifications. (For example, if the floral ware was what we hoped, it would turn up in association with American-made articles of various kinds, and that would be sufficient.) It was not thoughtful, however, of the Old People to provide their descendants with a set of religious beliefs that makes it extremely difficult — in many cases, impossible — to get permission to dig in their rubbish. You run into remarks about Dust Boy (whoever he is), references to the spirit of the past, and vague remarks about ancestors, and what you are likely to get in the end is a rather convoluted negative answer.

Yet, when they approached me, the lawyers seemed to think I would have little trouble getting permission. They had already met several times over the past year with the tribal council to go over the ins and outs of the case. The Indians understood that evidence from the trash heap could be crucial, the lawyers said, and were ready to talk with me. I had been working around San Leandro for several seasons and had used some San Leandro workmen. Several members of the council knew me, or had heard of me, and they would be prepared for my coming. I would be preceded by a lengthy letter from the lawyers, introducing me and setting forth, once more, the reasons evidence from the trash heap was essential. I was offered forty dollars a day for time spent in actual work, including a few days, if needed, for negotiations. Then, if the results justified it, I would be in line for what looked to an assistant professor like a very nice sum indeed for appearing as an expert witness.

When the offer was made to me, I went to old Sorenson, who, as I have said, knows the Pueblos better than any of us, and asked his advice. He said, "It can't do any harm. You know those people well enough to know you can't push them; all you can do is ask nicely and hope. Anyone in the academic line who doesn't pick up a little extra money when he can do so properly and legitimately should have his head examined."

I said, "I'm going on with my work at Rio Azulito, which is only ten miles away. If they'll give me permission, I can bring a couple of good students, and if we go in from the bottom I trust we can get into some older stuff while we're at it. It would be nice to get some contact material." (Contact material means from when the Spanish were first settling in.)

"You'll have to feel your way. Two helpers might look too big to them, but take your opportunities as they come, just so you don't get the Indians angry and foul things up for others."

I answered politely, but not without betraying some annoyance. "I hope I'm not utterly irresponsible."

Sorenson laughed. "One can't take anything for granted. But one thing — get out there as early as you can, right after exams end, and try to get permission firmly granted and work started before that July wingding of theirs comes up, the ceremony that ends with the Eagles Return Rite."

"The Eagle Home Dance?   When they sacrifice eagles at the end?"

"Yes. Only you know that's a thoroughly incorrect name. You'll hear some of them speak of it as the Pueblo Houses Dance. That's still not the real name, I'm quite sure, but it's suggestive. Considering that the principal chief or head priest of a Hopi pueblo is called Houses Chief, and that you have the idea of corporate power, which is created or amassed . . ." He was talking to himself at that point. I listened, trying to follow his thoughts; then the big bell rang for the first afternoon class and I had to hurry off.

I wasn't able to follow Sorenson's advice. One overcomes the obstacles one thinks are important, and I didn't know enough, and he didn't explain enough, for me to think I should take what he said seriously. The main thing I had gone to him for, after all, was his approval of my having a try at the work, and with that in hand I forgot much of the rest. Then, that year I had only one experienced man and three new undergraduates, one of whom had had one field season. On top of that, the Rio Azulito site is on private land, the ranch of a Spanish-American named Robles, and Mr. Robles had got it into his head, for the second time, that we were going to extract a fortune from the ruin. That meant that when we got there he was all braced to demand a new contract, with an enormous fee, and after that was smoothed over he, or members of his family, were always hanging around watching to see what we took out of the ground. They got in the way, and I was worried that they'd fall into a trench and mess up the strata, or be seized by an urge to dig themselves, or something like that. Give me a site on Indian or federal land any day, where everyone understands the rules and you have a binding permit.

Under the circumstances, I did not feel too free about leaving the site. I finally made it to San Leandro on a Sunday morning at the end of June, to find that the governor — the official head of the tribe — was away. The lieutenant governor was in the room they keep for an office, with a sign over the door that says "GOVERNOR" in large letters and under that, smaller, "GET PHOTO PERMITS HERE." San Leandro is what you might call a progressive-traditional tribe. The people keep up their ceremonies and other ancient practices with vigor, and at the same time they have TV, piped water, and things like that. They have a conscious program for hanging on to the old, Indian values while adapting to the modern world; it will be a neat trick if they can make it work. Part of the plan is to select each year's governor from among the older men, the lieutenant governor from among the younger ones — preferably a veteran — and let the two generations learn from each other. This year's lieutenant governor was Juan Rael, a Navy veteran. He had worked for me on Tsepo Ruin three years before, and he had read the lawyers' letter about me.

Juan was cordial. He explained the governor's absence and told me, somewhat apologetically, that the council had not formally discussed my business. It would require a regular council meeting, he said. Now that so many of the San Leandros were working away from home for wages, there was sometimes trouble getting a full council together. He said that one man, Anastacio Pérez, was in Denver, remarking, "He's kind of on the young side, but he has his specialty, you might say, so there are things you can't settle unless he's here."

I thought it worth taking time to strengthen my relationship with this man and to indoctrinate him as well as I could. He had made it clear that he considered the claim important, and he described the pueblo's plans for using the money — scholarships for young people going to college, a revolving system for purchasing registered bulls and renting them to tribal cattlemen, things like that. Twice while we were talking, tourists came in for permits to take pictures. Then another youngish Indian, named Eddie Ortiz, turned up. He wore an Indian Service police badge on his shirt, and Juan explained that he was the sheriff. They talked together briefly in Piro, then Juan said to me, "Suppose you show me where you want to dig. Eddie'll tend store for a while and we can have dinner."

We walked to the edge of the village and I showed him the place that looked best to me. It was simply a question of where the grade looked good and the trash was thick. He thought for a time, then he said, "Yeah. That ought to be all right. Here or this way" — he gestured to the east. "Not that way" — he moved his hand west. "There's something underneath over there; they won't want you to go near it."

I said, "Fine," looking down the slope. There was a twinkle of broken glass here and there over the surface, fragments of glazed, mass-produced ceramics, and tin cans, all more abundant toward the top. I saw a brass cartridge case, farther down the half-buried remnant of an old shoe, and near my feet a phonograph record and a plastic hairbrush without bristles. Over to the left, where I was to stay away, I saw the main parts of the transmission of a car. It was hard to believe that not far under such drab, familiar leavings were the evidences of antiquity.

Juan renewed his invitation to dinner and I accepted. It was noon, I was hungry, and Pueblo food is good. We started back. On the way, we passed the square kiva, a big, high-looming windowless ceremonial building. Most people don't look above eye level unless something attracts their interest, and I guess archeologists are even more inclined than most to watch the ground. It was looking at the high wall of the kiva that led my eye to where a young eagle was perched, tethered, on the edge of the roof of a two-story house. The bird looked ruffled and untamed.

I said, nodding my head toward the eagle, "I haven't seen that since I was in the Hopi country."

Juan said, "Yeah. Other pueblos used to keep them, but they've forgotten."

Asking anything about Pueblo ceremonies is tricky business, but, remembering Sorenson, I let curiosity out so far as to ask, "You need them for the dance you people put on next month? Like at the end of that dance the Hopis have about then?"

"Something like that. You seen that Hopi dance?"

"Yes. It — it had power."

The Hopis dance publicly in the masks that all the Rio Grande Pueblos keep secret. Sometimes you can talk about it, sometimes not.

Juan said, "It's a rainmaker. Hope we make rain." Then he led the talk to harmless topics.

Altogether, I counted six eagles on housetops. They are revered by the Indians, but to a white man they are simply wild creatures made captive, and it rather relieved me to think that in less than a month the birds would be sacrificed and so set free. You would not want one of these creatures to be kept tethered for very long. While my eyes were still directed upward, I saw in the west the rounded, dark green peak of Chompi Mountain, from which most of the eagles had come, and I wondered if they ever looked toward it.

The last thing Juan said to me before I left that day was to be sure and return the following Sunday, the first in July, which I did. The governor, who spoke pretty good English, was there and prepared for me. He was most friendly. He told me to come back for a full council meeting Wednesday morning. I wanted to put it over until Sunday, so as not to interfere with my work at Rio Azulito, but he said that would not do. "Everybody's comin' in now for the work we do around this time. Everybody be here by Wednesday. Couple days later, some of 'em too busy with that work." (The word "work" in such a context means ceremonial. Once they have a ceremony in hand, everything else has to give way.)

I had never before attended a tribal council. In the case of San Leandro, I would be encountering the ages-old theocracy, for which the lay officials are a front. I was curious and a trifle excited, and more than ordinarily aware of impressions, as I entered the village Wednesday morning and came into the large rectangular plaza, entering at the northwest corner, by the Catholic church, which, with its two low towers, rises a little above the other buildings. The plaza is an expanse of hard-trampled, clayey earth, dusty in dry weather, with nothing growing in it but one splendid cottonwood near the middle of the south side. The flat-roofed houses — some one story, some two stories high, some with porches — form a nearly solid enclosure. The native adobe is a warm brown with a slight sparkle to it, and under the porches — in New Mexico they are called by the Spanish name, *"portales"* — the walls are usually whitewashed. There is variation in the size of the houses, in the arrangement of doors, and in the windows, which range from tiny prehistoric apertures to modern metal casements. The whole, though uniformly composed of rectangles, is not at all monotonous. Adobe weathers into softness and the Indians build largely by eye, so that angles are not quite true and the most regular construction achieves naturally the irregularity that the Greeks used to plan for.

In front of the houses and close to them there are altogether eight *hornos*, the beehive-shaped ovens, standing about four feet high, that the Spanish introduced. They are the only curved surfaces; there are no arches. One of the much touted charms of adobe is how it takes sunlight and shadow, the sunlight absorbed and softened, the shadow luminous. The play of light and shadow around a plaza such as this is its principal beauty. On the *hornos*, the light blending into shade over the curves is a delicate and wonderful thing.

An Indian plaza is bare, harmonious, and snug. On an off afternoon such as that Wednesday, there will be some children playing in it, a few mongrels taking the sun, and in front of one or two houses pottery and other wares, usually tended by a girl, set out in the hope of tourists. Even with the chil-

dren and dogs, the village seems empty. Tourists are disappointed not to see Indians in costume all over the place. On
ordinary days, the men are busy in the fields — unless they
are in the kiva working up a ceremony — and the women
are at their housework or pottery-making. There's no reason
why anybody should be around, and when you come to think
of it, how is it that even in quite small non-Indian settlements so many people seem to have business on the streets?
What keeps them going to and fro? Hanged if I know.

   I said that a Pueblo plaza is snug. You could also say contained, almost fortified. When you work in the ruins the Old
People left, you keep trying to project yourself, and one of
the things you feel is this enclosed, self-contained quality,
whether it's in a cliff dwelling jammed onto a high ledge of
rock in the Navajo country or a little, open site near the Rio
Grande. The same thing is present in the pueblos of today,
and it goes back at least to Basket Maker III, a dozen centuries or so ago; we don't know how they placed their dwellings before that. The houses and the people, few or many,
stand close together, and perhaps that's why they are still
here after a couple of thousand years of droughts and crop
failures, of Navajos, Apaches, Comanches, Utes, and the white
man.

   Juan met me and led me to a building on what you could
call a back street, obviously a structure of some age, containing a large, bare room. There were somewhat more
than twenty men, most of them elderly, sitting along the
walls, some on a *banco*, an adobe bench built out from the
long back wall, the others on an assortment of chairs. I was
given a comfortable chair placed near the door, facing the
assemblage. At a plain table in the middle of the room sat the

secretary, a youngish man, and there Juan joined him. As it turned out, Juan was the interpreter, and the secretary took copious notes on a lined pad. The governor was inconspicuous in a corner. Most of the men wore their hair long, done in a *chongo*, a queue wrapped in a narrow red strip of native weave. There was a good deal of jewelry in evidence — turquoise or Navajo-silver earrings, necklaces of shell, turquoise, coral, or silver, and rings and bracelets. Several men wore moccasins. The rest of their costume consisted of ordinary work clothes, except in the case of one man — whom I took to be the man from Denver — in a business suit and bow tie, and the secretary, who wore lightweight slacks and a T shirt. Their expressions were friendly. The governor spoke a polite greeting in Piro and stated that all the proper people were here and ready to hear what I had to say. Juan interpreted, and added, after explaining that he was speaking on his own, that they all knew I wanted to do something to help them.

This group had met numerous times with its attorneys, the question of the El Cajón site had been fully discussed, and my mission had been set forth in a lengthy letter. With these people, however, you don't count on any of that. You begin at the beginning and tell it all. I don't know whether they require that procedure just because they like to hear familiar tales, or as a way of having a chance to think about a matter over again, or from a canny desire to see whether everyone tells the same story, but, in any case, you review the whole question.

I would say a few sentences, then wait to be interpreted. I was brief about the claim in general, but skipped no details on the potsherds and the conflicting evidence, and presented a full, careful statement of what stratigraphy can show and how something turned up in the rubbish could be tied to something more than ten miles away. While the interpretation went on, I planned what to say next and looked around. Once you adjust yourself to it, talking through an interpreter becomes a restful mode of operation. After a few minutes, I hardly noticed the jewelry or other exotic trimmings as the dark faces of the councilmen seemed to emerge and ceased to be the faces of Indians, of another race, and became the faces of individuals, some of them wonderfully lined, all of them full of character. These were men of authority, whose minds were stored with ancient knowledge, and they were healthy outdoor men, men of their hands — farmers, stockmen, and, in season, hunters. Physical condition, age, and knowledge joined to make their faces most impressive.

When I was through, a very old man spoke in Piro. Juan made no effort to translate but sat half turned, listening. Another man spoke. They did not seem to be speaking to anyone but to be thinking aloud and letting their thoughts fall into the room. It was quiet talk and I could tell nothing from it. I listened and looked at the faces, and dreamed away the modern clothing and wondered how many centuries back the ancestors of these characters were meeting in similar councils. Piro is a language of the Tanoan subfamily. How old was it? Had these same sounds once filled council rooms — kivas, mostly — at Pueblo Bonito, at Spruce Tree House, at Chetro Ketl?

Perhaps half a dozen of them had expressed an opinion when a medium-old man with a strong, broad face and a square jaw spoke at some length. When he finished, people all over the room made a humming sound that means assent. He spoke again, directly to Juan.

Juan said, "That's Crescencio Rael." (I estimate that over half of the San Leandros are either "Rael" or "Pérez." Having the same last name does not seem to mean relationship.) Juan went on, "He's high up in what we're getting ready for now, what they call Eagle Home Dance, and he's one of the *principales.* He says this is a hard thing you have brought up. We want to win our claim, and now, the way you tell it, I think we all understand about digging for those potteries. Only it ain't easy to say you can dig in there. It's kinda hard for me to tell it so you'll understand, what these old men been talking about just now. It's the old times, you might say, that are in the rubbish heap. Not the big things, like this dance we're bringing out next week, but — well, like the pottery. One time they made that kind for a while, right here in this pueblo, then they quit. So it's in the dirt there, along with what they used to eat, and, like the stuff they used to weave in old times, and all like that. It's part of what we're made of, and it's what the old-time people, the ones that are gone now, they used to know. What was familiar to them."

I have discussed Juan's words with several Pueblo ethnographers, who found them interesting. Note that he did not say anything about the Old People coming back or ancestral spirits hovering around. In fact, he did a nice job of getting an idea across without giving away any beliefs.

Juan said a few words to Crescencio, who answered in a few sentences.

"Right now," Juan said, "they are thinking about this

dance. That's what's in their minds, and this ain't no time for deciding what you're asking for. They say, let it go over until we're through with that work."

Crescencio added something more. I decided that he could follow English pretty well.

Juan said, "We're sorry to make you wait. We all know you came to help us. And he says, you come to the dance next week. You will see something good. Come and eat dinner at my house, and you can bring those boys you got working with you. Like at fiesta, we got plenty grub."

I could only accept the postponement. I tried to get a firm date for another meeting, but was put off. Then I got up and so did everybody else. Many of them, including Crescencio Rael, came up to shake hands with me, or touch hands — they do not actually shake. They said pleasant, noncommittal things, the older men in Spanish.

My attitude toward this job had originally been somewhat casual, but it had changed. The possible money would be very nice to have, and, beyond that, I was affected by the tendency in all of us to become partisan. I liked these Indians, the material the lawyers had sent me had convinced me that their cause was just, and I really wanted to see them win. In addition, there was the possibility of turning up scientifically valuable material, the desire to be one of the very few who had ever poked into the rubbish heap of an occupied pueblo. I imagined the tribe grateful to me, accepting me as a special friend, if I turned the trick. The postponement disturbed me more than I had expected, and I was worried enough to wonder if, in the end, old beliefs would make them refuse me permission. Until then, I had had little apprehension.

The dance was on Sunday week. As I understand it, this is one of the most purely Indian ceremonies that a white man can get to see among the Rio Grande Pueblos. O'Neil, a Pueblo ethnographer with whom I discussed it later, has a theory that the public part is an unmasked version of an older, masked ceremony. Yet it is held on a Sunday — one of those recent adaptations to their changing world that are a sign of the strength and viability of Pueblo culture. Wage work away from home has become important, and for the benefit of the wage workers they hold their affairs as much as possible on weekends. I had told Juan I'd plan on coming, and he had said, "All right. You stay and watch it all along, and maybe you'll understand better why these old men are having trouble making up their minds to let you dig."

The dance was performed by two teams of at least eighty men and women each, one the people of the Turquoise moiety, the other of the Calabash moiety. Each team was accompanied by a chorus with two drummers and about twenty male singers. Their performances alternated throughout the day. Juan was not in the dance, whether because his civil office required him to be on hand for secular matters (but no photographing was allowed that day) or because he did not belong to the right society I did not know. There were all sorts of visitors dropping in at his house, and for at least two hours his wife and several other women were busy serving table after table of guests with good, hearty food — mutton stew, chili, the bread pudding called *sopa*, and the necessary quantities of weak coffee and Kool-Aid. On the table was a large plate that was kept always piled high with bread baked in the *hornos* I've described. It is European peasant bread, the pure tradition out of Spain, and it's hard to find better bread anywhere these days. Everything was as clean as you could ask for. My boys got a big poke out of it and ate very well indeed. They got a lot out of the dance, too, having enough background to approach it seriously and to imagine the antiquity of the thing, projecting it, or something like it, into the plaza of the Rio Azulito ruin.

Wherever you were in the village, the drums followed you. The sound travelled through the earth. Often it seemed to come from almost any direction. In the open, or at an open window, even away from the plaza, you would hear the voice of the chorus rise at the strong parts of a song, and then it would fade again. In the plaza, actually attending the dance, you followed all of the singing and the sound of gourd rattles in the men's hands and the turtle-shell and deer-hoof rattles on their right legs, marking a time that usually went along with the drum but sometimes separated from it. If you watched, all of these rhythmic elements were interwoven with the visual ones — the men's feet, their emphatic steps and the general movement of their bodies and heads, the women's much gentler placement of their feet, even in passages of fast time, and, weaving over and through all these effects, the maneuvers of the dancers, in this particular dance very simple but occasionally marking a larger, slower rhythm that embraced the rest.

You listen, you stop listening; you look, you stop looking. You chat. You go in and eat. Except for a period of about two hours in the middle of the day, the dance is continuously with you. If you stick around, it increasingly binds you and the other people there together — the San Leandros and the visitors from other pueblos especially, to a lesser degree the occasional Navajos and Apaches who turn up, and least of all the whites, few of whom stay for more than an hour or two. A dance of this kind is a sophisticated, evolved form of art, which uses repetition and duration as essential elements. If you don't expose yourself to the repetition, you cannot get the impact of it.

We were there to spend the day. I visited several houses, Juan telling me what men would be at home. I felt that he wanted to help me advance my cause. I entered into no discussions of it, but I thought that the more these people knew me as a person, the easier it would be for them to let me pry into the repository of their past. I was well received wherever I went.

All the time, I was conscious of the half-dozen eagles on the rooftops, waiting to be sacrificed in the Eagles Return Rite. So then the prisoners are set free, I thought, studying the one on the top of the two-story house next to Juan's. He looked wild and hostile, not at all Puebloan. Another, farther away, was tearing at a gobbet of meat. It occurred to me that I had seen captive eagles flap their wings occasionally, but neither here nor in the Hopi country had I ever seen one seriously try to fly or break away. I wondered whether their wings were clipped. More likely, I thought, some of their pinions had been pulled.

I thought about the probable age of this dance and of eagle catching and sacrificing, and hence came again to the time-depth of the inward-turned, castellated quality of Pueblo life down the ages that I have already described. It was in the course of thinking thus, sitting on the low bench in front of Juan's house, soaked in the dance, relaxed, that it occurred to me that Sorenson might have meant that I should get my business settled with the leaders before their entering into all the complex of this ceremony carried them deep into their ancient psychological heritage, and that it really was quite possible that they would refuse to let me, one might say, make a crack in even a tiny edge of the pattern.

All day these people had been concentrating themselves, concentrating their power, building it up here within the village. You could feel it — a dynamic substance. I thought that the heart of Pueblo existence was retention, holding it all in, and that in this there was something almost morbid. There had to be a letting out, a spending, too, and in some sleepiness in the latter part of the afternoon, what with the heat and much eating and a slight lack of sleep from having gone into town with the boys Saturday night and sat up late talking shop over beer, it occurred to me that one outlet would come when the spirits of the eagles were set free at sundown to soar and wander as eagles should. This random thought comforted me and made me more hopeful of getting the permission I sought. As you can see, I had managed to get those birds on my mind.

A sharp change in the arrangement of sound jerked me into attention. The group that was dancing, the people of the Turquoise moiety, was not leaving the plaza, but the Calabash moiety dancers were coming in, their chorus singing its own song, drumming and dancing their own time. The enclosed place, the Piro center, became jammed with noise and people, with a new excitement of sight and sound. There really was not room for both teams of dancers, but somehow they worked it all out and managed to blend. A couple of my boys joined me and one of them said, "Wow! There isn't anything to say about this except 'Wow!,' is there, Doc?"

I said, "I see what you mean."

The sun was near setting and we seemed to be the only white people still there. I don't know how long that finale lasted, perhaps twenty minutes; then the two teams went off in separate directions toward their respective kivas.

Juan told me, "That's all now. It's over."

It was a dismissal. I had heard that the Eagles Return business and whatever else they did at the edge of the village after the dance was not for the public. I gathered the boys and we drove back to camp.

I wondered how soon I should return to San Leandro and see about stirring up another meeting. Not right away, I knew, as they had to have time to rest and to perform follow-up rites. They would need a little time. Next Sunday would be about right, and if things went well I could take as much as two or three weeks to work in, if I needed them.

To my surprise, Juan came to get me at the Rio Azulito site on Friday morning. We had just broken into what looked like a circular pit house dating from Basket Maker III, though I knew of no Basket Maker material from anywhere near there. I was all wrapped up in the engineering problems and the possibilities when Juan came climbing over the ruin and told me that the council was in session and wanted to see me. I had a moment's impulse to object that I could not go right then, but I thought better of it and climbed out of the hole I was working in and dusted myself off.

Juan, it turned out, had not come in his own car but had bummed a ride with a friend who was on his way to the Apache reservation up north. He remarked that his own car was a pickup and that the seat was in bad condition, so he thought I'd be more comfortable in my sedan.

Once we got going, I naturally wanted to get an idea of what awaited me, whether the council had come to a decision, and if so what. I said I hoped they'd let me dig for the evidence they needed, and he said, "You know how these old men are. They talk it over and talk it over."

The Pueblos — most Indians, for that matter, I believe — are not satisfied until they reach unanimous agreement. They could still be working on that, or Juan could be being evasive. I'd have to wait to learn the answer, and I hoped I was not in for a series of indecisive palavers. We drove on in silence for quite a while, then Juan began singing quietly and beating time with his open hand on the top of the car door.

I said, "That's one of the songs they sang last Sunday, isn't it?"

"Yeah. My uncle made it. He's the one that mostly makes up songs for our side. How'd you like the dance?"

"It was beautiful."

When we had gone a good bit farther, I came out with a question I could not help asking. "Now those eagles are all turned loose, aren't they?"

"Hunh? Turned loose?"

"I mean, when they were sacrificed, that turned them loose."

He thought that over for a while. "Well, no. You know how the Hopis do when they sacrifice them?"

"Yes."

"We do kinda the same thing. So their spirits stay in, they stay with us, until we send them back to go into little eagles. They're part of the pueblo, kind of, their nests and our houses. It goes round and round."

"Oh."

He started singing again. I was depressed. It's all part of the same pattern, or configuration; everything is kept in. The eagles never get free. Their spirits are sent back into the nests, which are all well known to the San Leandros and tied to the Piro center with all the strands of ritual, and there they hatch and become eaglets again, and are taken back to San Leandro to sit on those perches until the time comes to start them around yet once more. I glanced at Juan's profile. I didn't think I'd better ask any more questions; he'd gone pretty far in answering that last one. You keep it in. Once more my mind reached back across the centuries, back to the close-packed cliff dwellings. I thought of the ruin we were working on and the yet older Basket Maker site below it. Always the corn growing and the need of all the power men could gather in from every source to insure its growth, and always, you could be sure, roving hunters ready to swoop and steal. The fields were safe now. The Indians had machines with which to clear or improve their irrigation ditches, the modern tools of farming, and there were no more raiding enemies, but their way of life was under siege as it had never been before. Television aerials marred the antique lines of the flat-topped roofs . . . Against all the white man's destroying array of non-essentials they hoarded and massed the strength, and even this quite up-to-date young man beside me had behind him the captive souls of eagles. The eagles' forebears and his own had handed the strength down. We hit a chuck-hole and I decided to pay attention to my driving. Shortly the pueblo came in sight, the clustered, low buildings that matched the soil around them and the slight, centralizing accent of the facade of the church, with its little towers.

When we parked the car and walked on in, I thought that one ought to be conscious of breaking through a barrier of some sort, of breasting the strength of the people. I encountered nothing except the usual restful quiet. Although it was unnecessary, as we went along I glanced to see that there were now no eagles on the roofs.

We entered the old council room. I was prepared to make a circuit shaking hands, but Juan pushed the chair toward me, saying, "Make yourself comfortable," so I did. A very old man was talking, a shrunken old man wearing a bright, large-patterned factory blanket around his body. I supposed he had reached an age at which any ordinary room is chill. His voice was thin, his speech halting. God knows what he was talking about. Crescencio Rael, who had the final say before, interrupted him pleasantly and he fell silent. Then the governor welcomed me as courteously as before, expressing appreciation that I had dropped my work to come to the council without advance notice. After that, there was rather a long pause. Not knowing what else to do, I lit a cigarette.

Juan said something to the councilmen. The very old man said a few words. Then Crescencio spoke for not more than two minutes.

Juan said, "They have talked it all over, and they are all agreed. They are sorry, because you have taken trouble and they want to help our lawyers, but they can't let you dig in the trash heap. Not any part of it. Maybe we won't win that money. That's too bad, but we been getting on all right for a long time without it. It's like what I told you the other day, and Crescencio says maybe you understand better now that you were here all day for the dance. We sure thank you and we hope you come visit us often."

As he finished speaking, I was conscious of a change occurring in the gathering. Now, as I turned my eyes from him, I saw an expression of happiness and relief on the men's faces. They were all looking right at me, and I knew they wanted to see how I would react.

I guess my reaction had been building up in me, subconsciously, for some little time. I heard myself saying, "I think you are exactly right. I think the important thing is for you to keep everything whole." I rose, still surprised at what I had said, and knowing that I meant exactly that.

Everyone had to shake hands with me. It was as if we had accomplished something difficult and good together. We said friendly things to each other in English and Spanish, and one elderly gentleman with a face remarkably like a sack of potatoes taught me a Piro phrase that, Juan explained later, meant "All is well. Many thanks, friend." I was invited to stay for lunch in a dozen houses, but there was plenty of morning left and I had that site to play with, so I thanked them and drove on back to Rio Azulito. My little session with the San Leandro council had been, strictly speaking, a venture in ethnography, I told myself on the way. Sorenson might say I had muffed it, but if I had, by so doing I had uncovered a bit of simon-pure archeology that no ruin, no matter how complete, would ever yield up.

THE POT AND THE CUP

THE WORK was exacting to the point of exasperation, slow, absorbing, its possible outcome exciting. Spread out on a large tray that looked to be, and in fact had been, taken from a cafeteria were more than fifty pottery fragments, some no bigger than a twenty-five cent piece, the largest a crude triangle six centimeters wide at the base, five centimeters high. Sitting on a draughtsman's high stool, facing the tray, Juanita Caronal was trying to assemble whatever it was might be assembled from those fragments, working a three-dimensional jig-saw puzzle not made any easier by the fact that the edges of many of the fragments were somewhat abraded.

Despite her name, Juanita did not look particularly Spanish. She was a fairly tall young woman with dark brown hair and handsome, grey eyes, now in her first year of postgraduate studies in Talvert University's Department of Anthropology. She held a small fellowship, in return for which she was supposed to do a certain amount of work for the Museum of Man. At first she had put in a few hours a week at routine but instructive sorting, labelling, and cataloguing; then, to her great satisfaction, Professor Elvira Stafford had chosen her for her present task of reconstruction.

The sherds were covered with a smooth, earth-red slip. On some of them were parts of ovals outlined in black and containing within them what looked like a child's freehand drawing of a human face. On one long, narrow piece there was most of such a face, and, to the left of it, outside the oval, a black line, almost perpendicular, paralleled by a row of five dots. If you were a Maya scholar, you could not resist reading this combination as "10 Ahau," yet at the same time noting that the use of five dots instead of another line to represent the second five was wrong and, like the extreme simplification of the face, indicated that the hieroglyph had been painted on by someone who could not read the Maya writing and had simply applied the character as a decoration.

On some other sherds there was modelling in relief, bits of pinched-up clay and what seemed to be little rolls of clay pressed on. *If*, when assembled, these little bumps and lines formed a crude face and arms, and *if*, in addition, they were on the same pot as the pseudo-glyphs, that would be something quite new and possibly significant of hitherto unsuspected contacts between ancient cultures. It was Dr. Stafford who had seen the possibilities in this group of fragments all found close together. She had explained them to Juanita, and then remarked that there might be nothing to it and that it was better not to talk about it until they found out.

Juanita greatly admired Dr. Stafford, the only woman on Talvert's anthropological faculty. In that remark about not talking there was a hint of a secret to be shared and guarded, a bond between two women in a department that was definitely male-dominated. The student had been somewhat miffed when she learned that the professor had told Ox Terrel, who was also working in her laboratory, about it. But then, Ox had been enthused into a reversion to his undergraduate self and had swiped the tray from the university cafeteria for her, which made Juanita feel better.

Theoretically, professors do not condone the theft of articles from other parts of the university, but the tray really was ideal, the sherds were silhouetted clearly against the silvery metal, and anyhow, Elvira approved in principle of young men who did moderately forbidden things for the benefit of young women. Fourteen years ago a youth of similar inclinations, a man as tall but not quite as broad as Ox, had astonished her into marrying him between her master's and her doctorate. Despite the separations inevitably caused by her own career in archeology and his in paleontology, she had known eight years of thoroughly happy marriage before the treachery of an upthrust stratum of Algonkian shale sent him headlong from a cliffside and she was left a widow with a young daughter. Elvira said nothing whatever about the tray. She hoped Juanita had been nice about it. The girl was too often sharp in her dealings with her contemporaries.

Using a small box of sand to start with, Juanita had assembled three pieces of rim that plainly fitted together. These she had transferred to some of the modelling clay that is used in kindergartens, warranted not to grow hard or dirty the hands. After endless searching and trying, she had fitted a fourth fragment below and between two of the rim pieces. It was not apparent as yet what the shape of the original pot had been; the four sherds were stuck in a non-committal, thin strip of backing and set to one side. As Elvira came into the laboratory, the girl was in the act of fitting to each other yet three more fragments. One of these again had a portion of rim for its upper edge; from this the other two spread down and outwards. On these latter appeared the greater part of one of the illiterate 10 Ahau designs. Juanita knew the professor was in the room, but at the moment her concentration was too great to let the knowledge break into her thoughts.

Elvira went to a table across from Juanita's, to set down the basket of objects she used to illustrate the seminar session just finished. It was one in which she dealt with Middle American metalworking and the *cire perdue* process. Her exhibits included one small piece of authentic, hammered gold work from Oaxaca, one of cast gold from Panama, and one of the thin, quite useless, copper axe-heads that are found in the Soconusco region — where the Pacific coast of Mexico reaches towards Guatemala — and that seem to be trade articles from Peru. These were items that even advanced graduate students looked upon with some fascination.

She looked across at the girl. Juanita's gaze swept the tray, after the manner of anyone working a difficult puzzle who, having just fitted one piece, hopes that the next will suddenly become apparent. Her hands hovered over the pieces, unconsciously demonstrating, Elvira thought, the immemorial linkage between hand and eye that is the primordial factor in the evolution of men. The hands were finely formed, graceful. At the moment, Elvira thought, she's really pretty. The prim, sullen set that spoiled her mouth was gone; her expression was young, unguarded, alive. All she needed was to relax a little. Juanita gave an exasperated little sigh, rested both hands on the edge of the table, and looked at the professor.

Elvira said, "Slow going?"

"All but standing still."

"You've got two nice groups to start with. Can you estimate the circumference yet?"

"Not quite. If I can carry this section of rim along just a little farther."

The older woman nodded. Then she said, "A thing like this can hypnotize you, as I well know. And you aren't getting any credits for it — credit, but no credits. Ration your time — for instance, leave it alone this afternoon and attend to your reading. If what we think may be here is here, well, it's waited for around nine hundred years; it can wait a little longer."

Juanita looked at her with an expression faintly suggestive of disgust. Elvira laughed. "They used to say things like that to me, too, and I used to think, 'My God, how bloodless can you get?'" She saw Juanita smile. "All the same, archeology is a slow science — all good science is, I guess — and that's part of what you have to learn."

"I know."

Elvira looked at her watch. "Knock off at twelve-thirty. Any more, and you'll be getting desperate."

"Yes'm." The little girl form of assent was said with humor. Juanita went back to searching among the sherds.

As Elvira went to her office at the far end of the laboratory she thought, that girl is on the way to becoming married to her profession and it's not what she really wants, not what she was cut out for. What's eating on her? She entered her room and closed the door. She's got that thing — you can't name it — that make the worthwhile young men shy away, yet on points she has everything, including a romantic name. She's pursuing anthropology as if it were a drug.

The professor put her set of exhibits back in their flat box

and slid it into its place in the bank of boxes along one wall.
A number of these contained teaching adjuncts, others articles that she herself was studying. Having another lecture to
warm up for, she lit a cigarette and settled to her notes. Smoking was permitted in the faculty offices but not in other parts
of the museum.

Juanita had sunk back into self-forgetfulness. She found
Dr. Stafford an unusually easy person to be with, so that from
working her puzzle to talking with the teacher, then back to
the puzzle again were easy transitions. She needed a piece
with a dull hook on it — perhaps this one . . . The laboratory door opened and closed. She stiffened slightly, the piece
in her hand. She assumed, correctly, that Ox had come in.

He walked over and stood beside her, a very large, medium
blond young man, on the handsome side, with intelligent eyes.
His mouth suggested good nature and was quick to smile —
perhaps, a shrewd observer might suspect, because so far in
life everything had happened as he wanted it to.

"Hi," he said, "how goes it? Found any peculiar Peruvian
pottery portraiture yet?"

Juanita was conscious of her own heartbeat. She astonished herself by saying, "No, nothing but mousy, miserable morsels so far."

"It looks like one hell of a job. Well, good luck."

"Thanks."

She moved her hands over the tray again, enacted absorption. Ox probably stayed watching her for ten seconds before he turned away to his own work; it seemed a long time,
as long as she could stand. Self-forgetfulness was gone. At
the moment her unease was lessened by pleasure at the re-

mark she had made. She was not good at comebacks; she was not a wisecracker. The amusing alliteration with which Ox had led off was the kind of thing she admired and that dismayed her, making her feel stupid, excluded. It did not occur to her that, after attending Dr. Stafford's seminar, the young man had lingered on the steps of the museum for a slow cigarette, and during that time had carefully prepared his greeting.

The project at which Ox was working was not to satisfy the requirements of a fellowship, but one he had set up for himself in connection with an advanced course. Ox Terrel did not need scholarships. Ox Terrel could even afford to pay his own fare to Guatemala and return and spend the field season working for nothing at the university's big excavation at Popil. He belonged to about the best club on the campus. (Talvert was on the western, outer fringe of the Ivy League area and — a nice example of cultural diffusion in itself — always referred to fraternities as "clubs.") He had been a two letter man. He had also graduated *cum laude*, which Juanita did not know, and he had his M.A. That she did know, and it annoyed her, because she refused to believe that a spoiled youth of his kind could possibly be a scholar. She had to resist an impulse to throw a couple of bits of pottery that refused to match with *anything* against the wall. She quit work at fifteen minutes after twelve and headed towards her room, planning to eat a little later, when the cafeteria would not be crowded.

He did not even mind being called "Ox." Well, if you had become famous as an undergraduate because of your sheer size and strength, you'd probably think it a compliment. The pace of her walk became more rapid. It wasn't like —

not like — she would not complete the thought; inside herself she slammed that door shut. She was forever shutting it, and it was forever ajar.

At fourteen, she had won a scholarship to a pretty good boarding school. She was leggy and gangling, and that year she developed some sort of adolescent blemish on her face. Her name, a heritage from a Spanish grandfather, did not seem romantic to her classmates; they found it merely odd. Then a teacher, an irritable, inherently cruel woman, angered by some stupidity of the girl's, made a mean remark in class about her intelligence, her skin, the state of her liver, and the possibility that a good purge, perhaps calomel, might do wonders for her. Juanita never knew whether the woman's injection of the word "calomel" was done with real-ization of what effect it could have, or entirely casually. The teacher was old enough to have lived in the days of the com-mon use of calomel. Whatever the intent, her contempo-raries were far too quick to miss the obvious — Caronal, Calomel, Juanita Calomel.

There it was, and it lasted for four, long years. There was the word passed from schoolmate to brother to friend, there were the label, the brand, the joke you overheard one boy making to another, the agony of parties, the thing you could never explain to your parents.

She chose a western university so as to get away from it, and in fact the actual name, the tag, was left behind, as also the blemish was gone from her face. Yet she carried it all within her. She joined a fair to middling sorority. There were the desirable young men who dated her once and never came back. There was the silence, the blocked thing inside her that strangled small talk, the readiness to wince when there was no blow, to strike back when no one had struck. There were the second-rate men, the friends of her friends' dates, whom her pride would not accept, and then the occasional wolf who thought a lonely girl would be easy pickings and let himself in for a nasty shock.

After graduation she transferred to Talvert, reasonably enough, for she had already set her sights on Middle American archeology, and Talvert was strong in that field. Still, Juanita Calomel attended her. Talvert was nearer home. In the chapter of her sorority there was a girl who had been a year behind her at school. The girl never gave even the slightest hint that she had ever heard of the nicknames, of the jokes, but what Juanita knew she knew was an eternal threat of disaster, the mere sight of her a reminder that froze the older girl into silence and stupidity. She made only occasional use of the sorority.

She would assemble all those sherds, she would reconstruct a whole pot; it would have a stylized design derived from the Mayan and in addition a South American — Chibcha — face and arms. For a moment she toyed with the thought of an influence from Peru itself, and in rejecting it as hopelessly farfetched gave her daydream a quality of reasonableness, of common sense. The combination would be profoundly significant, much more so than the mere presence at the southern boundary of Salvador, where the sherds had been found, of a trade piece from the far south. More significant, she thought, than Peruvian axe-heads in Soconusco. Contacts, culture contacts. Skillful work would get her to Popil; she herself would dig in that ruin. Somehow (for the moment, her thoughts coasting happily, she did not interrupt them to imagine how) she would reconcile her parents to the idea of her changing her name. She would become Jane Carrol before she got her Ph.D., before she had put her name to her first publication. She would achieve publication before her doctorate — why not, if her skilled hands, her sense of form, her accuracy, won her responsible assignments? Jane Carrol, Dr. Stafford's — Elvira Stafford's — friend and co-worker, the young woman to whom Dr. Lancaster had turned over complete charge of Structure M-VI . . .

Within her mind a cinema unrolled in full color, accompanied by her own narration. Somewhere in the background Ox Terrel, who was unable to earn his doctorate, stood disconsolate and abashed, awaiting a sign of recognition, of acceptance. There were flashes of a sequence, somewhat out of focus, in which she worked side by side, trowel in hand, with Wally Caswell, who last season had discovered the Popil Bas-Reliefs, and, equally fragmentary, the assemblages, the Congress of Americanists, the annual meeting of the Anthropological Association, and the smaller, gay gatherings of the field men and women at the season's end, in Guatemala City or Belize, the learned oldsters relaxing with the young workers, where people who began by calling her "Dr. Carrol" soon called her "Jane" and Elvira Stafford looked on proudly. The girl's face became as feminine, as wooable, as it had been when she was lost in the puzzle of the potsherds, for Juanita whatever-you-call-her was totally forgotten. She entered her room, picked up *An Anthropologist at Work* and set to reading Benedict on the vision in Plains culture without any break in her contentment. What Ruth Benedict had done in ethnology, some day Jane Carrol would do in archeology.

Following a long-established tradition, the director of the Museum of Man, who was now Dr. Arthur Bogue, gave a reception for the anthropological faculty, graduate students, and the more advanced undergraduates, on the first Saturday in November. Long, long ago, the reception had been a tea; now it was a livelier affair, featuring a fish house punch which was Dr. Bogue's especial pride. His living room, extending the full width of the house, took the sun from south-facing French windows, and both he and Mrs. Bogue took pleasure in the sparkle of the fine, cut-glass punch bowl tinted by the tea-colored liquid and the surrounding, inexpensive (Mrs. Bogue was a hardheaded housekeeper) glass punch cups. Mrs. Bogue, occasionally relieved by another professor's wife, presided over the beverage and saw to it that no one took too much, for fish house punch is deceptive, heady stuff. The conversation was lively and often highly instructive. The affair created a sense of unity in the department and promoted informal relations between students and faculty.

Juanita did not plan to go. She flinched from a purely social encounter with numerous young men. That there would be half a dozen other woman students there did not make the prospect any better; rather the opposite. The girls were not beauties, but they were at ease with men. She could see herself sitting like a stick, forgotten, in a roomful of people chattering and laughing.

She, Ox, and Dr. Stafford were all in the laboratory shortly before noon that Saturday, when Ox got up from his work, stretched, and said, "Heigh-ho, the week-end. I'll see you at Dr. Bogue's."

Elvira smiled and nodded, Juanita kept silent. The professor happened to notice the little tightening of the girl's mouth, the following, momentary look of alarm and stubbornness. Ox left the room. Elvira wished she understood this girl, whom she liked, wished she felt as sure of her future as a natural woman as she did of her future as a scientist.

She said, "You're going to Dr. Bogue's, aren't you?"

"Why — I thought I'd give it a miss. I don't feel much like a party."

Fish house punch, Elvira thought. She had encountered the beverage once, at a reception given by the University of Pennsylvania Museum; ever since, it had been associated with delightful company, the perfection of the Maya carvings from Piedras Negras, and the beauty of the Oriental collection in the octagonal hall. A cup of that, she decided, is exactly what the girl needs.

"You know, it's really a command performance. I don't think it would set at all well if you didn't turn up. Macmillan will be there from California, and even if all you do is meet him, you'll be glad later to be able to say that you knew Macmillan. The chances are that he and Dr. Bogue will get to debating diffusion — in fact, I think I'll see that they do — and that will be well worth listening to." Intentionally, Elvira made no mention of Juanita's contemporaries. "Besides, you'll have a chance to cosy up to Dr. Lancaster — he's really a sweetie you know — and improve your chances of getting sent into the field next year."

Dr. Lancaster, chairman of the American archeology division, was personally in charge of the excavations at Popil.

"It's part of the game, you know, a simple, professional fact. When people are choosing people to go on expeditions with them, they pick the ones they like personally."

Juanita nodded. "I guess that makes sense. If you're going to work with someone, you want to work with someone you like." She flushed slightly, conscious of her admiration and liking for Dr. Stafford. Elvira thought that the becoming extra color related to Terrel, or possibly to Caswell. Give her a little punch, she thought, and she'll discover herself.

The girl smiled. "All right; I'll be there."

"And in your best bib and tucker. Elderly professors are highly susceptible."

"Yes'm."

Dr. Macmillan was one of the grand old men of anthropology. In his time he had debated, not unsuccessfully, with Boas, he had known Father Schmidt, and worked in the field with Lowie. He was enormously well read and a considerable classical scholar. He was large and round, with a round head and a large, almost white mustache; he looked more like a janitor than a professor. The glass cup looked lost in his big hand, and the way in which he tossed off the first helping of fish house punch and immediately asked for a refill caused all present who knew his legend to recall that as a young man he had lived and worked for some time in Czarist Russia. He liked to talk, he liked to teach, he knew he had not been invited just to sit, so when Elvira tossed out a remark about diffusion in Nuclear America (which has nothing to do with atomic bombs, but refers to the spread of ideas and traits through the region of the old civilizations from Peru to Central Mexico), he responded quickly, as Bogue then did to him.

The ensuing talk was spiced with such terms as configuration, ethos, and *Kulturkreis*, references to the Crow-Omaha kinship system, the distribution of grey-slipped pottery, and

the representation of similar pathological conditions in por-
trait vases from Peru (especially Trujillo ware), Northwest
Coast carving, and Iroquois false-face masks. Mrs. Bogue and
some of the other faculty wives dropped into quiet small talk,
the undergraduates found the going heavy at times, but the
older students listened eagerly.

Mrs. Bogue was a competent hostess. She enjoyed these
affairs and she had definite ideas about how they should go.
There was a departmental purpose to be served and the visiting lion should be made to roar for the edification of one and
all, but she did not intend to have the whole afternoon taken
up by a small group of performers while all the rest just sat.
She liked people moving about, chatting, making combinations. She liked being gracious to nice young people. This
year, too, a late, mild autumn lingered, its red-browns and
brown-yellow-golds glowing in sunlight that, coming
through the crisp air, made an atmospheric *chaud-froid*, and
her chrysanthemums were still splendid. Dr. Macmillan was,
among other things, a chrysanthemum man from way back.
Neatly, with nice timing, she interrupted the debate while
the sun was still strong in the west, thus forestalling Richard
Stronsky, an assistant professor, in his intention of bringing
up the subject of glottochronology, on which a number of
those present held pronounced views. She led her visitor
through the French windows at the back, onto the terrace
that led to the garden, enclosed on three sides by an old, brick
wall. Mrs. Lancaster moved into the chair by the punch
bowl.

There was a general releasing of people into motion. Cups
were brought up for refilling, a good part of the company
drifted out after their hostess. Elvira saw Ox get two cups of

punch, then join Juanita and hand her one. The girl looked as a pretty girl should look, relaxed, happy, at ease. Ox said something and Juanita laughed. They turned together, crossing the room. Ox, Elvira thought, was not well named; he was not clumsy, but moved with grace. She wondered if he would really make a scientist. Seeing his smile, she remembered suddenly, "My poor child, the best thing I can give you is a little misfortune." He needed tempering. But, she thought, he was an operator; he did not take Juanita into the garden, but led her the other way, through the front door to the long veranda on that side.

Elvira found herself talking with Stronsky and a graduate student named Landon. Stronsky suggested that he get her a glass of punch. She hesitated, having had one, and not much caring to be uplifted and then go on to a solitary meal and solitary evening. Her daughter was spending the night at a friend's house. Then she was annoyed at her own foresight and accepted. The man going to the punch bowl put her in mind of the couple on the veranda, and she looked towards that door neatly in time to see them come in. The manner of their return made her heart sink, as though she personally were responsible for whatever had happened.

Juanita came in rapidly, then checked her pace. Her color was too high, her eyes angry, her mouth set to match, her carriage stiff. Ox came slowly, behind her. He too was angry, but the effect was different, his face sullen, his mouth suddenly ugly. On his left cheek was a very red splotch that could not be accounted for by the effect of temper. The fool, Elvira thought, the spoiled fool. Everything came easy for him, including girls, and so — if two glasses of punch had been just what Juanita needed, then two, or however many he had managed to get, were just enough to make him ruin it. Stronsky handed her her cup. She smiled at him. There was absolutely nothing on earth to be done about those two at that moment, or perhaps ever, and it certainly would be a mistake to take special notice of the girl just now, so she had might as well relax.

In the end, Stronsky invited her to dine with him and she accepted. As she waited on the veranda for him to bring up his car, the bright day gone, winter imminent in the chill air, the overhead light harsh and sad, she saw the gleam of broken glass to one side, a punch cup shattered. Would an archeologist some day, she wondered, be trying to put that back together? They dined at the almost good restaurant just off the campus. He was younger than she, a good conversationalist, not confined to shop. It made a mild, agreeable evening.

Monday morning, Elvira had two classes, then a faculty conference that was renewed after lunch and used up half the afternoon. She saw Juanita at her nine o'clock lecture. Nothing could be learned from the head downturned over the notebook. The professor felt a moment of irritation with herself; good Lord, she was a university teacher, not a girls' counsellor. Later, in conference, she wondered what might have gone on in the lab. If those two were together there, things would be sticky.

It was after three when she herself got there, still carrying the notes of her ten o'clock lecture. As she closed the door, a trifle weary, shutting it with more noise than was usual for her, Juanita looked up from her puzzle. For a moment she was stiff, her expression spinsterish; then, seeing who it was, she smiled.

"Look," she said, "I'm really getting somewhere. Here's the circumference, and here's the upper part of the cross-section. I bet the bottom goes like this."

Elvira looked at the sketches Juanita had made, and at the now considerable area actually reconstructed and set in clay. "Good work," she said. "Now we begin to have a pot."

Young Terrel, she concluded, had stayed away.

"I haven't got to the modelled part yet," Juanita said. "Matter of fact, I think it's better to keep adding onto this part if I can, and sort of creep up on it."

Elvira said, "That's good method." She pointed. "Here's the known, the proven. There's the hypothesis, and there are the data yet to come. Work from the known, and as it grows larger, find out what happens to the hypothesis. You have science in a nutshell right here."

Juanita looked at her admiringly and smiled.

"When you feel like a break, come into my office for a smoke."

"Thanks, I will."

The professor went past the big table to her door. As she entered her room she looked back. Juanita held a small sherd in her fingers, turning it slowly, absorbed again. There, Elvira thought as she had thought before, is a young woman setting out to become married to her profession. As she closed the door, she remembered the broken cup. In this world, as she well knew, there is so much that can never be put back together.

THE LITTLE STONE MAN

Five San Leandro Indians sat in a row on the grass behind the Bonds' house. Charlie Bond, a pleasant-faced youth of twenty, sat facing them. One of the Indians, Agapito Rael (about a third of the San Leandros have Rael as their Christian last name), was elderly. His gray hair was tied in a queue wrapped with red material, his head was bound by a blue headband, and he wore heavy necklaces of shell, coral, and turquoise. The others were young, although all somewhat older than Charlie — the oldest, Juan Rael, being over thirty. Three of them had crew haircuts, and all four were dressed as any Westerner might dress on a warm day.

The pueblo of San Leandro was only five miles from Castellano, New Mexico, where the Bonds lived, and the Indians came to town for much of their shopping. It was not unusual for them to stop and visit. Some of them were Dr. Bond's patients, and, as so readily happens between Pueblo Indians and white people of a sympathetic disposition, he and his wife had developed friendly relations with yet others. Charlie's relationship with the San Leandro people had begun when he was twelve years old, when the Bonds first settled in Castellano, and it was far more intimate and less self-conscious than his parents'.

He had quickly learned never to inquire into Pueblo secrets, but in years of association he had picked up enough to know that Agapito was the Turquoise Cacique — that is, one of the two highest-ranking priests in the hierarchy — that Juan Rael was important in a society the function of which he did not know, and that Eddie Sota, recently returned from a hitch in the Navy, was Agapito's nephew and had started training to follow in his uncle's path. So far as Charlie knew, the other two were just young men who played good baseball and did their part in the dances.

They had refused an invitation to come into the house and have coffee, made themselves comfortable on the grass, and talked commonplaces for a time — about the green summer they were having after last winter's good snows, about last Sunday's ball game, in which San Leandro had trimmed a team from Santa Fe, and the state of the trout fishing in Chompi Creek. There was a pause, the moment of gathering themselves in, of letting everyone become prepared, without which it would be offensive to broach serious business, then the visitors began talking to each other in Piro. Charlie understood a little Piro, including the greetings, everyday expressions, and a number of things to be said to girls; when they talked as they were doing now, he could only catch words here and there.

Agapito said something decisive. Eddie looked at Charlie and said, "We think maybe you can catch another wild ball for us."

Charlie nodded. He felt a little prickle of excitement. Something important was up. At the same time, Eddie's reference called to mind his first encounter with the Piros.

Eight years before, his father, being new to New Mexico,

not knowing the difference between a Pueblo Indian and a Navajo, had taken Charlie with him to San Leandro when he went to visit a patient. Charlie had wandered about the village of golden-brown adobe houses arranged in solid blocks — a lonely boy, a boy who had not yet had time to make any friends in his new home, intrigued and rebuffed by the very picturesqueness of this place, trying not to stare at a man with his hair in a queue, at a woman in native costume. Hearing the crack of a bat against a ball, he drifted to the edge of the pueblo, where a young man was batting out flies to a number of boys. They were on a level strip between the last houses and a shallow cliff, below which the cornfields started. The white boy moved slowly to the edge of the cliff, behind the fielders, and stood watching. What they were doing he knew all about. They were mostly a few years older than he; still, they were boys, and he wanted like anything to join them. But they were talking in a strange language, he was of another color, and none of them even glanced at him. He stood watching and wishing, and thinking that the batter ought to have a bigger bat than the one he was using. A boy near the batter fielded a grounder, made a game of winding up, then pitched the ball underhand. Someone had said something funny, and the batter was laughing. Then he swung, really batting, and knocked out a line drive that went past all the Indians and would have landed in the cornfields had not Charlie caught it. It stung his hand like fury, and it was the beginning of everything.

Agapito was now holding forth. While Charlie waited, he thought of Professor McKee, one of the anthropology profs at college, and rather self-consciously wished the Professor could see him at this moment. Then Agapito said something final to Eddie, and Eddie turned to Charlie and spoke in English, while the others listened intently. "We got some trouble, and we been thinking maybe you could help us out. The old men talk it over at home, and they decided we could probably trust you. We know you've learned a few things about our — our old ways, our Inyan religion, you know, and we think you don't talk about it. I heard Telesforo when he was talking to Agapito here, and he was saying that you don't ever ask no wrong questions, you not trying to stick your nose into things, even if you have seen something or heard something that white people don't know about. I'm saying this part for myself, to kinda explain it to you."

He interpreted his words to his uncle in Piro.

The Telesforo of whom Eddie spoke was Telesforo Pérez, who was Agapito's opposite number, the Calabash Cacique. It was typical of Charlie's relationship with the San Leandros that they took it for granted that he knew who these men were, and they did not mind, because he never asked and never told.

Eddie went on. "Now, they say, we want you to do us a big favor, but first you promise you won't tell no one about it. Sounds funny to ask for a favor and then say that, but that's the way we got to do."

"Of course. I promise."

"Not your daddy or your mother."

"Not my daddy or my mother. Or anybody."

Eddie interpreted again. Several of the others nodded, and Charlie understood Agapito saying "Good. Go ahead."

Eddie said, "You know, we got a sacred place — a shrine, I guess you'd say, in the mountains north of here, on the edge of the grant?"

Charlie guarded his expression. He certainly did know about it, because a couple of years ago he had gone that way with a Piro girl, on whom he had had a crush, and her brother to pick wild strawberries. He got separated from the others and stumbled upon the shrine, with fresh prayer sticks around it. As soon as he saw what it was, he circled well away, and he had mentioned it to no one. Later, when his friends translated part of a rain-dance song for him and there was a passage, "Holy to the north, Holy in a mountain valley, Someone brings thunder," he guessed it referred to the shrine.

He nodded now, and said, "I heard something."

"We — we keep something there." Eddie seemed to run out of words. He turned and spoke to his uncle, who made an affirmative gesture with his hand — a bit of the old sign language that some older men used unconsciously — and said something.

Eddie faced Charlie again. "Well, it's like one of the images in church, only more like a *bulto*." He meant the primitive wooden statuettes carved a hundred years or more ago by the Spanish-Americans. "I mean, it's little, and the carving ain't so good; only it's stone, not wood." He went on to describe it — a human figure, definitely male, and decorated in a distinctive manner.

Then Juan spoke. "You understand, Charlie, this thing maybe don't look like much, but it's important. Ain't everybody in the pueblo, even, knows what it looks like. All of us here, we belong to the right club, you might say. And if anything happened to this thing — well, it's holy to us, and it's holy to a lot of other pueblos, too." As Eddie had done, he turned to Agapito and interpreted himself.

Eddie then said, "Well, this thing, it's gone. It's been gone now for eight days, and we think either Carlisle has it or else someone from La Aurora picked it up. They run pack trips up that way."

Carlisle was a dealer in curios, a talented fraud, who did in fact possess a fine collection of Indian goods. La Aurora was a guest ranch not far from Castellano. Its original name was Los Jiménez, since it had been the center for the old Jiménez family, but its present owners had given it the resounding, Mexican-sounding title of Hacienda la Aurora.

Juan Rael said, "We *say* Carlisle, because anyone like a sheepherder that mighta taken it would most likely sell it to him. I dunno about La Aurora. Long ago, when they first run pack trips through the grant, they went poking around too much. The War Captains and some of their staff went over and straightened 'em out. They sure don't want us to stop 'em from coming on the grant or visiting the pueblo, and their wranglers have instructions to keep their dudes in line. On the straight and narrow path, you might say."

Charlie nodded. He had heard something of that visitation, from the ranch end; it must have been impressive. And every year, when permission to ride on the grant was renewed, the governor of San Leandro reminded the ranch owners to keep their outfits on the proper trails. "Then it sounds like Mr. Carlisle," he said.

"Yeah. Him or someone. We been to his store, and a couple of our people been to La Aurora, selling curios, but we didn't see nothing. Trouble is, if anyone has this thing, as soon as he sees an Inyan coming he'll hide it and clam up. So that's where you come in. We want you to be our detective."

"All right. I'll try. I don't know that I can do any good."

When Agapito had been brought up to date, he nodded

solemnly and said, "Very good; thank you," in Piro. Then he said in Spanish, which Charlie spoke well, "If you find it, better you leave it alone and tell us right away. There is less trouble for you if you do not handle this thing."

Charlie said, "*Muy bien.*" He supposed the old man was referring to ritual contamination.

Jake Pérez, who up to now had simply listened, produced a pack of cigarettes, which was passed around. There was little said while they smoked. Charlie thought they ought to have produced the cornhusk cigarettes that are used on some ceremonial occasions. When the Cacique put out his smoke, the others followed suit and rose. They all shook hands with Charlie, some saying goodbye in Piro, others in English; then they filed off.

Charlie walked slowly about the yard. At first he was carried away by elation. The Indians had turned to, had called upon, *him*. Voluntarily they had opened the door to their inner life a crack more. If he could find that image, perhaps they might even initiate him, take him in. They had come to no one else but him; he was sure of that. At the height of his pleasure, he suddenly saw how ridiculous it was — the only white man the Indians trust. How childish can you get!

Because of his relations with Indians, he had taken courses in anthropology during his first two years at Talvert University, and was seriously thinking of changing his major to that science. His parents and some of their friends were well read on the Southwest, and he had heard them discuss the ethnology, among other things, of the local Indians. The outstanding white man to be received into a Pueblo tribe had been Cushing, at Zuñi, in the eighteen-seventies, and after he had learned all the secrets he could, he went home and published

them. The Zuñis had never forgotten or forgiven. Charlie
knew he would never betray anything told him in trust, but
the thought of Cushing was like a sudden shadow. If I ever
become an anthropologist, he thought, I won't do any field
work here.

All this dreaming along was well enough, but how should
he start trying to find that figurine? To bring his mind down
to brass tacks, he told himself, "I want to find a little stone
man, an anthropomorphic figurine about ten inches long, that
someone not an Indian is hiding." He walked in a circle,
thinking about Mr. Carlisle.

The curio dealer would be a tough nut to crack. He really
did know a lot about Indian crafts, was something of a connoisseur, and to the discriminating he offered things of quality
and value. Some of the best of these he kept in a cabinet in his
living room, and along with them articles that were virtually
worthless, such as Hopi kachina dolls that he had aged artifi-
cially and that he would offer to the gullible at outrageous
prices, alleging them to be sacred objects of enormous value,
the mere possession of which, here next door to Indians, put
him in mortal danger. The Indians knew about his frauds,
which made them suspect him. Still, he was no fool, and he
wouldn't let you search his place if he didn't want you to. He
knew how close Charlie was to San Leandro, and his own
dealings with the Indians had always been open and above-
board. If he really was hiding that thing, it would be a complete switch from his usual practices.

Still thinking about the problem, and not getting much
of anywhere with it, Charlie left the yard and started slowly
up the street. It was in his mind to go look at Mr. Carlisle's

shop. As it was past five o'clock, the place would probably be closed, but looking at it might somehow give him an idea. A block from Carlisle's place, he met his father.

"House call?" Charlie asked.

"No. Through, for once. Finished at the hospital, and no calls at the office. Cross your fingers. Where are you going?"

"Nowhere. Just bored."

They walked along together until they came to the Silver Dollar Restaurant, which was also a bar and a dispensary. It had a carefully frontier facade of logs that had nothing to do with New Mexico's tradition, and it was the only respectable drinking place in Castellano. Dr. Bond said, "Your mother wants me to pick up a bottle of sherry."

They went into the dispensary together. Curley Bostwick was behind the counter.

He said, "Hello, Doc; hello, Charlie. Say, you're just the people I was hoping to see."

The Doctor said, "What's on your mind, Curley?" His son knew he was braced for the usual try at getting a free diagnosis.

"Well, I understand you both know a good deal about these Injuns, and Charlie goes out to the pueblo" — he pronounced it "pew-eeblo" — "a lot, so maybe you can tell me." He paused.

Dr. Bond said, "Shoot."

"Well, a Spanish feller who's one of Sullivan's cowhands come in the other day, and he brought something he wanted to trade on. He said there was a break in the San Leandro line fence, and a couple of his cows had wandered in, so he went after them. While he was in there, he run into sort of a little stone house, and he found this thing in it. Wait a minute."

He went into the back room and returned with a package wrapped in newspaper. He looked out the door, then opened the package on the counter.

There it was. It was as simple as that.

"I give him a pint for it," Curley said, wrapping the little figure again. "Then I got to thinkin'. I hear sometimes the Injuns set a lot of store by things like this. I got customers from several pueblos; I don't want no trouble with them. And then, maybe it's worth a lot of money. What do you think?"

Dr. Bond said thoughtfully, "There isn't much money in a thing like that."

Charlie said to himself, "There's a man you can count on to say the right thing."

His father turned to him. "This mean anything to you?"

"Well, ye-es, it does. That is, I know that the Indians are all upset about something that's been stolen from them. They're pretty mad, too."

"Then it's dangerous to have this?" Dr. Bond asked. Lord, his father couldn't be doing better if they'd rehearsed.

"Yes," Charlie said. "You know they can get tough when someone fools around with what they think is sacred."

Curley looked good and unhappy. "What'd I ought to do?" Charlie said, "Get it back to them, as quick as you can."

"Here," Curley said, thrusting the bundle into Charlie's hands. "You know 'em; you get it to 'em."

Charlie did not see how he could refuse. As a matter of fact, he was glad to be put in a position to bring this object back to San Leandro himself, despite what Agapito had said about not handling it.

Dr. Bond said, "You mustn't be out of pocket on this. How much was that pint?"

"Three-sixty," Curley said.

The Doctor took out his wallet before his son, encumbered, could reach his.

"Let me pay it, Dad," Charlie said. "I've got it."

"I'll take care of it," his father said. "I have it more times over than you."

Curley accepted the money with thanks. Dr. Bond bought his sherry and they left.

Charlie said, "Thanks for saying all the right things. I guess I'd better take this right out."

"It's interesting. I'd like to get a photo of it."

"I'm sorry, Dad. You mustn't."

"The first winter you were in school here, your mother worried that you'd wind up speaking with a Spanish accent. Now, sometimes, I wonder if you haven't turned into an Indian. Will you be able to tell me anything about this?"

"I guess not. The truth is, I don't know much about it myself, except that it was stolen."

It occurred to him that it was odd that the Indians had not mentioned the break in the fence, which they surely would have discovered. Perhaps they did not speak of it because it was the War Captains' business, not theirs.

They took him into a house in which there was no furniture, they prayed and sang over him, making him safe from any harm that could have come from the power of the thing that he had carried. Without asking him to leave, they did what was necessary for the figurine itself, which took half an hour. Then they thanked him ceremoniously, and Juan Rael invited him to supper.

Shortly before he went back to college, there was a Turtle

Dance at the pueblo. He went to watch it and, as usual, ate at half a dozen houses, taking enough at each to show appreciation. In the middle of the afternoon, when women in full costume took presents to the dancers, two of them brought him round loaves of wheat bread and another a fat, flat cake of blue corn bread, which he knew to be delicious. Shortly afterward, a small boy came to him with a big paper bag in which to put the gifts. He felt singularly happy, and sorry he had to go East so soon, yet in another way eager, for now he knew he would major in anthropology.

Dr. Robert McKee, an assistant professor, gave an advanced course in Southwestern ethnology. Even though Charlie was now an anthropology major, he had to do a little talking to get admitted to it. Once he was in, Dr. McKee became interested in him, helped him adapt himself to requirements stiffer than those an undergraduate ordinarily must meet, and from time to time talked with him about Pueblo Indians, comparing observations as colleague to colleague rather than as professor to student. Charlie began to experience the unity, the closeness, that existed among the faculty and those students who were working toward a career in anthropology.

In November, Dr. McKee invited him to come to his rooms after supper to meet Dr. Sorenson of the University of Northern California, the author of the monumental study *Pueblo Indian Culture*. They would have, McKee said, a Pueblo evening. Charlie arrived at eight. He was the only student present and, not counting Dr. Sorenson, there were only two other guests — Dr. Stronsky, whose specialty was linguistics, and Dr. Elvira Stafford, the only woman on the anthropological faculty. The Southwest was at the extreme northern periphery of her field of interest. Charlie supposed that she was included to lend feminine charm — he himself found her surprisingly attractive for a woman who could not be less than thirty-five. Dr. Stronsky was dark, rather handsome, European-born, and distinctly cosmopolitan. The guest of honor was in his sixties — a tall, lean man with a mop of white hair, who disguised his erudition under an easy, casual manner.

All of these people were good talkers. Their respective educations went well beyond what suffices to earn a Ph.D. in a science, and in their talk they ranged widely. Charlie listened, not always understanding, excited to hear what he thought of as courses of study, topics with walled boundaries, discussed in the context of life and philosophy. He nursed a highball and kept turning his head from one to another of the speakers.

Dr. Stafford mentioned that Charlie was well acquainted with San Leandro. Dr. Sorenson said, "Oh?" and Dr. McKee answered, "Didn't I tell you that? I meant to."

"It's fifteen years since I was there," Dr. Sorenson said, to Charlie. "Is Cruz Rael still alive?"

"No, sir, he died about five years ago."

"Then did Agapito succeed him as Turquoise Cacique?"

"Yes, sir." So this man knew that.

Dr. Sorenson put a number of further questions — about various individuals, about how well the dances were being kept up — and flattered Charlie by asking whether he saw a connection between the San Leandro Basket Dance and the Hopi Niman Kachina Ceremony. He told some pleasant anecdotes of his experiences at San Leandro. At about this point, Dr. McKee, having freshened Dr. Stafford's drink, refilled Charlie's.

Dr. Sorenson said, "There was one lead I never had time to follow up. I'm interested in the distribution of anthropomorphic figures from the Hopi country eastward. Partly, it's their scarcity that interests me, considering how eminently capable the Pueblos have been at modelling and carving for the last couple of thousand years. Old Tomás Pérez said something one time about a 'little stone man' who relates to the Thunderstone Society. Have you heard anything about it?"

Charlie sipped his drink to gain time. To be able to tell the great Albert Sorenson something . . . He said, "I've heard of it. It's a small stone figurine."

"Male?"

"Yes."

"They don't keep it in the pueblo, do they?"

"No. It's in a shrine to the north."

"Oh. On Chompi Mountain, I suppose."

Charlie nodded faintly. He felt uneasy.

"And it does relate to thunder?"

"I think so, sir. Really, I don't know much about it — almost nothing. You know how they are."

Dr. Sorenson laughed. "I know."

He changed the subject. The gathering broke up at eleven. On his way to his room, Charlie was thankful that the scientist had, apparently, taken it for granted that he had not actually seen the figure. If he'd asked whether he had seen it, Charlie would have had to lie.

He returned to Castellano late on a June afternoon. As he was getting out of the car, three men from San Leandro went by on the other side of the street, but he was too busy greeting his mother to hail them. He took his things up to his room. On his desk there was a brown manila envelope with "Educational Materials" stamped on it. He would see what was inside later.

There was, always, so much to talk about. There was the pleasure, which never staled, of rediscovering what fun his parents were. It was a pleasant evening, and they had claret with dinner to celebrate.

The next morning he slept rather late. After breakfast, he got into his old car and set out for San Leandro. His studies had given a new depth to his understanding, had linked isolated items of knowledge in a pattern. He knew he would see his friends with new eyes.

He parked his car at the edge of the village and went in along a narrow street, past the back of the church and the square kiva, onto the plaza. He started across it diagonally, heading for Eddie Sota's house. Four men came out of a house on the far side of the plaza. The two in the middle, who wore their hair in queues, he recognized as the War Captains; the other two were younger and were carrying short staffs. Staffs were carried on certain special occasions by young men acting as a sort of ceremonial police. Charlie wondered what was going on.

Then he saw they were coming to meet him, so he stood and waited. As they came near, he greeted them in Piro, smiling. They did not answer. He knew them all, but their faces were the faces of strangers.

They stopped, facing him, and the younger of the War

Captains said, "You get out of here. You not come back. Not any time. You are our enemy. Now go."

"But — But — What on earth? What?"

The young men stepped closer, holding their staffs horizontally towards him. "You get out, Bond, or we put you out. We beat the hell out of you."

The hostility was a force in itself. He felt dizzy. Nothing made sense. He could not, in fact, take it in. He drove home, bewildered, and went straight to his room. His eye lit on the envelope on his desk. It had the return address of the university where Dr. Sorenson taught. An idea came to him that made him almost sick. He opened the envelope. It was a reprint from the April issue of the *Southwestern Anthropologist*, which he had not read. At the top was written, in ink, "With the author's compliments, Albert Sorenson." The title of the article was "Anthropomorphic Fetishes at Modern Pueblos."

Two boys from San Leandro, Charlie knew, were going to the University of New Mexico. He had been standing, holding the reprint in his hand; now he had to sit down. Unsteadily, he turned the document over. The footnotes were printed at the end, in small type, just ahead of the bibliography. The type was black, and bright against the white paper, and his name showed clear, even in the small characters. "Personal information of Mr. Charles S. Bond, of Talvert University." Without looking at the text itself, he could well imagine what a man of Dr. Sorenson's vast knowledge could build out of the little that he had let slip.

THE TIMELY DEATH
OF WALLACE CASWELL

Y OUNG MEN who have just been appointed to an instruc-
torship and who have no private means would be well-
advised not to become ensnared by campus queens, those
clean-limbed young beauties who move from classroom to
classroom as if unaware of the admiring eyes upon them,
then disappear into the privacy of their sororities, where their
sisters pretend to take them for granted and whence only the
most elite of males can draw them forth for social purposes.

Your brand new instructor, such as Wallace Caswell, with
whom this story deals, is less able to cope with one of these
creatures at his current stage than he was as an undergraduate,
all the more hampered if his mind is taken up with as abstruse
a specialty as Maya epigraphy and the correlation of Maya
and Gregorian chronology. His title of doctor is also shiny
new; he is at an apex of seriousness. He finds that he is at a
new beginning of learning, with wonderful new vistas opening before him, and that his doctorate — in Wally's case in
anthropology — is only a starting point. This phenomenon
is particularly marked at a university such as Talvert, where
Wally was making his career, at which the pressure towards
dangerously exclusive specialization is deliberately countered
by the senior faculty members, because of which policy the

young Maya scholar found himself involved in teaching Anthropology 4a, Introduction to Human Evolution.

A new instructor still cares about the next football game and the Big Game at the end of the season, but the quality of his caring is different; not even on the day of the Big Game itself is its outcome the supreme consideration. Other interests of a few years back have similarly changed, At this stage he is more removed than at any other of his life from ordinary concepts; he is, in fact, sometimes a bore to anyone but his colleagues, and even his seniors, the faculty members, may find his single-mindedness a trifle dull.

That was where Wally was, but he was also young, physically vigorous, a big, bony man, not handsome, not unattractive, and he was quite unable to avoid reacting strongly to Jessica Butterworth, who in her senior year, took Anthropology 4 to complete her minor. Until that year he had not known she existed. When she first entered his classroom, he was pleasantly aware of her moderate tallness — given his own stature, he liked a girl of good height — her long, graceful legs, good features, and honestly golden hair that shone as though a small light were trained on it. He recognized her for what she was, it was implicit in the assurance of her bearing, and suspected that she would not be a good student, in which he was wrong. The first he knew that he was in trouble was in early October, when she stopped to ask him a question as the class broke up, and in looking into her green-blue eyes he lost the thread of what she was saying and had to ask her to repeat. He felt his face grow warm, then was angry at himself and at her, for he saw that she recognized a familiar phenomenon and was amused by it. He answered her question, she said "Thank you, Dr. Caswell," and left the room. He gathered up his lecture notes jerkily.

It did not occur to him that far older and tougher teachers than he had been at least momentarily unsettled by those eyes. Although at that time his studies and his academic duties had him much preoccupied, he was not by nature monastic. In the last few years he had been rather out of circulation, but to respond positively to a pretty girl was not new in his life. He told himself with some emphasis as he went towards his room that the girl was not going to get an unearned A out of him by batting her eyelashes. Friday there would be a test. He thought, with a sense of satisfaction that was not a credit to him, that then he would see how she came out.

Unfortunately for his ideas, Jessica Butterworth, in addition to being a lovely creature, was intelligent and was interested in the evolution of man. She had not chosen an anthropology minor without purpose. Her combination of interest and intelligence was sufficient to carry her through the rather dry, opening lectures and reading on genetics, natural selection, and the anatomy of the skull, mandible, femur and pelvic girdle. At the level of that course, which was one of several aimed at undergraduates who might become sufficiently intrigued to turn to careers in the science or who, as graduates in later life, would be responsive to the financial needs of the Anthropology Department and the Museum of Man, the teaching was elementary. She mastered it well, and there was nothing to be done in honesty but to give her an A. As a matter of fact, an A plus could have been justified, but Wally remembered someone's remark that there was no perfection outside of mathematics, and what did A plus indicate but perfection? Thus he, who had been the recipient of that grade on a number of occasions from professors who were by no means easily pleased, denied it to Jessica, simply because she disturbed him in her simple capacity as a woman. Incipient love seemed to bring out the worser aspects of an otherwise excellent young man and promising scientist, the discoverer, only the year before, of Chamber 1-A-IV, more popularly known as the Tomb of the Two Priests, at Popil in Guatemala.

As an undergraduate, he had been attentive to three different girls at different times, had kissed two of them enthusiastically and fairly extensively, but had never pinned one. That was about the sum of his experience with nice girls. In Central America as a postgraduate student, as young men will after four to six months in the high bush communing with the monuments of the Ancient Mayas, he had sought out attractive girls who were not at all nice. He found these occasions pleasing, but the necessary, subsequent precautions depressing, so that he was disinclined to pursue researches in that field. He had, then, fragments of experience in a context of inexperience, and on the whole poor equipment for doing anything about having fallen for such a young woman as Jessica.

They came into November, and in class had worked past the fringe-finned ganoids, amphibians, reptiles, and the appearance of mamals, to consideration of tree shrews, lemurs and tarsioids, which would lead to the intricate and, to Wally, fascinating subject of the role of arboreal life in development of the upright posture and liberation of the forelimbs, thence to the truly beautiful interaction and matched developments of the hand, the eye, and the brain. In step with the progress of his course marched the growing realization of his feelings about his golden-haired student. He noted that she wore the pin of her own club, Athene, and none of any man's. (Talvert was west of the Ivy League zone, but near enough to it to refer to its fraternities as clubs and call them by names unrelated to their Greek letters, such as Wally's Bulldog or Jessica's Athene, the latter name betraying the greater willingness of women than men to be flagrantly serious.) It annoyed him that this pleased him so. The whole thing was ridiculous. Part of him greatly desired to see Jessica, whom he yet addressed, in proper instructor-to-student manner, as Miss Butterworth, in an informal setting, and was even capable of making tentative plans to this end. Another part of him rejected the very idea. The situation stank of folklore of a stale kind, the teacher who falls in love with his student, and it was made even worse by the fact that this condition, dangerously imminent if it had not already occurred, should appear in his very first teaching assignment.

The time of the Big Game drew near. This year it would be played away from home. A Bulldog undergraduate fell ill, leaving a ticket in danger of going unused. With the feel of late November in the air, it did not take much persuasion to lead Wally to use the ticket, accepting an offer of a ride to and from the game with a group of men who were going stag. Wally had played football energetically in high school and he would rather watch a football than a baseball game any day. He had a fine time. With the rest of the Bulldog crowd, he went on to a reception at the local chapter of their fraternity. When he entered the big living room, he saw giddily that the company consisted of a faceless herd, Jessica Butterworth, and himself.

She was there as the date of Cuss Biederman, a Bulldog senior. There was music. Wally danced with her briefly.

Ordinarily, he was a pretty good dancer, but now he seemed frozen and did so poorly that he was relieved when the record ended. He chatted with her, also briefly, and with no greater success; nor did this encounter get him past the barrier of Miss Butterworth and Dr. Caswell, for which he could blame only himself. He got home late at night, tired, depressed by the complete dying away of an earlier slight lift from drinks, and full of gloom. He sat for a long time in his armchair, just staring at a wall. Well, this would be ended soon enough. Right after mid-years he would join the annual migration of anthropologists to Meso-America, to serve as second in command under Dr. Lancaster for the second year of the big excavation at Popil. Before the rainy season drove them back to the States, Miss Butterworth would have graduated and left Talvert for good, and that would be that. A good thing, too, a very good thing. He went to bed. He could not sleep, and finally got up and fell to rereading a section of *Maya Hieroglyphic Writing*. This was his other love, his private world shared with a chosen few, exempt from the trespass of campus queens. He read intensely, thinking, balancing the arguments laid before him. Near morning he became sleepy, put the book down, and went to bed and to sleep.

In the quiet of Sunday he looked at the big book and thought, there's the answer. Stay deep in science, get ready for Popil after midyear's, and keep your mind busy. The idea was dandy until, on Monday at ten, Jessica sat before him in his classroom. With an effort he set his mind upon the developing frontal lobe of the sub-simian brain and the drawing in of the eyes to produce stereoscopic vision, got off his prepared joke about cross-eyed and cock-eyed, received a laugh, and continued. By the time the class had departed, his

confidence in himself was restored. A purely classroom, academic relationship with the girl was something he was sure
he could sweat out until midyear's.

The fates played hob with his plans and intentions, or one
could equally well say that Wally had not reckoned on Jessica's ablity to get around, without effort, without, often
enough, being in the least aware that there was anything out
of the way in being asked to wherever she was. Between his
work for his doctorate and his field seasons in the Maya
country, Wally had been distinctly out of circulation. Now
his total load was lightened, and being naturally sociable, he
went out more often. Thus, with one contact through anthropology, their respective orbits led to conjunctions.

The first of these occurred on the annual reception on the
Saturday after Thanksgiving given for the Department of
Anthropology by Dr. Bogue, the director of the Museum of
Man, and Mrs. Bogue. The affair was somewhat primly
billed as a tea, but, although tea was available, the principal
solvent was a mild stone fence in the big, cut glass bowl that
was one of the hostess's special prides. Over this bowl Mrs.
Bogue or one of the other faculty wives presided, their presence inhibiting too frequent returns. At the beginning of the
reception the level, ruddy, early winter sunlight poured
through the south windows and set up rainbow responses in
the punch bowl and glass cups. Upper class anthropology
majors and postgraduate students gathered around this professor or that, talk hovered close to their science, wandered
from it and returned. The jokes became a little freer, the
laughter readier, the debates a trifle more vigorous towards
the end of the occasion than at the beginning.

This was a party for those who were making anthropology their career; Jessica should not have been included, but she was. She attracted the most senior professors, and, her manners being very good and her carriage of herself modest, their wives liked her. When Dr. Bogue had suggested inviting Jessica, Mrs. Bogue, who loved to be surrounded by the young, remarked that that would be nice for the young men.

What should have been the high point of the occasion for Wally turned out the reverse. Mrs. Lancaster had spent the last field season at Popil with her husband. Now, finding a number of people, including Wally and Jessica, within her immediate range, with the world's best matchmaking intentions she asked him to tell how he discovered the Tomb of the Two Priests. Wally was all but struck dumb. He did not see how he could describe the wonder and excitement without making a total ass of himself, so he played it down, made the accident of finding the hole in the roof of the underground chamber sound dull, reducing the whole thing to an archeological resumé and exhibiting himself as a very dry academic stick. That was how he saw his performance, but then he had fallen into an inclination to think the worst. He did not allow for certain moments of vividness, his description of the limestone and mortar walls by candlelight, looking as if the masons who put them up had just left, of the figures of the two priests in plaster bas-relief painted with cinnabar, or the cool feel of a smooth, jade bead when his fingers encountered it under the dust.

For young men in his line of work who are not braggarts, there exists an emotional problem of which he had been somewhat aware and which now became acute. In his three field seasons with Dr. Lancaster he had ranged from the muddy, steaming rain forests of the Petén and the adjacent parts of Mexico to parts of the Guatemala highlands that reached above ten thousand feet. He had coped with all the perversities of pack mules, hacked his way with his machete, depended upon his rifle for meat. He had encountered the timid yet latently dangerous, wild Lacandones with their longbows, and had used workmen and bearers of half a dozen varied, machete-wielding tribes. Last season's work at Popil, in a permanent camp, had been comparatively luxurious, but even there he had experienced the quality of the massed, high-arching trees and the countless vines that preyed and depended upon them, had kept an eye out for venomous snakes, and in the early mornings had sometimes heard a jaguar mewing. His approach to his work was grave and scholarly, but in his heart, like many of his colleagues, he felt a romance in it that he would have been profoundly embarrassed to put into words.

Therefore he was dull and frustrated when Mrs. Lancaster gave him his chance to shine. So, too, on other occasions, when those whose travels and knowledge of wonders reached no farther than New York or Chicago were holding forth gaily, he was likely to sit dumb, not helped but hampered by the knowledge that he had done and seen so much more than they.

Jessica Butterworth was a beauty, a charmer; she was not Medusa to turn men to stone. Wally, entering a room and finding her there, or seeing her come into the room in which he was, stiffened, felt at once delight and pain, grew awkward, but he did not always sit a hopeless stock. An important ingredient in the art of making conversation is a talent for timely plagiarism, the use of a remark made in a similar context by someone else or by oneself. Of this Wally possessed a portion. Also, he had a fair degree of natural humor, although it was, at his present stage, suffering from desuetude. Humor, like affection, is best maintained by use. He did, on occasion, get away from himself enough to be amusing, and on at least two occasions had the pleasure of making Miss Butterworth laugh. He was, also, as good at lighting a lady's cigarette or fetching her refreshments as any man. In January, in the course of an informal evening, she called him "Wally," so he found occasion to address her as "Jessica." Doctor and Miss thereafter were reserved for the classroom. This was progress of a sort, but being on a first name basis merely made him one of many instead of an isolated exception among those near her age.

At that time, in Anthropology 4a, they had reached West African man, the recent finds at Olduvai Gorge, the first clear evidence of creatures — hominids or hominoids — who worked tools according to preconceived plans. Wally's own study of evolution had been made before those finds were published, but he had read on them extensively, the material coming out in one month or another to make an exciting serial story, and at the Lancasters', when there had been visiting firemen of stature present, he had heard a brilliant dicussion of the transition from man-apes to man. The question of where to draw the line and say that below this are man-apes, above this, *Homo*, man, is largely a matter of individual definition. Some, the most zoologically inclined, go largely by the state of evolution of the teeth; some by the appearance of the skull, or by the brain case alone; some, at the opposite pole from the tooth fanciers, demand evidence of speech. Wally went with the school that held that a creature that had reached the stage of knowingly shaping stone tools and of passing on this concept and the necessary techniques to succeeding generations had culture, hence were men, even if they did not yet bury their dead.

He felt that at this point, the definition of man in particular relation to the Olduvai Gorge people of the Lower Pleistocene, was an occasion for setting off some fireworks. He worked up his lecture carefully, keeping his wording as simple as possible, and practiced drawing several illustrations directly on the blackboard. From training in mapping, then in drawing decorated pottery, and then Maya Hieroglyphs and bas-reliefs, he had developed a fair facility with the pencil, which during the semester he had been learning to transfer to chalk. He knew that he was about to put on an act, but in the purity with which he served his science he did not think of this primarily in relation to Jessica, but to giving adequate expression to something strongly felt for the purpose of communicating its nature to the class as a whole.

The result was a thorough success. He could feel how completely the class was with him, the indescribable, different quality in their silence and their attention that successful actors know, he was aware of those remarkable eyes of Jessica's upon him, then dropping under their curling lashes as she wrote in her notebook, but he was carried away by his subject and his performance, so that the perception did not disturb him, did not really register with him until later. Then it occurred to him that being a scholar might not be the total handicap he had thought it.

In giant strides now the class would move through the Pithecanthropines to Neanderthal Man, the Swanscombe and

Steinheim crania, the Mount Carmel puzzles, and so, in a photo finish, would reach *Homo sapiens* in the last two lectures. Then he would stow his goods in pack boxes, take his machete out of the closet, and depart for six months at Popil. Professor Stronsky would teach Anthropology 4b. Thus the sweet torment of Jessica unattainable would be transposed into terms of distance and memory, and memory, he told himself, fades. Or did distance ever make the heart grow fonder? In his limited experience it did not, nor could he imagine himself wasting away for love while he was clearing the Plaza IV complex, which would be his principal assignment for the coming season. He did an earnest job of telling himself that imagining finding a stela with a long-count, intitial series date on it, which was not in the least improbable, successfully drove from his mind other imaginings about Jessica that he both loved and feared.

Immediately before the start of the midyear examination period, Bulldog threw a traditional winging, strictly stag, the stated purpose of which was to take everybody's mind off his troubles and, with all of Sunday for recuperation, send him refreshed to his exams. As usual, in the course of the evening Wally performed his specialty, which was Russian dancing, to a record kept in the club for just these occasions. Wally went into the act with *brío*. He may have had a highball or so more than he allowed for; knowing how soon he would be on the plane for Guatemala and what he must leave behind may have caused him to kick and leap with extra force; whatever the ultimate cause, suddenly he felt a sharp pain in his left knee, then found he could not straighten that leg. He sat in an armchair for some time while sundry young men conversed with him and acted as cupbearers; then a delegation helped him to his quarters and up the stairs.

The next day, when finally he wakened, in addition to a headache he had a swollen knee that was unserviceable. He finally managed to get hold of one of the university physicians. He said that he had wrenched that knee playing football in high school and spent a couple of weeks on crutches. The doctor said that he would have to have treatments of various sorts for several weeks, must spend at least two on crutches, and that for some months he would be in danger of a recurrence if he did not — literally — watch his step.

So there went his field season. Dr. Lancaster said firmly that, much as he would miss Wally, the young man should not attempt field work until he was completely healed. Dr. Stronsky, striking like a shark, set himself up a season in southern Mexico to do a really thorough study of the Chicomucelteco language, and Anthropology 4b landed in Wally's lap with a thud. With resignation he set himself to reading up on the later parts of the Old Stone Age, the Meso- and Neolithic, and the races of modern man. On the first Monday of the spring semester, his class was doubly surprised, first, at seeing him instead of Professor Stronsky and second, at seeing him on crutches. He thought, angrily, that he probably seemed ridiculous.

A few days after the term began he graduated from crutches to a cane, but he continued to avoid social life, punishing himself while giving all sorts of other reasons. Among his friends were a geologist, Ted Jensen, a few years older than he, and his wife, Sandy. Wally had come to know the man when he attended one of the digs in Arizona on which Wally worked as an undergraduate, for the sake of the interdisciplinary experience. After he had sulked for a couple of weeks, Sandy Jensen speared him on the telephone, reduced his objections, excuses, and alleged disabilities to nothing, made him firmly accept an invitation to dinner, then scared the living daylights out of him by saying that since he could not walk the distance, she would have Jessica Butterworth pick him up in her car. She didn't say she would "ask" her, she said she would "have" her, as though giving orders to the most delectable and most sought after female on the face of the earth were her daily practice. He protested, said he did not want to trouble Jessica, that, taking his time, he would walk it, that he could take a taxi. He got nowhere. In a gently firm, feminine way, Sandy knew how to arrange things as she wanted them. He should be at the door at six o'clock and Jessica would honk for him.

He knew that she drove one of those little MG's that are built to seat only two and also to last forever. Wally could not tell whether owning that was or was not an indication of wealth; those cars do not come cheap, but this one, although in fine condition, was definitely vintage. Early in the year she had driven it without a top, and he remembered her, hatless, a hatless youth beside her, her golden hair blown back. Like most who work in the tropics, he had the habit of hats and had wondered how she could drive thus in bright October without catching cold, a reflection in which he saw an indication of the gap between them, between the untrammelled undergraduate and one who (at twenty-six) had become older, cautious, less warm-blooded. At this season she had the top and side curtains on, although the sense of spring was beginning to be in the air. He would ride beside her, like a fellow undergraduate, only not at all like one, not knowing what to say, with the stupidity of his ingloriously injured knee and the cane with the rubber tip. She was ten minutes late, so he had ample time for such reflections as he waited just inside the door.

The sound of her horn, then, was a relief. He crossed the sidewalk and got into the car. She said, "Hi." He said, "Hi." She started off. Brilliant conversation, he thought. "How long have you known Sandy and Ted?" he asked after a time. "I didn't see you at their place last year."

"I met Sandy last summer. We were both counsellors at a summer camp."

Then she isn't rich. "Do you enjoy counselling?"

"Yes and no. At times, it's an awful lot of brats. This camp was for little ones, not teen-agers, thank goodness. But they have so *much* energy; you have to be peppy when you'd really rather not, and some of the things that fascinate them are totally boring. Did you ever do any of that?"

"No. I tutored a couple of boys the summer after my freshman year. I didn't like it. Spoiled, and naturally they resented being made to study during the summer, and the resentment turned against me. After that, I began summer field work, and so on. So I've been lucky."

"Mm, yes. I'd like to go to Central America and find cities in the jungle."

Calling the rain forest "jungle" was highly incorrect, and it is doubtful that the great Maya ceremonial centers were cities, properly speaking. He suppressed this knowledge. The high bush was no place for women anyhow. He said, "It gets a bit grim at times. Mosquitoes and all that. Sometimes the shut-in feeling bugs you. But it is fun when you're finding things."

They came to the apartment house where the Jensens lived. He was glad that she made no offer to help him, although he was a trifle awkward getting out and dropped the cane.

They were the last to arrive. The company already had that air of increased cheerfulness that begins when the first drink of the evening is in the hand. The other guests were Dorothea Linderman, a friend of Sandy's, not connected with the university, Clark, a graduate student in geology, an instructor in political economy named Le Grand, and Cuss Biederman. Wally was not too pleased to see Cuss; he was interested in Jessica, he was a leading senior, and Wally could not imagine that anyone could be interested in that girl without being her dedicated suitor. Le Grand was a stranger to him. There was something about him he did not like. The man had good looks, he was sure of himself, his manner smooth, and in these qualities Wally found another threat, the likelihood of another competitor whose attractions he could not match.

Le Grand, it developed, had recently returned from an extended visit to Thailand that had a connection with a State Department program. Cuss asked about the elephants and Le Grand spoke about them interestingly, commenting that he had not seen a white one. The talk veered, via remarks on Southeast Asia in general — Le Grand was well-informed — to the new administration's foreign policy. The discussion was lively. They went in to dinner, the main dish of which was good, roast beef with a California wine that Wally found delicious. Le Grand played connoisseur with his first glass, praised the liquid with a touch of condescension, and let it be gathered that he had spent some little time in France. The conversation drifted throughout dinner. Wally took some part in it — he had, fortunately, read the book that became for a time the center of discussion.

They relaxed in the living room for coffee and liqueurs. Dorothea asked Le Grand a question about Thailand to which he replied in detail. Wally felt rather defeated, seeing Jessica's interest. Thailand, Viet Nam, France, yes, these represented knowledge, travel to talk about, but where he had been — the sticks, very big sticks, but still the sticks . . .

Jessica said, "The girls — are they as attractive as you hear? Or as they seem in *The King and I?*"

"Some of them are; in fact, some of them are fascinating." He described their Oriental appearance, their slimness, their delicacy, and as he went on implied strongly that he had done a good deal more than just look at them.

Sandy said, "And what about you, Wally — what about those Indian wenches in Guatemala."

"Some of them look rather like the ones Le Grand described," he said.

"And when you get to know them well . . . ?"

"I'm afraid I never have." He sounded prim to his own ears.

Cuss said, "Oh, come on. *Tales of the South Pacific* and all that."

Wally sipped at his brandy. "Well — you see — those people don't practice birth control, and they do practice naming the children after their fathers. If the father was a foreigner, they'll point out the child. So you run into little, half-naked brats or a grown workman, with last names like Von Kramm or Stackpole — well, I don't want them pointing out any little Caswells. And if the father was fair, any doubt about the naming is answered when you see the product has a zoned eye."

"What," said Sandy, "is a zoned eye?"

"Well, when two Caucasoids — white people — marry, if one has blue eyes and one brown —" He hesitated no more than a second to discard about ten minute's worth of explanation about dominant and recessive genes. "They can have a child with blue eyes, or brown, or mixed. If they're mixed, the brown radiates outward from the iris into the blue, and if the mixture is just right, that's how you get green eyes." He looked directly at Jessica. Several of the others laughed. "But if a blue-eyed white man married a brown-eyed member of another race —"

"You mean," Jessica said, "that this is only possible if you have a license?"

"Mm — I understand that on occasion it happens without one. Anyhow, in a cross like that, if the eye is mixed, the brown in the center will form a neat circle with the blue in a zone around it."

Ted said, "So that's evidence that a German or blue-eyed American or someone like that was fooling around?"

"Yes."

"And you mean," Le Grand said, "that as a matter of curiosity you never sampled . . . ? And you an anthropologist?"

Wally finished his brandy. The time had come to take steps, and memory had served him up a key.

"I did have a rather curious experience once." Divesting himself of scientific correctness, he added, "It was in the Petén jungle of Guatemala."

Sandy said, "Give. That is, if it's reasonably decent."

"It is, reasonably. You know about the Lacandones, don't you?"

Several people said, "No" and "What are they?"

They had asked for it. He felt excitement. A little synthesis and a bit of imagination would do the trick. Keeping clear of any semblance of a lecture on ethnology, he said that the Lacandones were remnants of Mayas whom the Spanish had never subdued. He described their long hair, their greyish-white dress, in which they seemed to flit through the great forest like smoke or like ghosts, but above all like a natural part of it, which was, in fact, the way he thought of them. He described their stone-tipped arrows and their longbows, then, throwing away all restraint, credited them with the long spears used by the Jíbaros of Ecuador and from that, since he wished to add to the women's glamour, he told how the women adorned their black hair with the iridescent casings of certain beetles, as he talked seeing in his mind's eye the Jíbaro case in the South American Hall of the Museum of Man. He could feel that he had his audience's interest.

He had ridden with Dr. Lancastor, he said, on a scout north-westward from the Río Pasión, accompanied by four Christian Maya workmen. The forest was thick, the trail they followed old and often overgrown. They knew they were near a ruin of which Dr. Lancaster had heard from some of the men who go into the jungle to draw the chicle sap from which chewing gum is made. One morning, Dr. Lancaster suddenly halted his mule, dismounted, and, wielding his machete, went off the path to the right. He called to Wally. Not over five yards in rose the back of a — once again he wrenched himself clear of technical accuracy — a pyramid of cut stone and mortar.

On top of the pyramid was a temple in a fair state of pres-
ervation, facing away from the trail. From the temple, perhaps forty feet above ground level, one looked towards a plaza
entirely hidden by trees that overtopped the building. Beyond,
there would unquestionably be other structures, and in the
plaza itself there might be heaven only knew what altars and
monuments. This was what they had been looking for. With
their small force, all they could do would be to cut a number
of passages and sample the place. But, he said, there was one
path already there, and then he paused, asking for a glass of
water because the brandy had made him dry. Ted got it for
him. Jessica said, "Go on."

There was a foot trail, on which recent clearing had been
done, leading across the plaza and up the steps of the pyramid
to the temple. On the floor of the temple, in front of the
sanctuary, were Lacandón pots and offerings of rubber and
incense such as the prehistoric Mayas had made. Two days
later, the Lacandones themselves appeared — "As I said, like
ghosts, out of nowhere." The first visitors were an old man
and two young ones, all armed. They and the workmen could
understand each others' brand of Maya fairly well. Once they
were sure that the strangers did not intend any harm to the
temple and would not disturb their offerings, they became
friendly. There were exchanges of gifts, trinkets and salt for
tobacco and ears of fresh corn.

"What are left of the Lacandones live in small groups," he
said. "They want to increase their numbers, and they have a
problem of inbreeding, so sometimes they will offer one of
their women to a stranger if they think well of him."

Le Grand said, "Ah-ha." Jessica said, "Oh-oh."

Wally visited their settlement. The old chief had a daughter, probably about sixteen, something of a beauty. One day the chief came to him and between the few Maya words Wally knew, his few words of Spanish, and signs, Wally learned that the chief was offering him his daughter.

"It was pretty tempting under the circumstances," he said. "We'd been in the bush then for nearly four months, and that girl was really cute. I was working along a passage we'd cleared pretty close to the settlement, trying to make up my mind one way or the other." He stopped.

Le Grand said, "Well? What did you decide?"

"I don't know. That is — one of the young men, it seems, was in love with her, and knew of the offer the chief had made me. So he came out from behind a tree and stuck a spear in my back, right through the heart. I was buried at the foot of the main pyramid and Dr. Lancaster was mad as hops."

Laughter ran through the company. Wally sat back, flushing slightly. He had not guessed he had it in him. Cuss was inspired to tell a funny and somewhat relevant story. There were more stories.

Moving to sit beside him, Jessica said, "How much of that was true? Where did the fairy tale start?"

"If you leave out the business about the girl, the rest happened one time or another. I sort of synthesized, and I guess I put in a few extra licks here and there."

"And is it true that you got your bad knee doing Russian dancing at Bulldog?"

"Yes." He did not think the accident as entirely discreditable as he had.

It was beginning to be late and there were morning classes

to think of. Clark rose, then Sandy, then the others. Wally was a bit awkward getting up. Jessica put a hand under his elbow.

"You're a surprising guy," she said. "Shall I ride you back to your place?"

"If you don't mind."

She looked straight at him, smiling. "Of course not." For moments he could not take his eyes from hers. "Are they zoned?" she asked.

"No. But I've known that a long time."

She laughed at him. He knew then. In the briefest possible instant of privacy he knew, although of course there would be the necessary and ritually fixed interval of uncertainty that his culture demanded, even after he kissed her good night, as he would do. They turned from each other to say their farewells and thank their hosts, in the course of which formalities they concealed the visible evidences of the crashing event that had happened unknown to anyone but themselves.

THE REAL THING

As soon as Clare Turner heard about the "lost" Baron
Trenholm she knew that she was in luck. The one essential which her present trip had been lacking was now provided. Clare's travels followed a definite formula, out of which
were derived a series of books and of lecture tours before a
well-established chain of admiring audiences, all of which in
turn furnished her with a comfortable income and a pleasing,
minor fame.

The special quality of her travels and the resultant writings
derived from several factors. At college Clare had been studious and rather romantic, and had majored with honors in the
social sciences. From that training she retained the habit of
doing rather wide, quick reading on the exotic lands she chose
for her tours, so that she brought an effect of erudition to her
narrative. She was frequently introduced to audiences as "author and scientist." Then, she wrote well. The high aspira-
tions of her youth had been long since outgrown, her early
attempts at art had been replaced by a smooth, competent
style, cleverness in arrangement, and a fine sense of selection
which made each of her books easy, vivid, and at moments
exciting.

On her first major trip, on which she did a series of magazine articles which resulted in her first successful book, she covered North Africa. Partly in a spirit of taking a dare, partly out of real curiosity which had been aroused from one of her old courses in ethnology, she had gone into the Berber country in the high Atlas Mountains. From that side trip had come the best chapter of all, the one around which she built her book. She realized then that she had found the extra element for her formula which would distinguish her travelogues from those of most globe trotters. Thereafter she made it a point on each of her travels to go into the interior, upriver beyond the limits of civilization, into the high bush, the hinterland, to the point where tourists never ventured. Her second husband, who was an admirer of Leacock, used to refer to these adventurings as "going behind the beyond." Depending upon the pleasantness or unpleasantness of the climate and of the mode of travel, and on the availability of satisfactory points to be reached, these explorations might last two days or a fortnight. In her books and lectures it was difficult to determine the time element involved. Almost always her goal was some outpost of empire, occasionally an archeological camp or other scientific enterprise, and the sense of its remoteness could be very nicely conveyed by referring, rather humorously, to the touching surprise which the young Englishmen or Dutchmen or Americans manifested on seeing a white woman appear before them, and their rather delicious gallantry. These enterprises fitted well with the dual reputation of scientific endeavor and adventurousness which she had built up.

This year she had chosen the little republic of Alturas in Central America. It had turned out well except for the matter of the special expedition. Her choice lay between the high, forbidding Nimangil Mountains near the Guatemala border and the steaming, pestilential Ticab jungle on the Pacific coast. The latter, she gathered, was an extremely unpleasant area. Neither in the jungle nor the mountains were there any outposts. There were no young Britons (she preferred the British), not even an American oil camp. She could not figure out any specific objective, there was not even any important ruin, although Alturas lay within the ancient Maya country. There would merely be some difficult travel, a view of some wretched native settlement or other, and return. Such an undertaking would not make copy up to her standards, and it promised no pleasure. Clare Turner was still attractive, but she had reached an age, five years after her second divorce, at which the rather worshipful admiration of the lonely young men was a keen delight, and there were incidents in her memories which did not appear in her narratives.

Then, at dinner at the Salvadorean legation in the capital, she heard of Baron Trenholm, and she knew that she had found her objective. The Baron was a Norwegian aristocrat who made a very serious hobby of ethnology. He was Curator of Middle American Anthropology at the Royal Museum at Oslo. He was in his late thirties, and the society of the capital had found him quite a beau during his brief stay there before he left for the Nimangil Mountains. He had gone in in December, at the beginning of the dry season, and everyone took it for granted that he would come out, as all scientists did, before the hard rains began in June. He had not come out. The rainy season passed, the dry returned, and now it was near the end of April. He had been in those mountains for more than a year. No one had heard from him since the courteous thank-you notes he had sent out from Sacabil, where the narrow gauge railroad ended. His disappearance had received no official attention, but it was much in the minds of hostesses to whom a distinguished European with a title was an important prize.

Clare knew even better than the people around her how distinguished Trenholm was. She had read a number of his scientific publications, especially the formidable and very inclusive monograph on the Rashti Indians which had come out in 1940, just before the invasion of Norway ended his researches. Among ethnologists, he was an international figure. Obviously, she must go and look for him. Such prominent men do not simply disappear; she would probably find him well and happy but she had no intention of ignoring the tragic possibilities. In any case, this was the most romantic quest that she had yet dreamed up. She thanked heaven that he had chosen to study the Rashti in their cool mountains, rather than the Tishaniles who occupied the dreadful coastal jungle.

Since her readers might well think that it was a step which should not be omitted, she went to the Norwegian Vice-Consulate, dreading lest that office explode her whole project at the start. The vice consul's position was largely honorary. He himself turned out to be an elderly storekeeper whose grandfather had been a Norwegian. He was supremely uninterested in Baron Trenholm, knew nothing of him, and pointed out, defensively, that since no inquiries had come from Norway, there was no reason for him to trouble the Altureño authorities. Clare was satisfied, and reserved the possibility of an acid little paragraph about the man. She packed her camp gear and took the train to Sacabil.

Sacabil was the capital of the province of that name. Five miles to the north of it the mountains rose like a wall, an unbroken, steep ascent of over six thousand feet to a pass at eleven thousand feet above sea level. The lower slopes were brownish with pale green washes of grass or cultivated land, the top was richly green, and in the clear air, even from the plaza at Sacabil, one could see how the mantle of tall evergreens made the edge of the ridge seem fuzzy. In the late part of the rainy season and in January and February, the highest levels were sometimes white with snow. The inner slopes caught the moisture-laden north winds coming from the Caribbean. It was a fertile country, she understood, which remained poor only because it was so difficult of access. From the maps and the descriptions of scientists she knew that beyond the first ridge there was a succession of similar ones, separated by deep, steep-sided valleys each with its river at the bottom. In there there were nothing but Indian settlements, a couple of small garrisons of troops who were themselves mostly Indians, a priest in one village, a scattering of Ladinos — Spanish-speaking Altureños — either officials or merchants. Assuming, reasonably, that the Ladinos all had a good deal of Indian blood, she could claim that no white men lived there. She foresaw a difficult, uncomfortable trip and was disturbed by the necessity of going in entirely on her own, but business was business.

The only hotel in Sacabil was run by Don Miguel Carrera. Her presence intrigued Don Miguel, and he was glad to enter into conversation with her. At school, Clare had learned Italian, and reinforced it by early travels in Italy. From this she derived a curious substitute for Spanish with which she could maintain extensive conversations. Like most people who have learned Italian as an accomplishment, she rather despised Spanish, and had no idea of how grating was her constant injection of Italian pronunciations. She brought Trenholm's name in casually. Yes, he knew of him. He called him "Don Esteban," which was what the Altureño tongue had made of Sven. He remarked that Don Esteban had great practice in this country. He had gone to San Mateo to live, and instead of hiring local people to take his gear in, had picked up half a dozen Indians from that village in the market and hired them as bearers.

Clare said that it was a coincidence, she, too, was going to San Mateo. Don Miguel said that the scientist now was not there. A friend of his had gone to San Mateo on business a few months ago, and said that he had gone. He did not know where. Clare remarked that it was odd he should have stayed so long in the mountains. Don Miguel said that probably he had found himself a pretty little Indian girl — at times, one encounters them beautiful — and established his residence somewhere. As he said this he eyed Clare curiously. She said that what Trenholm might be doing was not of importance to her. She must go to San Mateo in any case, to make scientific observations.

Don Miguel urged her not to make the trip. He said that those mountains were not conformable to the travelling of a North American lady, that there might not be peril nowadays, but there was much discomfort and inconvenience. She thanked him, and told him that it was necessary for her to go.

The hotel keeper told her then that she should not attempt to take the direct route from Sacabil. That route, which was strictly a road of horseshoes, ran for many leagues over the high central plateau of the mountains, where there fell much hail with great violence, drinking water was hard to find, and one might encounter bad characters. She should go by motor from here to Santa Catalina, where tourists occasionally came and there was a guest house. The proprietor of the guest house could help her to hire mules and a guide who was practiced. From there she could reach Uyalá, where also people of reason were to be found, Ladino people, and on the second day arrive at San Mateo. There she would be well enough, there were numerous people of reason and even a store maintained by a Turk. Clare thanked him again.

By a "Turk" Clare knew that he meant almost anyone from Asia Minor, most likely a Syrian or an Armenian. The presence of such a person there was reassuring. He might be good copy, or she might have to suppress him, if telling of him took the glamour off San Mateo. A man like Trenholm, she thought, might take a native "housekeeper," but he would hardly allow her to alter the scheme of his life. It could happen — she remembered a Dutchman in Sumatra — but it was unlikely. The main thing was to get to San Mateo and start inquiries.

From Sacabil the motor road extended to the crest of the mountains, where the "road of horseshoe," the narrow horse trail, took off over the highest country. The motor road continued west four leagues to Santa Catalina, a rugged Indian village near the head of a steep, green valley, with a number of white-painted, tile-roofed Ladino residences along its main street, one of the largest of which was the guest house. Clare studied the village. As a jumping-off place it was most satisfactory, for it was primitive enough in itself to impress her audience with the thought that to her, the explorer, this was still civilization.

The proprietor found her a guide named Pablo, a muleteer

by profession, who worked for his sister-in-law's brother, from whom Clare hired five mules. The hiring took some time, for the sister-in-law's brother raised his prices steeply. He worked on the simple principle that staying at the guest house cost the equivalent of two dollars a day, and that any reduction his customer might hope to get by refusing to accept his price would soon be cancelled by her expenses. Clare bargained for form's sake, as the sum involved was inconsiderable. The owner gave her a fractional reduction as a matter of courtesy, and she closed the deal. Then he produced Pablo.

Pablo said that he knew San Mateo well. He was dark and rather squat. He wore a large sombrero, a blue shirt, tight-fitting trousers, sandals, and a spur on one bare heel. Over his shoulder he carried a brilliant serape from Oaxaca. Muleteers wander the earth, to wherever they may be hired to take a cargo, they have homes and wives, but they know the trails and the women of three or four republics. They are poor men, but they are free, and it is always wise to treat them with respect.

There was little to be learned of Trenholm in Santa Catalina, as that village did not have much traffic with San Mateo. Some people knew vaguely that a "German" had been there, or was there. Some six months ago he had spent a night at the guest house. That was all.

Near sunset she looked out from the portal of the guest house, across the deep valley, its lower portion filling with purple shadow, to the gold-touched ridge beyond, and another ridge beyond that. She visualized the steep climbs and long descents, and wished that Trenholm had chosen leveller country. She thought of Pablo, uncouth, unknown. Never before had she gone in alone like this; there had always been white men, Sahibs, and deft retainers.

Clare hated discomfort. There had been a time when she would have welcomed real adventure; a little of that spirit had remained in her when she made that first side trip among the Berbers. Long ago there had been an undergraduate, romantic, eager, unafraid. Life had destroyed her. It began with the failure of her first marriage, the dragging, tortured final years and then the desperate decision to break, the love freely and innocently given and now buried deep under the hardness of the years and still a pain somewhere behind consciousness. There had been the years of poverty and the frustration of her belief in her ability to live by the kind of writing she had dreamed of in college, before she found her formula and hit her stride. She was through with insecurity, with being unguarded. She intended never again to suffer pain. Her second marriage had been smart, reasonable, cynical, and doomed from the start. When that ended and she was freed from the torment of her husband's clever tongue, she took life in hand and shaped it exactly to her liking. She had done so ever since. She had had lovers; she had no true friends. Now she looked out over the darkening mountains, feeling the chill in the air as the sun left the high ridges, and the prospect of her voyage repelled her. Business was business. She wasn't going to like it, it violated her instinctive avoidance of rugged reality, but the end was worth it. What material!

Even her alarm at the morrow's prospects was good material, toned down and properly handled. It was a new angle. She would make something of Pablo, he lent himself to good description. And Trenholm — if ever her appearance startled the white men in the outposts, it should do so this time. What

would he be like? They had found him attractive in the capital. Yes, she looked forward to meeting him. If she found
him. Tied up with a native woman, gone in drink, perhaps?
Unlikely. Sick with fever, or merely following up some remarkable bit of research? Trouble with Indians? They said
that these Indians were meek enough nowadays, but they had
an old history of uprisings, and Trenholm himself in his monograph told of two young Germans who disappeared without
trace after they had entered a sacred cave and stolen some
idols from it.

It is an ethnologist's business to pry into the innermost
secrets. These Indians might be meek, but they looked capable
of almost anything, small, quiet, unreadable. The men's dress
had a wildness to it. Some tribes wore brilliantly striped
trousers, most wore woolen kilts with red and green or red
and black checks; their shirts, woven of rough cotton, were
usually decorated with bright colors. Unlike the Ladinos,
they wore small sombreros, low on their foreheads. In addition, it would not be far wrong to describe their machetes,
the wide-bladed knives about three feet long which they carried, as part of their dress. Except when they came in to
Sacabil, one seldom saw a man who was not so armed, and
here in Santa Catalina she noted that many of them, instead
of wearing their machetes in a sheath, carried the naked blades
casually in the crook of their arms.

It could happen. They could have waited, for instance,
until he left San Mateo for some unspecified destination, and
caught him on the road. That way he would not be missed.
It could be. She began framing her speculations, building the
opening of her chapter. It was full night now, and too
cold on the portal. She went to her room, lit the two candles

on the little table, and began making notes. Her plan — she would go to San Mateo, and there make inquiries, delicately, carefully, among the Indians. If they were too blank, if nothing could be learned, then there would be the dreadful supposition of tragedy. She put down her pencil abruptly. She had missed a bet, such a simple, prosaic bet.

If there had been no inquiry for Trenholm from his museum in Norway, there was an excellent chance that he was in communication with it. Very probably she could have learned his present location from the post office or the telegraph office in Sacabil. Well, she could learn as much at San Mateo; he must have made some arrangement for forwarding his mail. She would inquire of the Indians just the same, if only for the sake of the material, and with good luck the information she would pick up from them would enable her to ignore the less interesting inquiries when it came to her account. She went back to her notes.

At this point, when she described how she was about to penetrate the unknown country, it was her practice to refer to the brief list of scientists and explorers who might have proceeded her. It was part of the scholarly effect, gave credit to others, and by its very brevity added to her own credit. She omitted from consideration, of course, a few thousand Spaniards, Altureños, Guatemalans, and Mexicans, as well as countless generations of Indians. In this case there had been Stephens and Catherwood in the 1840's, then Seler in 1910, Trenholm's two expeditions in the late 1930's as well as his present visit, and Martha Pine in 1946 and '47.

Clare frowned. The matter of Martha Pine troubled her. She visualized the Pine woman as flat-heeled, mannish, and unprepossessing, but even so, if she could live in these mountains for two whole seasons, her little expedition looked like nothing at all. She tapped her fingers on the table. Trenholm gave her the answer. She was going to play him up, and in any case his monograph was the most complete work yet issued on this area. It came out in 1940, when La Pine was still an inky-nosed undergraduate, and naturally said nothing about her. Thus in all innocence she could fail to mention the woman. She was beginning to feel fond of the baron.

She laid out her things for the morning, boots, jodhpurs, a good, tough, yet smart gabardine jacket. She unpacked a neat little .380 automatic, checked the clips, and gave it an extra cleaning. Worn in a shoulder holster the weapon did not show at all, but it threw a good solid slug and was accurate up to fifty feet. More than ever before, it was a comforting article to have along. Weighing it in her hand, the thought that she could actually have occasion to use it seemed over-dramatic, faintly ridiculous. She felt less concerned about the morrow.

They left Santa Catalina just before nine. The air was chilly, but Pablo said it would be hot by noon. He rode ahead, then came the three pack mules, while Clare followed behind. Her ample outfit and supplies made a fair load for all three animals; Pablo's entire equipment was rolled in the serape on the back of his saddle except for his machete, considerably longer and wickeder than those carried by the Indians, which was slung from his saddle horn. For nearly an hour they descended to the bottom of the valley, where the trail forked by the river. They crossed the river, the swift-moving water, blue-green from passing through limestone, swirling just beneath their stirrups, then for two solid hours they climbed. The long periods of going up or down held her cramped in the saddle; when they stopped for the noon meal she was stiff, sore, and tired. She would have liked to have taken a nap, but somehow could not let herself fall asleep with the muleteer sitting so near her. She smoked and rested for half an hour, then they mounted and rode on.

She had to admit that the country was as beautiful as any she had ever seen. The bottoms of the valleys were lush and rich with water. The heights were forested with magnificent trees. From the slopes and shoulders of the mountains extraordinary vistas kept opening, full of wild grandeur. She had seen something like this in Wales, but here the scale was greater, and to the cold country vegetation was added tropical lushness, and here and there the ever-exotic touch of orchids.

From time to time they passed groups of Indians, most of whom carried heavy burdens resting on their backs and suspended from tumplines passing over their heads just above the forehead. The Indians would step off the trail and stand in a row to let them pass. The weighted tumplines made it impossible to turn their heads on their necks, so they would move their whole bodies slowly while their shiny, expressionless black eyes followed the travellers. Clare found herself acutely conscious of their scrutiny.

Twice more they came to forks on the trail. At each there was a crude altar at the base of a moss-grown, primitive, partly rotted wooden cross. On the altars there were offerings of flowers. At these forks, Pablo studied the trails carefully before he made his choice. Clare asked him why he did this, and he answered that at times one deceives oneself, and it is always well to consider.

In the middle of the afternoon they were travelling along the side of a great slope. It rose several thousand feet above them on their right hand, on their left fell equally far. Further to the left were a series of lesser ridges and valleys, and far in the distance there rose the blue line of other mountains. Pablo pointed towards them and said, "Guatemala."

Clare studied the view, enjoying it, and mentally arranging it for description. Shortly she noticed a white mass ahead of them, which seemed to be spreading out along the slope and across the lower country. She puzzled over this until she recalled Trenholm's passage on the climate of this area. The northerly winds bring clouds from the Caribbean over the low country, until they reach the mountains, where they form — she remembered his exact words — a clammy mist of exceptional density. She did not like the idea of having to travel through that sea of grounded clouds. She called Pablo's attention to it. He said, "Do not worry. The trail is open and sees itself clearly."

They and the mist drew together. It stood before them, a wall, on which the afternoon sun threw shadows of trees, sharply blue against the brilliant white. Then it engulfed them, and the brilliance changed into a thick, greyish whiteness. The air was wet and cold. She could barely see Pablo up ahead of the mules. She felt lonely, uneasy. How simple to lay an ambush, she thought, how easy to bring about the disappearance of a man who had violated the dark secrets of the Indian religion. She shivered.

She called to Pablo, "How long will this mist last?"

He answered indifferently, "We may be in it till morning, or we may pass through it in five minutes."

She breathed a hearty "damn." She was uneasy, tired, sore, and chilly.

Another cross loomed in the mist. Pablo stopped. Here a second trail crossed their own. He studied the ground at length, looked around, peered into the mist.

"*Señora,* I feel it very much," he told her. "We have equivocated ourselves of the road. This crossroads was not in the description given to me."

"Description? I thought you had been to San Mateo."

"Yes, *señora,* precisely, but by the direct road. It is that my sister-in-law's brother gave me the most careful directions, very adequate in truth. Unfortunately I equivocated myself somewhere in the mist, so now we must go back until again I see a landmark of confidence."

"You offered yourself to me as a guide when you had never been over this road? Is that your usual way of doing?"

Pablo flushed. "The directions were adequate, but in the mist anyone can stray."

Clare felt a flash of pure temper which was partly a reaction against a feeling of despair. Keeping her voice soft, she relieved her feelings by calling him a very ugly name in English. His countenance underwent an astonishing change. A moment ago he had looked ashamed and placative; now his mouth set like a trap, and his eyes hardened.

In quite clear English he said, "To hell weet you." He wheeled his mule, dug in his one spur, and went down the back trail at a gallop. She sat listening to dwindling sound of the animal's hooves. She could not bring herself to call after him or to chase him. Then there was silence, broken by the sound of the mules' grazing and the drip of wetness from twigs. What was she to do now?

She dismounted, keeping hold of her mule's reins, and sat down on a large stone. She lit a cigarette. The cross, taller than a man, looked ominous, hostile, its wood black and shining in the wet. Go back — what good would that do? She had no way of recognizing the right turn if she found it, and it would be night in a few hours. What happened when night came? She knew nothing of making camp for herself, or of unpacking mules, or even how to keep them from straying. Stay put, go forward, turn back, whatever she did led to the hopelessness of nightfall in this dreadful country, inimical, brooding, strange, peopled by savage louts. In the grey chill of the mist, at once confining and infinite, with occasional spurts of rain falling about her, she felt completely lost and afraid. Now she really was in the interior; there was no element of fraud about this. An old, well-buried, forgotten guilt returned to her, a sense of shame, and she was hysterical enough to think of retribution. She rose to her feet, feeling that any motion would be a relief. On an impulse which ordinarily would have shamed her, she gathered a little handful of flowers and laid them on top of the wilted ones on the lichenous altar. She stood before the cross, almost praying, and resisting a primitive impulse to drop to her knees. She also had a childish wish to put her arms around her mule's neck and cry. Then she heard a sound behind her. She whirled about, and quickly stepped back.

Three Indians stood in single file, looking at her. Over the usual costume they wore long, black, woolen ponchos, open at the sides, which made them loom angular and somber in the mist. They had the inevitable machetes at their belts, and carried long staves with simple, decorative carvings at the upper ends. Two of them were elderly, these had sparse beards and mustaches; the third, young and smooth-faced, carried a long, narrow burden on a tumpline.

Instinctively she stepped back again, drawing the mule with her. The Indians went past her to the altar. They moved quietly. Their machetes hung like swords, they gave the impression of armed men from some ancient time. Leaning on their staves they knelt at the altar. The oldest one made a slight gesture of his hand toward the fresh flowers and said something, then all three prayed in a low murmur. She wondered, were they as uninterested in her as their expressions seemed to indicate? Would they, could they, help her? Natives were people who served one, under the orders of Sahibs, but here, natives were simply people. Could she communicate with them? Did they speak Spanish, could they understand her alien Spanish? Should she offer them cigarettes?

They rose, and again stood looking at her.

She held out a hand. "I have equivocated myself of the road," she used Pablo's phrase. "Can you help me to arrive at Uyalá? Or can you tell me if any white people live near here?" She said "white people," *gente blanca*, translating literally from the English, forgetful of the local phrase, *gente ladina*.

After a pause the oldest Indian spoke in Rashti. The young one pointed towards him and said in Spanish, "He is white people."

This was pure surrealism. She did not know what to say.

The old man spoke again in the ugly Rashti tongue. The younger one listened, then interpreted. Because of the tumpline, he swung his body from the waist as he turned from the old man to the woman, his head remaining rigid even when he spoke. He wore his hat over the broad leather head-strap, so that it perched high with a comical effect. To Clare he seemed grotesque, and this quality, on top of the mysteriousness she felt in the three men, and the mist, and that unreasonable, meaningless first answer, all belonged in the one nightmare.

He said now, "Are you looking for Don Esteban, *señora?*"

For a moment she felt giddy. This could not be true. She stammered, "Don Esteban —" and then, remembering as best she could how Don Miguel had pronounced the name, "Don Esteban Trenholm?"

The young man repeated, "Don Esteban?" He paused. "The blond. A very high man." He searched for a word, then completed his description. "The scientist."

"Yes, yes."

The old one spoke again, the young one interpreted. "You have not equivocated yourself. You are precisely in the road."

The third Indian had remained quiet, staring at her, his clasped hands resting on his staff and his cheek against his hands. Now he spoke, and again the young one interpreted.

"Where are your servants? It surprises us to see you so alone."

Although Clare was still thoroughly astonished, she was more collected. The man used the plural; multiple servants would be of greater credit to her. "They believed that they were lost and they fled themselves."

The oldest man, the leader she thought him, spoke again, at greater length. Clare gathered that they understood Spanish, even if they could not or would not speak it, since her answers were not translated.

The interpreter said, "We others are in road to where Don Esteban encounters himself. There we are going. That you come with us."

While he was speaking, the quiet Indian went up to one

of the mules. The interpreter followed him. They arranged them in line, tying each one's rope to the pack of the one in front. The quiet Indian took the rope of the first mule.

She asked, "How far is it?"

"It's not far. Four leagues, perhaps."

Her heart sank. As a rule of thumb one figured an hour to a league, and it was now after four. Still, she seemed to have no choice.

"Put your pack on one of the animals," she told the young man.

"Thanks." He used the tone in which the word is a refusal. "The wax must go with a man."

The old leader had already started along the trail to the left, the west. The young one followed him, then the quiet one started, leading the mules. They were in charge. She mounted, and as she settled herself once more in the saddle, felt reassurance in the weight of the automatic under her left arm.

"The wax must go with a man." What on earth did that mean? "He is white people — *el es gente blanca*." What could that mean? When the mist came down she had entered another, mad world in which people disappeared and appeared, and did, and understood, and said, everything unreasonable. She pressed her mule so as not to lose sight of the others fading ahead of her.

The level ended, the trail pitched sharply down, twisting to right and left, down into mist, into nothingness. The man leading the mules was too far ahead to question, even if he could answer. How long would they descend? She remembered the view before the cloud covered her. This might go on for hours.

Unrelieved downhill riding becomes agonizing. Clare rode well, she habitually kept herself in good condition, but she had not been on a horse for several months, and that day she already had had six hours of rough going. The Indians travelled at a fast, gliding pace, almost a trot, which kept the mules at a running walk. On the irregular trail which disappeared so short a distance below her, their rate of travel seemed alarmingly fast.

The proportion of rain in the mist increased. Clare took her slicker off the back of her saddle and put it on. Her jacket was good and damp; under the slicker she was too hot and her clothes steamed. She could not imagine being more miserable. She had no idea when this ride would end, nor what the ending would be like. Her professional self recognized that this was such material as she had never had before. This was real. All she had to do was to describe it adequately and she would have the best chapter she had ever written, far and away the best if she were really being taken to Trenholm — if.

Ordinarily, when confronted with good material, her observation and recording of it was highly conscious. She formed phrases for later reference and determined upon the appropriate emotions, establishing her own role as she went along. It was as if she wrote and acted a play for herself, which later she would describe as experience. This time she was not verbalizing, but merely feeling and storing. The difference was caused not only by her fatigue, but by the impact of true experience. The situation was out of her control, it had long since gone past the boundaries she always set, it had, one might say, a personality which was stronger than her own.

It grew dark but the air became warmer, not cooler. She

rode on in pure helplessness, not in faith nor even in determination, letting her mule pursue the dimly seen rump and white pack of the one ahead. Her appreciation of the story in this became mechanical, something she clung to as a means of holding herself together. The ground began to level off. They were under the mist now, and the rain had stopped. She could tell faintly that they were in a valley, she made out the form of a palm tree against a bit of sky and from this knew that they had descended far.

She heard dogs barking and her heart lifted. They travelled on. She remembered in the past being irritatingly surprised by the distance at which dogs in a native village could be heard at night, but never before had she realized quite how great that distance was. Then she saw the spark of a fire. She made out a second fire. One of the Indians called out a sentence in a loud, chanting voice. Many lights appeared and gathered ahead of them, spots of dancing flame like an unearthly gathering of fireflies, and she rode into confusion. There was a sea of Indians and torches, a marimba playing for all it was worth, and a drum made of a big log carried by two men and beaten, not on its end but on its side, by a third. The pack mules stopped and fell to grazing, and Clare's mule stopped beside them. With great ceremony the young Indian's bundle was opened, and from it there was taken a candle at least three feet long and eight inches wide. So that was "the wax." Clare sat in the saddle, wondering if they had forgotten her, wondering what might be done to her in the midst of this unknown ritual, in the midst of the incomprehensible, small, dark people.

A man came towards her, conspicuous as though under a

light because of his stature, bearing, and costume. Relief rose in her along with an excitement which lightened her fatigue. It was he. It was really true, it was he.

He approached her with a curious, restrained eagerness, peering towards her, then when he was near he checked his gait and came up more slowly. She could see that he was puzzled. She did not wonder.

He said, "I do not think I know you." Clare wanted to giggle or to say "Dr. Livingstone, I presume." It was so odd a greeting.

"I'm afraid we haven't met. I'm Clare Turner."

He brought his heels together and bowed stiffly. "Sven Trenholm." To the North European form he added the Spanish, "*para servirle.*" Clare said "*gracias*" and extended her hand. He took it and bowed again.

A number of Indians with torches, mostly boys, gathered around them, staring. He looks as if he'd been through the wringer, she thought. She had heard that he was a heavy man, but now he was thin, his head skeletal, his eyes hollow. Fever? The old tropics-whiskey-woman formula? He was clean-shaven. His clothes were clean and fresh, although his khaki shirt was faded almost white and had been clumsily mended in several places. He wore an old straw sombrero which looked more than ripe to be thrown away.

Trenholm said, "You must be tired."

"And hungry."

"Of course. Excuse me." He turned and talked at some length in Rashti with one of the older men present. The man in turn sent several boys running. Another boy took up the rope of the lead mule. With inexpressible relief she realized that now there was someone of her own kind to take care of her. She was infinitely thankful at having found him; never was a quest more sincerely completed.

Trenholm said, "If you will come with me."

He was a scarecrow and his hands trembled, but he was clean, clean-shaven, sober. He had lost nothing of the formal courtesy of his kind, there was nothing about him to suggest any disintegration of fiber. Clare gathered herself together; she must impress him well, each move must be right. As he walked beside her mule, she said, "There seems to be a ceremony going on. I don't want to keep you from observing it."

"The bringing of the wax — this I have already fully notated. Later there will be matter of interest. You are an ethnographer?"

"I — I have read in ethnography. I have read your monograph."

By the glow of fires in doorways and by the torchlight she saw that they were crossing a wide, clear space around the edges of which were scattered a few palm-thatched huts. At one side, behind them as they were going, stood an unusually large one, into which the people were moving in an irregular procession, following the music and the bringers of the candle.

"I see they thatch with palm here," she said. "Are we in *tierra caliente?*"

"On the edge of it. Here the altitude is just under a thousand meters. From where the men found you, you have descended about fourteen hundred. As the Ladinos say, this country is very upright."

From about seven thousand to about three thousand feet, she figured. That was a good phrase, "This country is very upright."

Trenholm continued, "The Indians thought you were my wife."

Clare said, in English, "They equivocated themselves."
Trenholm laughed. "I knew your name when they asked me, so I suppose they jumped to a conclusion."

They stopped by a small house. "This is not very good," he said, "but it is the best we have. At least it is unoccupied. Have you a hammock?"

"I have a cot."

"Good. More suitable, I think. Will you dismount?"

Several Indians fell to unpacking her mules. A woman brought a torch which she placed on a flat stone in the middle of the floor. They went in. The hut was completely bare except for the stone for the torch, and three firestones at one side. The boys lugged in her gear. She was not going to give in to fatigue; without consciousness of any reason, she was deeply determined to live up perfectly to this occasion. The scientist helped her set up her cot, folding table, and camp chair. She got a pair of fat camp candles out of one of the packs and set them on the table. She considered him by this clearer light. For all his gauntness, his features were good. He was attractive, his eyes were perceptive, thoughtful, and his mouth was strong.

"You came from Santa Catalina today?" he asked.

"Yes."

"You should be tired. That is a good ten leagues, and the *bajada*, the descent, is hard going. If you don't mind my saying so, that is a remarkable ride for a woman to have made."

This mild praise caused her unexpected pleasure. At the time she made no comparisons, but the fact was that her usual situation was reversed. The lonely young men were grateful for her presence, astonished that she should appear, eager to please her. Here it was she who was grateful, and if either of them was surprised, it was she. This man to find whom she had gone through so much, and who seemed so well worth finding, was valuable to her. His respect, his friendship, had become essential.

She said, "I am rather tired. I think I'll have a drink. I have some decent brandy, will you join me?"

"With pleasure."

She dug out her flask and metal cups. He accepted his drink with a slight bow. They sipped. She felt the pick-up and the warmth of it.

"It is long since I have tasted such as this," he said.

The music of the marimba and drum reached them clearly, although it was a good hundred feet to the big house into which they had gone. The sound made a vaguely harassing background. A woman brought in a jar of water, another followed with a basket covered by a napkin, from which she set gourds containing black beans, a tamale, and tortillas on the table. A half-grown girl following her stepped up shyly to add a tin pot of coffee. Clare got out eating utensils, sugar, and canned milk. In doing so, she also brought out her sizable medicine chest and set it on the ground. Trenholm noted it.

"You will be long in these mountains? Excuse me, go ahead and eat. I have eaten."

Clare waved her hand at the cot. "Please sit down." She took a few sips of hot, black coffee. With that on top of the brandy, her appetite awoke. As she ate she answered him.

"I can stay only a day or so."

For the first time he showed surprise. "You do not sound as a scientist."

"No, I'm a writer. Travel books."

"May I smoke?"

"Please do." The amenities, in this setting.

"Even for a popular book, you should stay longer. One cannot grasp these people in a day or so."

Was it only the scientist, or was it also the man? She wondered how she looked, and was sure her hair was awful. Men are lucky: Trenholm was her age, yet he did not have to work himself over periodically in order to look presentable.

"I wish I could stay on," she answered. "My time is not entirely my own. Perhaps I can stretch it out a little."

"You should, you would find it rewarding."

His tone was disappointing, but then, he was formal by habit. She asked him about the ceremony. He explained, with rather dry precision, that here there was held a dance portraying animals, of great importance for hunting. Although there were many Spanish elements in the costumes, the dance itself and its purpose were part of the ancient religion. It was based upon a very old myth about how the deer were kept locked up by a god until another god, the culture-hero, released them. He believed that no scientist had witnessed it before. She noticed that he did not say "no white man"; to him, that would be immaterial. He was the kind of man who would be interested in data, not in "firsts." She hoped that she could write her impression of him without being offensive.

"This time there may be yet another element, a sad complication but not without interest," he told her. "There is, you understand, the Chief of the Dance, who owns it."

She nodded. "You described the dance organizations in your book."

"Quite. That large house belongs to this Chief. We are far

from the main village of this group, but the dance belongs here, it can be performed only in that house. His son, who was to have been one of the monkeys, has a severe fever which I do not recognize. He is likely to die. What effect that will have I do not know. They are preparing for the dance in there now, and also he is there. I have told them to move him to a quiet place, but that they will not do."

"Won't they think that I brought bad luck, if he dies?"

"I think not. He has been sick for some days. The wax — the candle — was late, they had trouble getting it in Sacabil. It arrived just in time, and you with it, so in that way you have brought good luck."

She nodded and brought out her cigarettes. He accepted one, commenting on the North American brand, then he said, "Since you will return so soon to sources of supply, might I look over your medicine kit? Perhaps there is something that will ease the child. One never knows."

"Of course. How about yourself? You look as if you had a spot of fever, too."

He smiled slightly. "Malaria. It is inevitable. My stock is low, though. Have you Atabrine?"

"Yes, and quinine bisulphate." She set the box on the table. "Help yourself." She pointed to two sizable phials. "There's lots of quinine."

He picked up one of the phials. "Thank you. I am old-fashioned, and I dislike turning yellow. You must take it yourself while you are down here — ten grains at this time, after dinner, is excellent. Many take it with their digestive drink."

"There's plenty of coffee left. Won't you join me in *café, cognac, et quinine?*"

He smiled with real amusement. *"Enchanté."*

He had humor under the dryness and formality, humor and, she suspected, sophistication. As she poured coffee he cocked his head, listening to the music.

"It is still the music of El Toro," he said. "It will be perhaps half an hour before the main ceremonial begins. You would care to witness it? Perhaps you are too tired, you have had a hard day."

She was not going to let go now. "I'd love to witness it." She used his slightly stilted verb. "They won't object?"

"Not if you are reverent." He washed down his quinine pills with a sip of coffee, then put more sugar in his cup and added his brandy. "Do you know Miss Pine? I believe she is still 'Miss,' though she should have her doctorate soon."

That was why he so calmly accepted the idea of her having entered this country. Of course, La Pine had lived here. "I haven't met her, I'm sorry to say. I knew that she had been here." That was that. She could no longer eliminate the woman, for Trenholm must read her next book and find it honest. It was going to be a different kind of book.

"She has an excellent article in the last number of the *American Anthropologist*." He paused, calculated, and laughed briefly. "The next to last. They reach me slowly here. The woman's point of view is so valuable in ethnography, when they are not ashamed to be women, as some of them are. I would lend it to you, but the ants destroyed my copy."

So La Pine was not ashamed to be a woman. La Pine had been all one dry season in these mountains while he was here. La Pine was definitely becoming a menace. "I'll read it as soon as I get out."

"Do — 'Survivals of Chinamit Organization among the Northern Rashti.' Now, let us see if we can help the child."

He studied her medicine kit. "Sulfa — perhaps if we try this — it cannot do harm, and who knows?" He spoke partly to himself. "May I take this over? I can speak to the authorities at the same time, and then come for you."

"By all means."

"By your leave." He made his little, formal bow before he left.

She looked at her watch, eleven o'clock. If she had good sense she would call it all off and throw herself on her cot, instead of whipping out her vanity box with the mirror in the lid, setting up her electric lamp, combing her short hair like fury to bring back the curl, patting this and that on her face, deciding on no rouge as she was deeply and becomingly tanned, and then the satisfaction of lipstick well put on. Considering everything, she looked well. She shut the box and lit a cigarette.

Even if she were not interested in Trenholm himself, she would not miss this. Without any pretense or dressing up of the facts, she was really going to witness a hitherto unknown, ancient ritual. Ambitions she had had during her college studies revived in her. All of this, right from the start, from Santa Catalina, could be, must be, written honestly, the kind of work she had once hoped to do and turned from more and more as her audiences and her readers kept pulling at her to make everything a little more, to fulfill for them a facile dream, a fatuous dream. This time control had entirely slipped away from her, and she had entered upon an exploration to which she would never have consented. It was a double exploration, of these mountains and of herself, and she would not knowingly have let herself in for either.

Trenholm came to the door. "Shall we go over?"

As they walked, she said, "Now that you have given the boy medicine, if he dies, won't they blame you?"

"No. Among these people, medicine men may fail. I explained to them that there was no assurance, only a hope, and then, I took some myself, to show them that it was harmless. Who knows, it might be good for me?"

At the door, her first impression was of a congestion of people sitting on the floor, the men in white shirts with red and yellow stripes down the front, above which their faces and heads seemed darker than usual, and the lesser number of women in their bright blouses, in which a deep red was the predominant color. A young man indicated an empty bench against the wall by the door. She saw that there were a few other benches along the walls, occupied by men who wore the same black ponchos as had the three who found her at the cross. She supposed it to be some sort of robe of office. Trenholm drew a leather-covered notebook and a sharp pencil from his pocket, opened the book, and set it on his knee. He studied the room and then, as though he were isolated from all that went on around him by a bathysphere, set to work on a neat sketch-plan.

Clare, too, was absorbed, so much so that she was only secondarily aware of the security she felt in the baron's presence beside her and of a touch of annoyance at his instant obliviousness of her. The big house formed a single room perhaps forty feet by twenty-five, with stick walls seven feet high. Above the walls crossed the round, smoke-blackened beams, and above them towered the enormous, pitched roof, so high that the ridgepole was lost in darkness. In the far corner to her right stood an altar with a figure of a saint upon it, in front of which the big candle was burning. Against the back wall, opposite the door, a heavy table formed another altar carrying a cross with stubby arms, hewn out of a single piece of wood about four feet high. The upper portion of the cross had been carved into a stiff, expressionless, elongated face. In front of this burned a row of slender, black candles. From her reading she knew that these were made of wild beeswax, and that their use went back to the ancient Maya. On either side of the altar, in simply made, wooden chairs with arms, sat two old, bearded men. They wore the black ponchos, and purple head-wraps. There were a few other men along the back wall, in smaller chairs.

Before the altar was a clear area, covered with mats, on which was a multicolored heap of costumes and masks. This area was lined with black candles. At several points in the room stood breast-high poles on top of which were fastened flat stones, on which torches burned. Near the saint's altar the marimba, played by five men, and the big drum poured their volume into the room. All the rest of it was jammed with seated people. All the rest of it, she thought, until Trenholm, interrupting his sketch, pointed with his pencil and said, "The family and the sick boy."

She looked to the far left corner. Behind the surrounding fence of people she made out a relatively empty space, in which several women sat with their backs to the room.

"With all this going on," she said. "How dreadful."

"Yes." He sighed. "I tried to get them to move him. Sometimes people will not let one help them." He turned a page and made some notes.

The music went on and on. The tunes, although pleasant, were slight and repetitious, and the drum was oppressive. Three young men, two carrying trays and one a torch, stood by the altar. One tray seemed to be full of tiny, earthenware cups, the other was piled with what looked like little golden sticks. The attendants knelt before one of the priests. He took one of the little cups and drained it with a quick, tossing motion, then he picked up one of the little sticks. The third attendant held up a torch, and Clare recognized then that the sticks were cornhusk cigarettes, such as she had seen on sale in native markets. The young men passed to the second priest, and then continued around the room, offering their wares to the various black-robed men, but without kneeling.

As if the drink had been a signal, one of the priests leaned forward, extended one hand, and began praying in a loud, monotonous, rising and falling voice. The words stumbled out at great speed. Trenholm listened intently, pencil poised. Occasionally he made a note. The music continued unabated. Hoping that this portended a change, Clare brightened, but soon she decided that there had merely been added a new source of sound in the room.

Trenholm said, "It is their pride to be able to race their prayers. I can understand only fragments. Later I shall try to have one of them recite to me slowly, in private, but I shall probably not succeed. I think, when I am home again, I shall study shorthand. Rashti in shorthand would be original, no?" He listened again. "There!" he made a note. "Did you catch it? The old names — you have read enough?" He continued listening, his head cocked. From time to time he wrote down a word, and as he did so spoke it to her. "Ahau . . . Imosh . . . Lambat . . . Ben . . . Do you recognize?"

She nodded. The Lords of the Days, she had read enough for that. "I thought they were long dead."

"Not entirely. They are here — or their ghosts."

The phrase "or their ghosts" caught her ear. One could quote that. She began calculating, trying to call up what she had read about the old Maya.

The three attendants approached them. Trenholm said, "The first time, you must partake. It is *aguardiente*, very rough, but happily not much of it. After this you may refuse."

He accepted a drink and a cigarette and she followed suit. The cup held less than a standard jigger, but the rough, green liquor, distilled from sugar cane, gagged her and burned in her stomach. The taste and feel of the cornhusk wrapping of the cigarette were pleasant, but the smoke was harsh and sharp.

Trenholm nodded to her with a faint smile. "You would make a good ethnographer. You do not need to finish the cigarette."

She returned to her calculation. She had been glib enough about the ancient Maya when she wrote *Lost Palaces*. If the inscriptions go back to about 300 A.D. and you allow for all the time it took for that elaborate system to be evolved, and the Lords of the Days came first, then those names were, say, twenty-five hundred years old. Older than Christianity. Buddhism? She could look that up. She couldn't be merely glib, she wanted to be sound. She'd ask him tomorrow. Despite the discomfort of the bench she drowsed uneasily. There was a new sound, the sound of rain, and with it a smell of wet earth and leaves and, if you could call it that, a smell of coolness. The patter grew steadier, louder, became a solid, mechanical noise which pulled her awake. At moments drops came in through the stick walls. The freshened air was welcome. She glanced out the door; there was solid blackness there, with glints of silver where the downpour caught the light. She remembered that she had left her hat and slicker in the hut.

Trenholm said, "This comes early. I think, though, it will not last." She saw that he was concerned.

"It's only April."

"The last day of April, and down here the rains are different. Still, I trust this will not last."

He was deeply worried; she wondered why. Her wondering became vague. She nodded, woke, nodded. The uncomfortable bench supplemented the aches of her day's ride, the assorted sounds were a persecution, the cycle of simple tunes had become abrasively familiar. She longed for her cot, but there would be a hundred-foot waterfall to go through. More than that, she was determined to stick it out. He had said "You would make a good ethnographer" because she had kept a calm face over the vile drink and smoke. She wanted to prove that that was true, and to complete this genuinely.

The attendants came by several times with their trays, but she and Trenholm waved them on. At one point she must have fallen completely asleep for a few minutes, for her eyes started open and she felt a moment's freshness followed by a more lasting, dried-out wakefulness. The priests prayed in shifts; as soon as one came to an end and dropped his hand, the other started his prayers tumbling out. The effect of haste, almost of interruption and competition, was incongruous. It seemed to her that they had been doing thus for ages. Trenholm was making notes again. She noticed that his hands trembled more severely than they had earlier in the evening. The effort he made to write neatly was almost painful.

He closed the book over his pencil and glanced at her. "I have been able to catch a large part of one of the main prayers. They are very repetitious."

The attendants were coming round again. "Don't the officials get drunk?" she asked.

"Oh yes. It is necessary. It puts them in communion with the higher powers." The attendants were near. He looked at his watch. "One twenty, this won't last much longer. This time I shall indulge."

He took the phial of quinine pills from his pocket and shook out two of them. Poor as the light was, she thought he looked feverish. It was a form of heroism, she thought. How long had he been driving himself like this, in his condition, before no audience, thinking nothing of it? What did any experience of hers, even this past, fantastic day and night, amount to in comparison? This was really something to write about. He took the little cup of *aguardiente*, popped the pills into his mouth, and downed it.

"That is primitive," he said, "but effective."

She offered him one of her cigarettes. Then she asked him, "Why do you write so carefully? Can't you read your own writing?"

He answered, as if it were the most natural thing in the world, "In case it should be necessary for someone else to exploit my notes. One should always write them so that a colleague could take them over and use them without any explanation — if anything should happen."

She was digesting the implications of that, when she heard a sound which shocked her into full alertness, a long, high pulsating scream, a sound of the purest agony of heart, which broke and ended in sobbing words. She jerked erect.

"That is too bad," he said. "The little boy has died. I am sorry."

She had heard keening before, a strange sound from distant native huts, and had described it effectively, but she had never expected to be locked in with it, so to speak. Her chief impression of what was going on about her was one of confusions. There was the confusion of faces and bodies, ruddy light of torches, the pool of clear, gracious candlelight around the bright costumes, shadows, and the great blackness under the roof. There were the smells of bodies, damp clothing, tobacco, the pleasant odor of the beeswax candles, pine smoke, and a distinct undertone of crude liquor. Above all there was the confusion of sounds, the marimba, the drum, the praying, all continuous against the background river-sound of the rain, and cutting through all of these at intervals the tearing, heartbreaking lamentation. It might be formalized, for all she knew it might be insincere, but it was set in an expression of wild, unbearable, passionate grief.

Trenholm said, "Look — that man in the third chair, had you noticed him? The Chief of the Dance. It is his son, but until the dance 'has been broken' he is dedicated, he is not supposed to allow himself to be disturbed by any personal matters."

"Poor man."

"Yes. They are good people and he was a fine boy. Eleven years old."

She watched the Chief. He beckoned an attendant and spoke to him. The attendant took a demijohn from under the altar — so that was where they kept it — and made his way through the crowd to the corner where the mourners sat.

Trenholm said, "Now begins the wake. It is a catharsis, they pour out the shock, but it is messy. Listen, the rain is letting up."

The crepitation of individual drops was audible. Clare felt less imprisoned. She glanced back at the Chief of the Dance. He seemed to be praying. The attendants came to him, and he tossed down a drink. As he did so he raised his eyes, and it seemed to Clare that when he handed the cup back he was staring at her. She could not really see, but she felt that his eyes were baleful. She remembered all the tags she had heard about drunken natives, drunken Indians, religious frenzies, running amok. The automatic under her arm seemed futile. The people in the room were unarmed, but the huts roundabout were full of machetes. Not for anything now would she have left Trenholm's side. The calm, sick man beside her making his precise notes was her only confidence.

The music, the drumming, the praying, all stopped at the same moment without any coordinating signal she could perceive. The sound of the rain had dwindled to the plopping drip from the eaves. The sudden silence was startling, it was a genuine physical relief. Also, since she had no idea of its cause, it was frightening. She turned towards Trenholm, and as she did so slipped her right hand under her jacket until it lay near her pistol.

He looked at his watch and noted the time in his book. "That's over. It will take about half an hour for them to put on their costumes. There is coffee at my place. Will you do me the honor?"

People were already moving out of the door.

"I certainly will."

The wail of the keening tore through the room, more piercing than ever in the quiet.

Trenholm lived with the family of the woman who had brought them supper. There was definitely no sign of a beautiful native girl. The woman set out coffee, tortillas, and delicious, very small bananas. The coffee was a great comfort, and Clare found that the dark brown, almost black sugar, which one scraped off the loaf with a knife, went surprisingly well with it. They sat on a straw mat, and while they sipped and smoked, the scientist explained various points of the ceremony. From time to time the sound of the keening reached to them.

"So far," Trenholm said, jerking his head towards the Chief's house as one wail ended, "that does not seem to have affected the ceremony at all. Perhaps it will not. It is a curious situation; the mourners also have their ritual position, the wake involves dancing, both ceremonies require a certain drunkenness, and the two are, one might almost say, wrapped in one package."

"So long as it does not involve us," Clare said.

"One thinks of that. But no, we should have been able to feel that definitely by now."

A flame appeared a short distance in front of the big house. It grew into a large bonfire, and as it spread an uncertain light through the open area, the music began again beside it. They went together to see the dance.

Clare was too drained to get much out of it. Many of the costumes, clumsy imitations of old Spanish modes, seemed tawdry. The lion, jaguar, and deer, realistically costumed and masked, were rather impressive. There were twenty monkeys, their parts taken by little boys, forming a sort of chorus line. Their costume was vaguely reminiscent of an old military uniform, with broad stripes on dark blue trousers and elaborate, tacky chevrons on the sleeves, but their masks, which caught the wizened monkey look, were appealing. There were also some royal-looking characters representing, Trenholm had told her, the sacred beings who once held the game animals locked up or the ones who caused their release. Absurdly, these wore a travesty of seventeenth century court costumes, knee breeches trimmed with elaborate edgings in memory of lace, mirrors sewn on their coats for jewels, bemirrored, tri-cornered hats. Their masks were of bearded blonds, pink-skinned, smooth-featured. Somehow these blond masks were the most grotesque and inhuman of all. One turned almost with relief to the deer or the rather sweet-faced lion. All the dancers carried rattles. Their only step was a monotonous jig. Clare had seen the Yaquis dance once in Mexico City and the Pueblo Indians in New Mexico, she had seen native dances in many parts of the world. This, she concluded, was the poorest of the lot.

A woman entered the dance space, moving with the same jigging step. Trenholm touched Clare's arm and said, "The boy's mother. The two rituals are getting involved after all."

The woman was soddenly drunk. She was old and wrinkled. Her blouse had come out of her sash and hung loosely about her. She must have been pulling at her hair, for the braids wrapped around her head and held with bright ribbons, ordinarily so neat on these women, were disordered and there were loose ends. She danced with a curious, erect limpness, her back straight, her shoulders slightly forward, her arms hanging loosely, her knees slightly bent. She jigged as though the music were strings attached to her heels and she had no volition of her own, but soon Clare noticed that she kept trying to intercept the line of monkeys.

"Poor thing," she said. "Why don't they take her away?"

"They are sorry for her, and it is necessary for her to dance, too."

The bemused, jerking woman sought the monkeys. The faceless little monkeys, the appealing, humorous, blank masks paid no attention to her. They flowed around her and went on. For a moment she danced facing one of the sacred beings with his slightly oversized, smug, incredible pink and gold mask; then she turned, sought the monkey again. Each time they went by as if she did not exist.

"She's looking for her boy," Clare said.

Trenholm nodded. "Yes. It is tragic."

Which was real, which was fantasy, the masks or the woman, or whatever nightmare was working in her tormented mind? What did the uncertain, flickering light, the faceless little ones, one of whom should have been her boy, the compulsive music, create for her? She danced through the line again and then reeled, almost falling against Clare. Clare jumped back, her flesh crawling. She stayed slightly behind Trenholm. A little later an Indian came forward, took the woman by the arm, and spoke to her gently. She partially collapsed. He led her away, supporting her by her elbow. As she went, she broke into the dance step at intervals, and just before she went inside the house gave vent thickly and vaguely to the mourning lament.

The east was turning white. Blissfully the music stopped in its abrupt fashion. Trenholm said, "That is all. They rest now, and dance again during the day, over and over. There is no variation, I believe."

They walked silently across the open space and parted near their huts with a brief word. Clare had the fatigue-sense of being a shell within which a faint humming noise and echoes of the music went on. She found that her hut had a door; she dragged it shut and piled some of her gear against it, took off her shoes and jacket, put the pistol within reach, got out a blanket, and threw herself on her cot. For a few moments thoughts churned slowly in her mind. She had not really believed that things like this could be. This made all her former little trips look cheap. A different kind of writing, a true kind. He was a man . . .

For a time she slept profoundly. As the heat of full day at this lower altitude began to press down, she threw off the blanket, and became conscious of the discomfort of sleeping in her clothes. A little later the music started up again, and this, along with the tumult of thoughts which slithered around in her head when she was drowsing, finally made her give up. About noon she went to Trenholm's hut. He was away, but the people there gave her coffee and food.

She got through the afternoon by watching the dance at intervals — by daylight it had much less quality than when it first began — resting in the relative coolness of her hut, and making a few notes, mostly of the ethnological items Trenholm had told her and a rough outline for her description of the ceremony. Sitting in her camp chair, she considered the rented *alforjas* and saddles on the floor. Eventually she would have to make some arrangement for getting back to Santa

Catalina. Trenholm would find her trustworthy guides. There was no hurry. She was tired now, but one quiet night would take care of that. Her publishers expected her book in time for late fall publication, but she was a fast writer, and she could easily stretch her time a week or so. It would be worth it, in so many ways. Perhaps he would come out with her.

If she could spend even a little time among these people in Trenholm's company she could have at least the beginnings of a real insight into them. So far, she did not like them, but she was curious, memories of her long-past studies were awakened, and this time she did not want to do one of those jobs of pseudo-penetration which came so easily to her pen. When she passed through the mist she had, truly, ridden into another world in which the dominant element was a man of true integrity. From here she looked back. She did in fact look through her door to the circular patterns of the palms behind the farther houses, and beyond them to the piling up of mountains, green, then green-blue, then truly blue against the horizon. In her imagination she saw this lower, tropical part, and the cool highlands above, and the twisting trail with a barrier of white cloud, a barrier which divided two worlds and through which one could pass only by the magic of pure chance. Beyond lay the world she had chosen, the world of her wrecked first marriage and her ugly second one, the calculated relationships, slick books, reputation, the applause of persons she despised. My dear public, she thought. My dear public, and my ego.

She had carried that world with her wherever she went, until she lost it in the mist. She felt rather afraid of what would come next, but that feeling was countered by the deep assurance of what kind of writing she could do this time, and once she had started in that vein, surely she could continue. What would it be like to be an ethnologist's wife ("ethnographer," he always said, keeping the old distinction), to work side by side with him, provide the woman's point of view? She wondered what La Pine really looked like. She wished he would turn up soon. She needed to see him by daylight and talk with him under calmer conditions. Until that happened, there would be suspense.

He came back late in the afternoon. He told her that he had watched the first repetitions of the dance until he was sure that there were no variations, taken some photographs, and then carried his hammock to a shady place by the river, out of earshot of the music, and after a bath and more quinine had slept for a couple of hours, returning in time for the rituals which ended the ceremony. "These ceremonials become so passionately dull," he said. The remark pleased her. He had seemed so devoted to his work, and there was that touch of dryness in his approach to it, so that she hadn't expected he could admit to boredom.

She invited him to dinner, and asked him to find a girl who spoke some Spanish to help her. The girl he provided spoke very little Spanish and was almost immobilized with shyness, but at least she was able to keep the fire going and boil water. Clare did not contemplate any difficult cooking, merely the preparation of good coffee and warming and seasoning some of her more choice tinned goods. She set the table, with a rather pretty oilcloth cover, and the two camp candles placed as if they were formal table candles. She pulled the foot of her cot up to one end as a second chair. There was an excellent effect of ingenuity, improvisation, and an almost humorous elegance to the result. She figured that by combining her supplies with native foods she could give variety to at least half a dozen dinners.

Trenholm was pleased and amused. He ate well, relishing the delicacies. They talked, starting from the food, of France, and of Denmark, which she had visited. It was civilized, easy conversation. She poured the coffee, set out the quinine and brandy. They lit cigarettes. Their relationship was familiar, the man and woman at leisure after a good dinner. She had caught a little of the atmosphere one encounters, for instance, on a well-run safari, when at the end of the day the exotic is pushed to arm's length and becomes a background instead of a dominant consideration.

Trenholm asked her how she came to be lost and alone by the cross, remarking that he had not wanted to trouble her for explanations last night, when she was tired and there was so much distraction. She decided that she would have to know him better before she told him that she had come to look for him; she said that she wanted to see a bit of the country beyond the usual traveller's circuit, and added that, hearing that he was somewhere hereabouts, she had hoped to meet him. Then she told him frankly about the incident with the muleteer.

He said, "You are not the first person to make that mistake. You never can tell who may have picked up English, it is a most unsafe language. The most unsafe of all is swearing English, so many of these people may have worked for oil men or such. The Finns are the people who can really speak their minds, and they say Finnish is a fine tongue to swear in."

Then she told him about the Indians, and the curious remark about "*gente blanca.*"

"They took that to show knowledge on your part. You were looking for 'white men' — that is, men of ceremonial wisdom. I think I mentioned the phrase in my book." Clare nodded, remembering. "You had made an offering to the cross first, then you said that, and you gave them confidence. After that you arrived with the 'wax,' just in time, so that they feel now that you are a person of good influence, although they are disappointed that you are not my wife. They are looking forward to her coming."

So they are looking forward to his wife's coming. Clare put out her cigarette and lit another. This was really unexpected. "Your wife is coming here?"

"Yes. She is an orchidologist, you know. Some time ago we were briefly in the valley country over there, towards Guatemala. The indications were that the hunting would be good there. By good luck, this year she received a sufficient grant, so she has started over on the Guatemala side, and when she arrives opposite here," he pointed westward, to the true, low country, "she will join me. That is why I stayed on these last few months. Then we shall return to Norway and put on weight." He smiled. "She is due any time now."

"That's why you were so worried about the rain last night."

"Yes. It makes the going slow and unpleasant."

"I'm afraid I disappointed you."

"I must admit, a little, although I could not imagine how she would be coming from that direction."

Clare smoked and stared out the door. The lost Baron Trenholm was merely keeping a date with his wife. He even received scientific periodicals, a trifle late. Baroness Trenholm would reach here after three or four months in the deepest lowland jungles, the country marked "*despoblado* — uninhabited" on the maps. The farthest point which she, the adventurous Clare Turner, had reached, the wildest place to which she had ever penetrated, would be for the baroness the threshold of coming out. It would even, as a well-established settlement in higher country, seem in itself to have aspects of civilization. The joke, she thought, is certainly on me.

Oblivious, Trenholm went on: "I think you would enjoy meeting her, if you decide to stay on. There is much to be seen here."

Something in his expression as he talked of his wife, the way he had come towards her last night, his worry when it rained — lucky woman. "I'd like to stay, but it's out of the question. I have to meet a deadline." She saw that he did not understand her. "My publishers must have my manuscript by a certain date, and my time is limited."

"That is a pity." He thought a moment. "Several men are going to Santa Catalina tomorrow. There is a direct trail from here, much shorter than the one by which you came. The men with the 'wax' did not follow it for ceremonial reasons. If you wish to go with them, they will handle your mules. You can trust them, and they speak fair Spanish."

The sooner the better. "Good. That would be fine."

"It has been very pleasant having you turn up. One does not expect —" he made a wide gesture. "There are fine people, but there is a loneliness —"

"I can imagine." His feeling towards her was impersonal, the relief of a moment with one's kind. He liked her well enough, that was all. She had to exert some form of power. "I'm overstocked on delicacies," she said. "I have much more than I can possibly use. Won't you let me leave them with you? I'm sure your wife would enjoy them."

"You are very kind. I cannot resist the offer. She will be sick to death of beans and rice and heart of palm." His last words underlined the contrast between her expedition and the baroness's.

They talked for perhaps half an hour longer in a desultory manner. Clare was empty of small talk. When he said that she must be tired, she said she was. After he had gone she sat for some time, smoking, making mental adjustments, then she turned in. She lay staring up at the blackness of the roof, and gave vent to a hearty, "Oh damn!"

The mules were lined up on the trail, accompanied by half a dozen men who were going to Sacabil. When she and Trenholm drew near, they lifted their hats respectfully. She thanked him for all he had done for her, and especially for the insight he had given her into the meaning of the ceremony. He replied, "Oh, no, it is I who should thank you. I am grateful for your visit, for medicines, and for all the luxuries. You must come to Norway, since you are such a traveller, and let us repay you."

She mounted. Then she said, "If you don't mind my stealing an expression of yours, I'd like to call my chapter about all this 'The Ghosts of the Old Gods.' "

" 'The Ghosts of the Old Gods'? Oh yes, when you said the other night that you thought that they were long dead. Yes. It is very good."

She gave him her hand. He bowed over it, and said, "*Vaya con Dios.*" The men started off, driving the pack animals. She followed. From some distance up the trail she looked back, and saw him still watching her. She imagined that he found her puzzling.

Through the day they worked their way back up to the high country. Clare decided definitely that she had seldom travelled in such beauty. She no longer thought the Indians' machetes menacing, but instead found amusement and some romance in these medievally-armed footmen attending her. Then it came to her that she was travelling with simon-pure natives who were not anybody's servants, without even a hired muleteer for intermediary, and not concerned about it a bit. If this had happened at any other time, she would immediately have planned on making great use of it, but she did not see it that way now. They were quiet, respectful, friendly. They were good people, as Trenholm had said, although she imagined one would not want to push them too far. They were his friends, and through him and because of certain good omens accepted her. The Indians called him *"Cham Shtevan"* adding their own corruption to the Altureño version of his name. *Cham*, she understood, was an honorific which they did not ordinarily apply to white men. She would write about this ride, of course, and about these nice Indians, but not in the old manner. She breathed deeply of the high air and looked about her, wondering if she could carry this world with her into the old one, as hitherto she had carried the old one wherever she went.

At Santa Catalina they had cold beer. The beds had mattresses laid over springs of woven rawhide. At Sacabil there were real beds and one could have a hot shower for ten centavos extra. In the capital, the Hotel Helvetia was genuinely luxurious. She was asked to dinner at the North American Consul General's, and of course she was questioned about her trip. When it came out that she had gone into the mountains alone and had seen Trenholm, there was no evading telling a fairly complete tale.

She tried to tell it lightly and briefly, but what little she said produced a rain of questions. There was no use trying to say what she had really felt and thought to these people; she knew their kind well enough, you found such colonies all over the world. "Natives" to them were a myth, at once a source of servants and a dangerous race of unpredictable subhumans, while the true interior was somewhere beyond the limits of belief. They clung to these concepts aggressively, especially the women, because only thus could they justify the narrow circumclusion and prejudice of their own lives, and maintain in their little routines the essential myth, basic to all the rest, of their superiority. Automatically, from long habit and simple tact, she adapted her tale to their expectations. Two luncheons and three dinners later, when she left the capital, she herself had built a myth, and in certain matters she was uncertain just what the facts were.

New York has its own greatness; its towers defy other grandeurs. She saw friends, spoke lightly and amusingly of her trip, returned to familiar ways. The writing went badly. Something was thoroughly off key. She preferred to work in the city, finding the country distracting, but she was ready to give up and try a few weeks in Westchester when her agent called up to say that if she could get her copy in soon there was a chance of serialization. She determined to get herself in hand and really turn out work.

A good way of breaking a jam, she had found, was not to start at the beginning, but to write first the chapter which set the key. That would be "The Ghosts of the Old Gods." Her notes for that chapter puzzled her. They did not sound like her, and there were one or two drooly statements which reminded her of lines she had read in one of her old diaries she had found once and burned in disgust. She put the notes aside. This was the best stuff she'd ever had hold of, she knew she was a competent, experienced writer, she was going to do it just right.

Let's start fresh. Not a quest for Trenholm, but have him in the reader's mind. Plant him a bit in an earlier chapter. Primary reason for going in — these Indians retain gobs of the old religion, possibility of witnessing some ceremony derived from very ancient times. Cite Lothrop. Yes. But get word of Trenholm at Sacabil, those speculations, yes, good stuff, but not overemphasized. With a sense of deep relief and relaxation she moved into the familiar groove. She knew her business, she shaped, rejected, selected, feeling the story take shape, and as it did so, take hold of her. Her publishers described her as an author-ethnologist, she should play that up this time. Give Trenholm his due, of course, once she got to him; he was a perfect character, his quietness, determination, devotion, lack of drama. Of course a single day's ride was too little, she would have to blur the time element again. It came as pure story now, as Pablo grew more and more uneasy and finally, when she rebuked him, took that as an excuse to desert her there in the mist, deep in the country of the fanatical Rashti. She made a tactful offering to the cross, she talked with the Indians, with the feel of the pistol under her arm she decided to take a chance and go with them.

The thing ran smoothly from there. You could do something nice with the medicines, his appreciation of the dinner, the rather stilted parting. Handle all that underplayed and let the reader put more in between the lines. The ceremony, of course, took care of itself, with the sticky moment when the child died and they did not know just which way the natives might jump. They both showed calm faces. When she looked back on the trail he was still standing, looking after her. Mood of restraint and understatement throughout, gorgeous stuff. Now she had it.

She went to her typewriter, then gave an exclamation of annoyance. La Pine? To hell with La Pine. She didn't matter. The baroness? You could not leave her out entirely. In the distance — his wife was a noted orchidologist, then on an expedition herself. Suggesting some leather-faced, long-striding wench. That would do. Now she was in the clear, and she knew that she had a perfectly gorgeous story.

She sat down and put paper in her machine. "The Ghosts of the Old Gods." No, that would not do. She needed something a lot more punchy than that, something to lead off the best material that had ever come her way. She reflected a moment, then put her fingers on the keys and typed rapidly:

CHAPTER XII
THE REAL THING

CAVIAR REMEMBERED

I N Dr. MacMillan's opinion, dinner in the middle of the day was something of a barbarity, even on Sundays. He was a tall, broad, solid old man, commonly accepted both in this country and abroad as one of the deans of anthropology; he was of an active mental and physical habit, and he enjoyed his food. The big meal of the day should be accompanied by wine — in this word he embraced everything from vodka to Vouvray — but drinks at that hour shortly left him in an unpleasant torpor. This effect had become much more marked since he passed his seventieth birthday; as a young man, he had suffered from no such disability.

Still, the food had been excellent, *sans* alcohol, the talk very good. They had been discussing the evolution of man and whether Zinjanthropus, recently discovered by the Leakeys in East Africa, was man or a tool-using man-ape. Now he relaxed in an armchair while his hostess, Dr. Warren, poured coffee. She had joined the anthropology faculty since his last visit here. Considering her, he thought that the day was happily past when learned women were *ipso facto* repulsive. Dr. Warren was charming. Holding the porcelain coffeepot, she showed a shapely forearm. She was, he thought, remarkably young to be a full professor. Then he thought that his thinking so was a sign of his own advancing age. Turning fifty had depressed him, sixty had inflicted on him the conviction that he was all but finished, but seventy had struck him as an achievement and it seemed to him that he was in many ways younger now than he had been twenty years earlier.

Put yourself back in the middle way of life and you saw that this woman was no mere girl. A widow, he understood; Alicia Warren. He accepted a cup of black coffee. Thank goodness, she had demitasses, and the china was good. Something, whether in her smile, or her dropping in of a lump of sugar, or some turn of head or body, made him recall Princess Svetlana across the chasm of time and horrendous change. As a matter of fact, it had never been true that brilliant and learned women could not be delightful, but in those days one rather assumed that no woman would hold a Ph.D. unless she was deformed. He wondered what Warren's husband had been like.

MacMillan could see that O'Donnell, the youngest faculty member present, was getting ready to pitch. At table he had been rather quiet in the company of his seniors, as had the girl — a graduate student of La Warren's with a teaching fellowship — whom, he presumed, the young man had been invited to balance. The others present were John Cottrell, Chairman of the Department of Anthropology, Sidney Levine, close to Cottrell in rank, and their wives.

In the talk that followed, arising from O'Donnell's question about the role of the use of tools in shaping the human mind, MacMillan introduced quite appositely a comment on the monstrosity of the name Zinjanthropus, a hybrid of Arabic and Greek, and remarked that the making of such a compound by an English scholar was a sad index of the decay of knowledge of the classical languages. It always interested him to see who among his juniors were conscious of such matters. Alicia Warren pleased him by saying, "It began with 'automobile' and it's been going on ever since."

John Cottrell said, "How about Minneapolis? Sioux and Greek, but of course, that was the work of some semi-lettered frontiersman, I suppose."

MacMillan smiled and sipped coffee. The woman did not really resemble Svetlana at all, and yet there was something . . . They returned to their main topic. Under Macmillan's influence the talk was better than usual. It was natural to treat him as a sort of chairman, and before him Cottrell forebore to indulge in monologues, nor did Macmillan abuse the deference they showed toward him; he talked well and generously, but did not hold forth. Alicia Warren thought of Renaissance men who embraced all knowledge. Dr. MacMillan did not do that, but he certainly embraced all anthropology and his interests reached beyond his science.

The visitor had then been at the university a little over a week, taking part in seminars, giving two lectures, meeting with the anthropological faculty and acting as the center of occasions such as this one. He relished being a lion and was the most energetic professor emeritus it was posssible to imagine, but one should not demand too much of him. At a pause in the talk, Mrs. Levine said that she and Sidney had to be going. The Cottrells said they must, too. Everyone rose.

O'Donnell said that he was supposed to have a conference at his quarters with an undergraduate major. From his voice it was plain that he would be glad to be talked into skipping it. Alicia had invited him to make a partner for Elsie Durand. She was pleased when Dr. Cottrell remarked, "Well, then you're hooked."

Alicia said, "After all, Dr. MacMillan will be here until Tuesday." But it was not MacMillan, she knew. As she diagnosed the trouble, Bill O'Donnell had studied and worked only in all-male, Ivy League colleges until he came to Hampton; daily contact with a reasonably presentable female colleague had thrown him off balance.

Gamely, the young man offered MacMillan a lift to wherever he was going, but the latter said he thought he'd like to stay on a while — if Dr. Warren did not mind. She said she would be delighted. So Bill drove Elsie back after all, and did not sulk about it.

When the others were gone, Dr. MacMillan drifted about the living room, remarking that he was past the age of disguising curiosity, the mainspring of science, and that he liked to see what books and furnishings his friends chose. "Or is this your own furniture?" he asked.

"Mine — or my husband's. The best of it doesn't reflect our tastes, though, but only that our parents and grandparents were fairly well off."

He scanned the bookshelves, thence came to the north window. He glanced out casually, then stood still, looking. The character of his interest became more serious.

"The formation at the end of your garden — alluvial terrace?"

"Yes."

"Do you know what period it is?"

"Approximately. Hennessy, of the Geology Department, has done a study of this region. That terrace was laid down at the end of the last glaciation — "

"The Mankato."

"Yes. What's now the Quoshaw River flowed there. Then the river shifted this way, cutting this level and leaving that terrace, then south again, to level the valley the campus is in."

"I see. That is just the kind of place where one should look for early man. Paleo-Indians have never been found in this part of the country. There are a number of explanations, and one too seldom thought of is that no one has had the luck to look in the right places. Have you ever poked into that terrace?"

"We have a sort of joint digging seminar that's put on by Archeology and the Division of Paleontology together. They plan to work this part some time. Judson is in charge, and he really has the technique. They've tried the terrace further over and got mammoth, dire wolf, and such, but no signs of man. Paleo-Indians aren't my line, but I've looked around for things on the surface. What I've found is pretty straight Woodland, but I did pick up one piece last fall, and you know, I'd about forgotten it."

She went to the semicircular table against the east wall and from its shallow drawer took out a small fragment of worked flint. MacMillan examined it with care.

"There's not enough for me to want to commit myself, but this *could* be the base of a pretty early projectile point. Let's not say Sandia. It *could* be, and that would be astonishing this far East. You know, I grew up partly in Saint Petersburg — before I left they changed the name to Petrograd, but that was so transitory."

Alicia nodded, puzzled by the abrupt shift. His Russian years were part of his legend.

"When I was boy — I thought I was a man — there was

a fad of archeology there. As a matter of fact, there were some excellent archeologists about." His smile was full of memories. "You could make a general rule that any man higher than a count was too impetuous to be a good digger."

She thought that he gave the word *man* a special inflection as though there had been a woman who broke the rule.

"They went out in their frock coats and got the knees of their expensive English trousers dirty, and the ladies in their high collars and long skirts came along, mostly to watch. Hiring a muzhik to dig was *infra dig*." He laughed.

Alicia smiled, not sure of the Latin tag.

"Sunday archeology," he said. "It can be a lot of fun." He weighed the stone in his hand. "Where did you find this?"

"Where the garden ends at the terrace. Over there. I was cultivating the peonies."

"Why don't we poke around a little bit? You must have some equipment handy. Trowels? Graph paper? It's a very long time since I've opened a site."

"All right."

Judson, she thought, would be annoyed, but to be able to say one had worked with MacMillan, even for a few hours . . . He smiled at her, and for a moment she thought that in the smile was too much personal appreciation, then she was angry with herself. This was not Bill O'Donnell.

She produced a small shovel, a proper archeologist's trowel and a narrow gardening one, a couple of stainless-steel spoons, a reel of steel tape, graph paper, thumbtacks, and a drawing board. While she was assembling these things, her guest went to her woodpile and shaped a number of stakes, handling the axe easily, the implement seeming small in his hands, against the bulk.

At the end of the peony bed, he said, "We might as well start here. It may be a pure waste of time, you know. You can run upon something almost as soon as you start, there may be nothing at all to find, or, like the patient Leakeys, you can keep taking out stuff for thirty years that makes you hope and at the end find one of the four most important skulls in the world."

"I know. Of course, I'm used to working where you can see structures showing aboveground, or at least definite surface signs that there's something underneath before you start. I've often wondered how the people who work on the really old stuff can have the patience."

It was not at all cold out, at least at this hour, when the sun, still high, poured over the southward-facing terrace. MacMillan spent some time in measuring and staking out an area and preparing, on three sheets of graph paper, what would develop into an elevation, a cross section, and a plan. He removed turf with the shovel, then, each taking a small area, they worked with the trowels. At a slight depth the soil became gravelly. It was worthwhile to be doing fieldwork with MacMillan, Dr. Jonathan L. MacMillan, but Alicia also began to be slightly bored.

"Those Russian women who watched you dig," she asked, "were they really interested?"

"We were mostly fooling around a few sites that were pretty rich. Neolithic, largely. And then there was a lot of social chatter, and there would be wine — Rhine wine usually — and caviar, or buffalo-grass vodka if someone was along who had an in with the Czar — things like that. I remember one time I was a bit high, and I was talking to a girl and digging at the same time, not watching what I was doing, and a very fine stone blade fell between my knees. Fortunately, she noticed where it came from."

"Your technique improved later, I take it."

"Yes. Also, the circumstances were rather more monastic."

The sun was lower. The shadow of the leafless birch tree made cool lines over them. Alicia's trowel rasped on something hard. She scraped carefully, uncovering a greyish object.

"Looks like a fossil," she said.

"Definitely." On the graphs, he marked the site of the object in three dimensions.

Slowly she defined it. It was six inches long and nearly two inches wide. She sat back on her heels.

MacMillan said, "This end is broken. This looks like the spine of a cervical vertebra of a large animal, a mammoth as like as not."

"Well, then we're not completely skunked."

"No, but still, we haven't come to archeology. Let me try here." He worked delicately to the left and slightly below the broken end. "Ah-ha!" Part of a curved bone came into view, faintly suggestive of a napkin ring. "The vertebra itself, I'll bet." In a few minutes it was clear that he was right.

The sun dipped to the tips of a row of tall evergreens to the west.

Alicia said, "We'd better let Judson see this *in situ*. He'll name the animal right off."

The old man looked at her. "You're cold, and so am I. This sort of thing is no fun with goose pimples. Let's call it a day. Have you any free time tomorrow?"

"I can be ready at two-thirty."

They rose, stiffly. As they walked to the house, MacMillan

said, "This is a lark for me. Let's work along both ways from that bone and see what we may find. I feel lucky. We'll leave everything in place, of course, and you can call in your pale-ontologists and geologists later. After all, one fossil bone in post-glacial gravel isn't going to have anyone jumping up and down with excitement."

"All right. Have you time for tea, and how about a spot of rum in it?"

"Perfect! I'm due at Hendon's at six-thirty; until then I'm free."

The sun still reached through the west window, almost level, to light up the strong black and red Oaxaca serape on the floor in front of the fireplace. The fire burned briskly with birch logs. From where he sat, MacMillan could see out the north window to the terrace and to the fine-twigged, tall birch that had cast its shadow upon them. Alicia served him his tea — he took three lumps of sugar — and handed him the decanter of rum. He laced his drink generously. She, in her turn, measured a couple of teaspoonfuls into her cup. As he sipped his drink he seemed to expand and grow younger.

"Birch," he said. "It's several years since I've seen birch. These logs and that tree out there — so much today has re-minded me of Russia. Of couse, I saw and enjoyed the happy upper crust of it; underneath there was a lot of misery in those days, but whether more than there is now I don't know. Birch, tea and rum, and snow in the north shadow of the house."

He emptied his cup. "Of course, at this time of year the snow still lay heavy and we'd never have gone digging."

She offered, and he accepted, another cup.

"I ought to serve your tea in a glass," she said.

He laughed. "That's hardly necessary. My samovar days are far behind me." He paused, reflecting, then he looked at her with an expression of tender cannibalism that recalled the moment's suspicion she had had earlier. "You were asking about the ladies who came to watch us dig. There was one young woman who really took an interest. She had a fine mind, and under a different dispensation she would have become a scientist. It's odd; earlier today you reminded me of her. You still do. You don't actually look like her, but there is something."

At this moment, she decided, the conversation must be kept going briskly. "And was this young woman a countess or lower?"

"Eh? Oh, I'd forgotten I'd said that. No, she was the exception." He sipped at his tea. "There was a tumulus near her father's *dacha*, which was one of those modest little cottages with about sixty rooms. We dug there together. We took her little brother along, otherwise it would have been improper. We got some nice Neolithic stuff out of it, as far as we went. She had technique. This afternoon made me remember it."

He gazed at Alicia.

She asked, "In the revolution — what happened to her?"

"I don't know. Disappeared, as so many did. I saw her cousin later in Paris when I was working with Abbé Breuil. He was dressed like a muzhik, playing the balalaika in one of those Russian nightclubs. He wasn't able to tell me a thing."

"Breuil and Paris — that sounds like quite a combination."

"Mostly Breuil and the Dordogne. He was working a Mousterian site that season."

The term, Mousterian, the name of a fairly advanced tradition of Old Stone Age flint-working, was a natural lead for turning the talk back to shop. He talked very high-class shop. The woman listening knew he was putting forth a special effort for her benefit, and could not but respond. At exactly five minutes after six she glanced openly at the clock, exclaimed, and spoke of his dinner engagement.

At the door he took her hand. "Two-thirty tomorrow, then. We can get in at least two hours before it turns too cold. We should uncover a couple of square meters in that time, unless we're lucky and find something."

"Fine." You could not quite snatch your hand away.

"And we'll do it right, in the old style." His heels came together and he bowed over her hand, his lips barely touching it. "Many thanks for the tea and everything. *A demain*."

"You're welcome. *A demain*."

She stood in the hall, thinking. When he bowed over her hand, she could have sworn he was wearing a frock coat. She was making a lot out of nothing. "And we'll do it right. In the old style." Meaning what? Reminiscent caviar and wine, or an old, imperial-Russia seduction scene? That woman's younger brother went with them, otherwise it would have been improper. A younger brother or the equivalent might be a good idea; that would depend on people's schedules. She hoped that she was indeed making something of nothing, but there had been the look in his eye, and, as she knew, sometimes old men forget themselves.

Schedules for Monday afternoon worked out badly for her; she had to take whom she could, and for a later hour than she would have liked. At two-thirty that afternoon she was ready and suitably dressed in warm slacks and a sweater. She had brought from the museum another trowel and some brushes.

MacMillan arrived on time, bringing with him a bottle of excellent Rhine wine, a large jar of domestic caviar, and a tin of English biscuits.

"Here's our picnic," he said. "Will you get us a knife to spread this with? I'm sorry I couldn't manage real caviar, but little dabs of the stuff, and salted the way it usually is, are no good. We can stick this bottle in the snow to keep cold; I suppose the refrigerator is really better, but the snow is a matter of sentiment."

She got a knife and glasses.

"Why three?" he asked.

"My mother always had at least one more teacup on the tray than the number of people she expected, so that if someone dropped in, he wouldn't have any reason to feel that he was causing trouble."

Dr. MacMillan accepted that readily enough. They arranged the picnic things, with the bottle bedded in a rather dirty-looking remainder of snow, then they went to the dig. He marked off areas for them on either side of the fossil vertebra. As she watched him, it occurred to Alicia that she had not thought of this man as an archeologist.

As though he had heard her thinking, he said, "Before my father was stationed at Saint Petersburg, he was in Berlin. I had two years of college at Heidelberg. At that time I wanted to be a geologist. We had a young instructor who took some of us to the sandpit at Mauer, where Heidelberg Man was found, and later I was introduced to Dr. Schoetensack. " Seeing that the name did not register, he said, "The man who found it."

Alicia began to uncover another bone. He made some suggestions, then went on as he worked with his trowel. "The idea of visiting a sandpit every day for twenty years and in the end being rewarded by the oldest human jaw in Europe — the second oldest in the world, we thought then — was romantic to me. The very young, I think, have an inclination toward sainthood, toward self-immolation — usually in violent conflict with a lot of other inclinations."

"Yes. I see what you mean."

The bone was another vertebra, surely of the same animal. Dr. MacMillan remarked that they — or the paleontologists, to whom such fossils mattered most — could hope that the whole skeleton would come out. So often, where water has been at work, bones are hopelessly scattered.

Then he said, "Anyhow, that started me on early man, and so into anthropology in general. We were transferred to Russia. That was fun, and the program looked so simple — my vacations there, and study in Germany, with, my father insisted, postgraduate work at an American university to keep me from becoming a total foreigner. Then the war started. There was no proper school of anthropology in Russia. I played archeologist and enjoyed myself, and came home in 1915 to find, to my surprise, that there were some very good anthropologists indeed in the semicivilized United States."

From time to time as he talked he stopped work and turned to face Alicia.

"Then, afterward, I had the luck to put in a session with Breuil, at the peak of his fame. So, doing a thing like this is full of associations."

"Of course."

His tone made what he told of himself seem unusually intimate and she knew, as a woman can know, that there was only a narrow line between that intimacy and another that she did not want at all. Her wristwatch told her that it was nearly half-past three. Definitely, her bone was another cervical vertebra, intact.

Studying it, MacMillan said, "The head should be over this way and the body on your side. The axial vertebra was the place to aim for; if we could find a man-made weapon close here, we'd have something."

"At the best, pretty recent compared to what you worked at. What's the accepted date on Heidelberg Man?"

"Right now the received date is 300,000 B.C. But the oldest I ever worked on was that Mousterian site — not over 100,-000."

"And if we get anything here, it will be less than 20,000. We celebrated our hundred and fiftieth anniversary a while back. They had a couple of guests from Oxford."

"Which some say was founded by Alfred the Great."

"Exactly. In this country everything runs true to form."

"From the point of view of the deceased, I don't think it makes much difference. Anyhow, age isn't the point, it's finding out what did happen to some people at any place and time in the past. Hey! I think I've got something."

Alicia looked. "Flint, isn't it?"

"Yes. Like that washed-down piece you have in the house." He took out his penknife, opened the small blade, and worked delicately immediately above the bit of stone.

It turned out to be an inch and a half long, thin, with an edge marked by irregular corrugations where flakes had been taken off.

"This is it," MacMillan said. "What wonderful luck!"

"Yes. Wonderful! Hadn't we better get a geologist here right away?"

His expression of resistance was almost childish. "Not quite yet." He looked at the sky. "The weather is set fair. We can safely leave all this overnight if need be. I want to uncover this a little more, so that it will show well when it's photographed."

He worked slowly, carefully, removing a miniature, shallow cave of earth from above the flint, then uncovering its upper surface. It was definitely a point.

"I wish I didn't have to leave here tomorrow," he said. "You get your people to do a thorough job around here. This isn't actually in contact with a bone, but the association is good. I think you've got early man here, all right. Beats that one hundred and fiftieth anniversary." He sat back and stretched. "Well, we've made our point, you might say. Now, let's celebrate."

"Isn't it a little early?"

"It's nearly four, and after all this is only wine."

He went to the shade of the house and got the things. From his overcoat pocket he produced a corkscrew, with which he opened the bottle. He poured with formality, putting a few drops into his own glass, sniffing, and tasting, before he filled Alicia's. She opened the jar of caviar with the point of a trowel and spread the dark stuff on crackers.

"Here's to the original Hampton Man," he said, raising his glass.

"To Hampton Man — oh, goodness, it sounds so official!"

He quaffed, she drank. It was delicious wine.

"I suppose that one should wish that his bones rest in peace," he said, "but since we're ghouls by profession, here's to his disinterment."

"Right."

She drank again. He emptied his glass, refilled it, and ate a well-spread cracker.

"My, but this *is* like old times. And with that bit of flint there . . . Isn't it strange, you find that little piece of worked stone, and someone says to you across thousands of years, 'I was here, I was hungry, I hunted'?"

"Yes. And then I suppose his wife helped him butcher, and they made camp and cooked meat." She considered. "The low ground was the high ground, then; he killed his prey at the river's edge, then they made camp where it was higher — perhaps about on the roof of my house."

He smiled, his eyes full of sentiment. "You know, you do sound like Svetlana — the girl I mentioned. It always annoyed me that Stalin's daughter was given the same name."

"The girl who was higher than a countess?"

"As a matter of fact, she was a princess. Of course, princesses were much commoner in Russia than in other countries. You would make a good princess — Princess Alicia — I like the sound of it." He took some wine. "You know — since we've worked together like this, it seems silly to go on be-doctoring each other. Do you mind if I call you by your first name, Princess Alicia?"

It was old-fashioned, it was absurd, she did not think that she could ever bring herself to call this man Jonathan, they were sitting much closer to each other than she had intended, and in his eyes was folly. His hand, the hand of the sage, the master, the respected one, fell upon her arm. At that moment, ten minutes late but still, by a hair's breadth, on time, William O'Donnell came around the house with a camera slung from his neck.

"Hello, there!" he called. "Are you finding anything?"

Dr. MacMillan looked furious and frustrated.

"You bet we are," Alicia said. "Come and look."

When he had studied the objects he whistled. "This kind of thing is way out of my line, but it looks hot. What is the animal?"

"Mammoth, I think," Dr. MacMillan said. His voice was cold.

Alicia told him, "Get your camera going." She rose and went to fetch the third glass. When she returned, MacMillan was instructing the young man what pictures to take. She thought, you hear how dogs can smell hostility — these two don't smell anything, it's extrasensory perception that makes them bristle at each other. She poured a glass of wine and spread caviar on another cracker. O'Donnell sipped and photographed, taking altogether twelve pictures. The sun had dipped below the birch tree and once again reached the edge of the evergreens. Hands grew cold. They went into the house. Alicia asked the men to lay and light the fire; each one's part in doing so became a competition. She got tea.

The business of pouring tea, of passing it and the toast, of circulating the little decanter, created a pause. MacMillan felt as if he saw the group, including himself, from a slight distance. It was a familiar phenomenon, going back to his first ethnological work, when, as he questioned his informant, he tried to gauge that man's view of himself, the extent to which his very presence and his questions discolored the data. (As he had written in his most famous book, the field worker must never forget that he is not only an observer of the ethnographic scene, but, willy-nilly, an active and affective participant in it.) Now, viewing himself, he felt a moment of shame, then a thoughtful sadness because one can never turn back the clock. That morning he had looked up both Warren and O'Donnell in the faculty list, and from the dates of their bachelor's degrees decided that she must be thirty-six, he thirty-two. He told himself that seventy is not quite twice thirty-six, but it comes mighty close to it. And she was not encouraging O'Donnell's interest in her, but on this day had arranged for him to come — *faute de mieux*, unquestionably — because she had read his own fatuousness. If you are seventy and looked upon as the grand old man of your science, the only thing to do is to live up to your age and image. It was nearly five o'clock. He was due for dinner with the president of the university at seven, a formal affair. So he had time.

Referring to the tea, he discussed briefly the division of the world between tea and coffee drinkers. This country, he said, was fundamentally a coffee country, but where tea was served in the old, colonial-East Coast manner, it was something of a rite. He contrasted the detailed solemnity of the Japanese tea ceremony with the relaxed, social ritual of the Anglo-American custom. From the coffeehouse, a men's institution, arose Lloyd's of London and the English system of men's clubs; tea remained in the parlor with a woman pouring. He quoted Pope and Henry James.

Via references to the general subject of the ritual consumption of various drinks and solids, he made a smooth transition to the plant peyote. Up to this time he had maintained a monologue and entertained himself with the associations and transitions by which he reached the point that he had aimed for from the start. O'Donnell's specialty was North American ethnology, Warren's was Middle America. With the mention of peyote, he entered their areas.

He gave some details of peyote ceremonies he had seen in the northern Plains tribes, then asked O'Donnell about his observations, citing a paper the young man had written. O'Donnell responded eagerly.

The ritual use of peyote began in northern Mexico; hence it was easy to carry the conversation over into Warren's field and involve her. Soon they were discussing the origins of farming in the New World and the probable spot at which maize was first cultivated. The old man egged them on with questions and at the right moments he held forth, offering new combinations and interpretations of knowledges. His two companions were enchanted and he was quite happy. Rivalries, the question of male and female, were forgotten. Suddenly it was after six and past time for him to get to his hotel and change for dinner. O'Donnell said he would be glad to drive him there, and he accepted.

At the door Alicia — Dr. Warren — gave him her hand, smiling, thanking him for his company. He thanked her for her hospitality and the fun of the private excavation, and told her to be sure to let him know what developed about Hampton Man after the specialists had worked on the site. He did not hold onto her hand nor bow over it. He got into the car with the young professor.

It was all right now, he thought, he had made it all right. Memories can trap one, but one cannot go back, any more than one could once again lavishly spoon up the remembered caviar. He laughed suddenly, just as O'Donnell was about to speak to him, and covered it with an evasion. He had told her

of Svetlana's younger brother chaperoning them, and realized
that Dr. Warren had cast O'Donnell in the little-brother role,
which, surely, the young man would never have chosen for
himself.

THE DOOR IN THE WALL

DARTS OF AWAKENING began to enter the dream, the awareness that it was a dream, the sense of light beyond his eyelids, red, clashing with the clear light within his mind. It was a delightful dream and he did not want to let it go. Cayetano had somehow become a benevolent Pan, and the Dark Goddess was surely the most beautiful woman he had ever known and he loved her with a love entirely happy and pure, and besides, the answer to his months of fruitless seeking was in her hands, and already without words she was enabling him to understand the mystery of the axis.

Daylight, sound, and the natural completion of sleep were too much. Morning light coming directly through the high, unglazed east window was a bright bar passing above his cot, its shaft striking the whitewashed, adobe west wall to throw a softer reflection back into the big, bare room. Light spread into it also from the west window, and seeped in under the thatched eaves, which were carried on rafters that projected well beyond the walls.

Bert lay on his back, the dream still confusedly with him. He stared up at the inverted reservoir of darkness in the high pitch of the thatched roof, a sample of night permanently retained to join with each returning night and to give comfort to the family of bats that lived secretly up in the roof tree; a thinly mysterious, temporary refuge from waking, from planning work, and an aid to the disentangling of dreams. Cayetano had been important in this one, and had at last revealed a benevolent, friendly self, which was obvious enough wish fulfillment, but the goddess, what did she stand for, whence did she come? It was she who had revealed to Bert the nature of the axis, which turned upon itself and became a circle, or rather a long oval, embracing all the Indian people of Rosario, and by means of which they became one and comprehensible. Waking further, he remembered the goddess in the Dresden Codex, the bare, young body and the bird of prey growing out her head, the cruel face. His goddess was all goodness. She was dressed, he realized, not as an Indian but in what he took to be the latest, North American high style. Did Freudians realize, he wondered, how clearly people often dream? This one was a simple compound of the ethnological quest that had so far proven vain, mixed with a somewhat sublimated sex, quite obvious after all this chaste time and with so many attractive, golden-brown women within reach.

He heard an axe chunk heavily into wood, the sound quite different from that of a machete striking, which could also be heard, but from a greater distance. Don Rafael's boy, next door. Listening to the heavy impacts and the long pauses between, he could visualize the long, perfectly straight helve, its distal end projecting more than a handsbreadth beyond the head, the whole raised to the full extent of straightened arms at each stroke and brought straight down, as though brute force alone must serve to split the wood.

He sat up on his cot, throwing off the light, bold-patterned, native blanket. Another day, another dollar. The Lip Woman would be here shortly and the horse must be fed. So forward, back and breast as either should be. Something accomplished, something done . . . The night had been heavy, stuffy. Everyone had told him that muggy weather came in March and April, to cool off again in May, but at two thousand meters and after the brisk, fresh months of the early dry season, he felt insulted. He leaned down, picked up his sneakers, shook them out carefully, and put them on. The earthen floor was bare and well swept, but bare earth in the tropics is never quite lifeless and you never set your unshod foot on it.

He stripped, poured cool water from the red clay jar into his basin and washed down, feeling better, brisker as he did so. Dressed, he went out to feed his horse. It was a good little animal that spent too much time in its shelter, eating corn-stalks. As bored as I am, he thought. Ethnology is a slow process of gaining acceptance. And if you don't gain accept-ance? You just go on and on being friendly with everyone, even the ones you'd like to haul off and kick in the butt, like Cayetano, the slippery cheat, you just go on and you hope. In May it will cool off and there will be a little rain, then in June the real rains come, *el invierno*, the winter. Depending on the extensibility of his money, and the deep need to be once more with his own kind, talk once more with an Ameri-can girl, he would go out to teach Anthropology 4 at sum-mer school. With nothing more to show than observations on material culture and technology containing nothing whatso-ever new, and a command of the language called Raxti (or Rašti in proper, phonetic script) and more commonly re-ferred to in Spanish as The Tongue?

He looked to the north and west, where the mountains rose, soft-edged ridge behind ridge, green going into blue, knowing the fragrance of the great evergreens up there in the cold country. They said there was quite a ruin at Yumbalán. It might be a good idea to go up there, get away from here for a while, a day or two on horseback, a week of good, clean, impersonal archeological scouting. You don't have to be a diplomat to clear bush and make a map, you just see a job and go to it.

He had built a fire in the three-stone, Indian fireplace (one of the great advantages of a dirt-floored, thatched building was that you could have a fire inside it) and put the coffee water on to boil by the time the Lip Woman tapped gently at his open door. Her name, actually, was Malín Palín, but that was not how he thought of her. She was between old and young, small-boned and slender, always neat — as most of the Indian women were — and afflicted by a pair of buck upper incisors that, through the years, had battered her lower lip into a state of acute tenderness and swelling. Bert knew better than to set up shop as a doctor in a tropical village; one would wind up doing nothing but tend the sick, but she was related to Cayetano in some complex way — always Cayetano, wherever he turned — and the very oddity and simplicity of her affliction prevented refusal.

The Lip Woman spoke no Spanish at all. She greeted him in The Tongue, "*Ah in-tat.*" Almost no other Indian save Cayetano would use that language with him. He answered, "*Ah in-nan.*"

She stepped inside the doorway and far enough to one side to be out of sight of anyone passing along the road, and stood in the penumbra like a docile child, her hands clasped against her sash with a package in them wrapped in green leaves. In the tribal style her hair was done in two braids, which were wrapped in multicolored, bright bands of local weave, then made into a crown around her head. The effect was gay and somewhat royal, above the worn face and the striped blouse faded to dimness by sun and washing. The sash at her waist was new and fresh; below it hung the narrow, calf-length skirt, blue, green, and white with fine touches of yellow. As he squeezed ointment onto a bit of cotton wool, Bert thought that these women aged remarkably well. From the habit of carrying loads on their heads they stood beautifully erect and walked with an interesting, gliding walk. They seemed to spread hardly at all as they grew older, and their wrists and ankles stayed neat. He dabbed ointment on the woman's lip. More than two months of this treatment had worked visible improvement. Less of the Ubangi effect.

She said, "Thank you," and held out the green package. "There was no egg today. Here is a banana."

He took it and thanked her.

At the door she turned to say, "We have seen each other."

"We have seen each other, then."

That was the *despedida*, the goodbye. It was an automatic, set form, but each time he heard it he had to record that it was a lie. Not with any of them had there been mutual seeing, the meeting of two human beings, but only good manners and the formality of smiling, and, on his part the unending, gentle search for the aperture that they, gently and expertly, kept hidden. He was as near to a real personal relationship with the Lip Woman as he was with anyone in the community. He could have had another tube of that excellent ointment shipped to him within a fortnight and have given her one with which to treat herself, as he would do when it was time for him to leave, but he counted on that morning ritual. They never said more than they had said today, yet it was a moment of simple, human contact that meant more to him than he realized.

He set about getting breakfast. His other meals he ate at Doña Candelaria's, but breakfast he cooked for himself, preferring something approaching his home style. The Lip Woman had brought him a *platano*, a cooking banana, which, sliced and fried, made an excellent tropical replacement for bacon. As he cooked and ate, a solid North American breakfast with two fried eggs and yet exotic to the extent of the fried banana and the shortbread lightly flavored with anise, his mind mechanically went over the day's routine. Out of order, he thought first that Cayetano was due for a session with him in midafternoon. If he did not fail to turn up, as sometimes happened. I am getting a Cayetano complex, he thought. It was the man's curious charm, his elusiveness, and the stubborn feeling that he, Bert, would have suffered an intolerable defeat if he left here without having discovered what his informant really was, sorcerer, soothsayer, healer, or priest of the old religion, or — the thought laden with anticlimax and ridiculousness — just another Indian, a little better educated, a little smarter, than most.

He had hired the man to teach him Raxti and guide him in observing the open, permissible things, such as the crafts of weaving and pottery-making, the manner of building a house, the farmer's cycle and the crops, and to arrange for his supply of firewood and feed for the horse. The ethnologist, working with a rustic innocent, had the advantage of all the decades of study of ancient and modern Maya culture, the survivals in Guatemala and in Chiapas that have been so well described, Bishop Landa's remarkable account of Yucatan in the sixteenth century and all the other early sources. So when you looked at a field you casually referred to the "holy corn," in talking of planting you mentioned prayer, in discussing the structure of houses you referred to the four directions, and as you worked on your vocabulary you asked how one said "year bearer," or "days without name," or "watcher of the soul." According to the rules, the naïve Indian would be so astonished that a stranger from a far land should know enough to speak of such things that he would answer unguardedly. Thus the door was open and the scholar's foot was in it, and you went on from there. But Cayetano, sober, was merely blank, and Cayetano, tipsy, assumed an amused, flirtatious, wily expression that made you want to shove his teeth down his neck. And Bert was sure that it was this same Cayetano who had made it impossible for him to get into any real talk with any other Indians.

As a normal part of linguistic work, you collect texts. You ask for stories, tales, and if you don't get anything but thoroughly dull personal experiences, you suggest as though it were but a random fancy that your informant tell you about the beginning of the world, before the sun rose, or how the mounds at Chuultún, Holy Stones, the ruin at the edge of the village, were built. All Bert got for his pains were simplified Bible stories, and as to Chuultún, the same "Who knows?" that had been Cayetano's refrain when the two of them went there. You could see where they had burned the incense, where the thick smoke of the fat pine had blackened the stones and where the resin had run down, spots of beeswax from a type of candle that had been millennially old when the Spanish first landed, and that nobody in the village admitted to ever having heard of. Cayetano knew nothing about any of it, not a thing. Oh no, not he.

The Ladinos, who were amazingly ignorant about the Indians whom they exploited and among whom they lived out their lives, all thought Cayetano had some esoteric position but no one was sure just what. Don Pedro, the *alcalde*, said he was a *zahorín*, Don Rafael that he was a *brujo*, Don Angel, the telegraph operator, that he was a *chimán*, and Doña Candelaria that he was a *curandero*. Try to pin them down, and about all you got was that the other Indians held him in respect, addressing him as *Cham — Cham Caitano —* and he was some sort of witch. Perhaps in fact there was no hidden hierarchy here and the man was nothing special. Perhaps. But the Catholic priest thought he was, which was why he objected to Bert's using him as an informant. And then, the very fact that he often turned up slightly drunk but under control and never got really drunk strongly argued some form of Mayan priesthood.

Some of this Bert reviewed in his thoughts, concluding, well, I'll have another session with him and it'll probably be the same old nothing. In the meantime, more of the same old stuff, they're due to thatch Juan Manuel's house today, the market, lunch at Doña Candelaria's, and so on, and on. Lunch would probably be cold minced mutton chopped up with mint again, since they'd had hot mutton last night. It was an agreeable dish, the first forty-five times. Late this afternoon, he might be able to get in a ride. Change of scene — he knew all the scenes. I chose ethnology because it was live, a game of human contacts. I should have been an archeologist straight out, and be busy now at some nice, acquiescent, productive ruin.

He took pencil and notebook. It was better to leave the camera behind. For some reason, they didn't mind his sketching, in fact, they were amused to see what he produced, but the camera, with its single, intense eye, made them extremely uneasy. It was common to hear the Indians speak of people looking, or even thinking too much about someone, and from their tone of voice he gathered that such looking and thinking had evil power. The camera, he thought, was a machine for intensified looking, while a drawing was a neat and clever trick. The same verb, *ts'ibli*, served for drawing and writing, which took one back to the ancient Mayas with their fine arts and their hieroglyphs. *Ts'ibli* was permissible, as it was not, for instance, with many Indians of his own Southwest, and when, as he sometimes did for pleasure, he worked up a sketch into a crude water color, those who saw it were entranced. To the equipment in the handy, *ixtle*-fiber pouch he slung from his shoulder, he added a sketchbook and a couple of HB pencils.

At his doorway he was stopped by two half-grown boys. In this warm weather they had shed the black wool tunics he had come to regard as a fixed part of the native costume, retaining the pajama-like, white cotton garments with the fine lines of red and blue decoration on the fronts of their shirts. That decoration, laboriously woven in by the women, was hidden during most of the year, to be revealed in this brief period when wool was uncomfortable.

They raised their hats and greeted him in Spanish, the Indian Spanish, lilting, monotonously musical in its rise and fall, high-pitched, with a limited vocabulary and the phrasing often directly translated from The Tongue.

"Good day, señor. Forgive the trouble, señor. Big your heart, señor, that you let us look into your gun that loads from behind." Strangers to him, they did not call him Don Alberto.

To people who had little acquaintance with anything but muzzle-loaders, the brilliance of his shotgun barrel when you broke the gun and held it to the light was a first-class marvel, the fame of which had spread wide. He was in no hurry, and anyhow, it is part of the ethnological game always to be obliging. He got out the gun, a single barrelled 16-gauge, broke it, demonstrated. They looked, were duly impressed, thanked him at courteous length, and departed. Of such things were his day composed. He looked up. The meek, musical, almost whining approach, the effect of almost servile friendliness, like the farewell, "We have seen each other," were deeply false and close to taunting. What would boys that age know? Not much, probably, but whatever they did know they would keep masked from him, from the Ladinos, from the priest.

He looked towards the church, whose hexagonal, buttressed apse rose blank and high a hundred feet west of his door, solid, with the old, conquering, Spanish solidarity that carried an echo of the strength of Rome, the domes, the arched bridges, the towns laid out in the rectangular plan of the *castra*, the last flicker of the tradition of the Caesars carried here, to Central America. Draw a line west from its altar for half a mile and it took you to the center of Chuultún. The

Maya Caesars had their staying power, too, and they had chosen for their temple the spot with the better view, looking across the valley to the distant volcano, Tsacuinic, looming on the horizon, too regular a triangle to be quite credible in nature.

It was that projected line that had generated the idea of the axis in his dream, but he could see no source or logic in the mystery of the oval. Somewhere along the common line of the two hostile antiquities there was a division. On this side of it lay what was known to all, on the other, what belonged to the Indians only. This division existed within the people themselves. Why was the line so uncrossable in this particular village? The Indians came to mass with moderate regularity, made a great and traditional thing of the major feasts, dug out of their penury the gifts of food, fuel, and services that maintained the churchly establishment. They were distinctly more devout than the Ladino men, even though they liked to pray in front of the church and then, inside, to the dark figure of the "Old Virgin" in the corner rather than to the altar, upsetting the unfortunate German who had been dropped here to take care of their souls. In their devoutness was a paradox. An axis is nothing but the name for a spatial relationship. There was the altar in the church of Nuestra Señora del Rosario and an altar, or several altars, at Chuultún. Was there any connection between them, and if so, what? There, he thought, in a nutshell are my goal and my frustration. If I knew that, I'd have a center on which to build an ethnography. Nuts.

He turned west, wondering whether it was the young and earnest German priest, living in this village that had for centuries been a mission, visited only a few times a year, that had caused the Indians to clam up especially tightly. Or was his own technique just not good?

On this part of the central street, close to the plaza, the way was wide and straight, its reddish dirt unrutted, since wheeled vehicles could not travel the long, twisting, climbing trail, the *camino real*, that led to Rosario. On either side stood the houses of the Ladinos, twelve in all, including the vacant one he had rented, rectangular, precise, well whitewashed, brightened by brilliant reds and blue on doors and shutters. One other, like his own, had a thatched roof; the rest showed the red-brown of tile. They stood close to the roadside, several of them extending high, white walls to embrace a larger, outdoor area. They gave definition and an almost urban trimness to their stretch of street.

Doors in several houses opened onto tiny shops in which a dozen or less kinds of articles might be offered for sale, nails, priced by the dozen for little ones, so much apiece for the biggest, tallow and paraffin candles, *aguardiente* or the more highly prized, pale yellow liquor, San Lázaro (it would revive a corpse, the inevitable saying went), an empty Cinzano bottle, which was accepted all through these parts as a standard measure for liquids, with its cork carefully attached by a string, brown salt from Ixtepec, a bolt of cloth, links of highly spiced sausages. The title of a book came to his mind, as it had done heaven knew how often in the past three months, "Penny Capitalism." The Indian women in the market place were penny merchants, as were the Ladinas in their houses. Two networks of minuscule trade wove through the village and reached beyond to other plazas, other markets, coffee and grain from Rosario for woolen goods from San

Miguel, salt from Ixtepec, and wheat flour from the cold country. He had enough material to do a nice chapter on trade and economy. There were clear distinctions between what Ladinos and Indians dealt in and how they offered their wares — except for Antón Luch, whose house, tile-roofed and long, was the last on the right in the little urban parade and who maintained the only real store in Rosario.

Antón was Indian, although obviously of mixed blood. Rumor gave him a Swiss father. To his emporium, Bert thought, I must now wend my way or run out of cigarettes. Giving Scylla a wide berth, I tack towards Charybdis. The thought, like the thought of penny capitalism, had been amusing the first time and had grown stale and inescapable. When one depends upon one's self for one's amusement, how dull one becomes, how repetitious. The mind insists on bringing up over and again the thought of which it has grown weary. He was protected from any danger from Charybdis by the unyielding chastity of Antón's daughters, or at least, by the fantastic price set upon them, and as for Scylla, it was no temptation.

Scylla was a small house on the same side of the street as his own, the domain of La Concha. La Concha, not Doña Concha, when the Ladino men spoke of her among themselves, was said to be a widow. Over the rough counter of her little shop she sold, among other things, liquor by the drink without benefit of license. In the back of the house, it was well known, she sold her favors when anyone turned up who would purchase them. Actually, no one had flatly told him that, but it was there by inference, in often repeated jokes, in a tone of voice, an occasional snicker. If she had ever had charms, they were long gone; from the standpoint of

Bert's less than thirty years, she was old. She served the drinks in little shot glasses, badly in need of washing. One visit to her tavern was sufficient for him, and she herself, he thought, was well enough symbolized by the glasses. No, not a temptation. His Scylla and Charybdis did not amount to much; he could hardly claim that his strolls down Ladino Row were fraught with danger. He crossed to the other side of the street before he reached La Concha's house, mechanically, thus avoiding the chance of having to exchange greetings with her. It seemed silly, but her over-friendly manner gave him the creeps.

He turned into Antón's store. The older sister was on duty behind the long counter. She had waited past her time; you could see that a few years ago she had been a beauty, but now the hooked, Maya nose had begun to dominate her face and her cheeks had lost roundness and smoothness. Her mouth had bitterness in its curve and all her expression was underlain by resignation.

She said, "*Buenos días, don Alberto*," excused herself, and ducked quickly out the back door of the shop.

Bert understood. Antón, whose optimism he considered pathological, must have given orders as soon as he settled in Rosario that the *norteamericano*, or the *gringo*, or whatever he called Bert (to many Indians he was a German, *un alemán*, the generic for tall, fair-skinned people, just as *turco* embraced the whole Levant, including Armenians), the distinguished foreigner, the scientist, was to be waited on by the younger daughter, she whose charms were at the perfection of their bloom.

The girl came out promptly, modest, eyes downcast. Her costume was the same as the Lip Woman's, except that it was made entirely of silk. Her blouse, sash, and skirt glowed, her hair wrappings were brilliant against her black hair. Her skin was golden, with a warming, red flush in her cheeks. Her upper eyelids had an exotic, Oriental curve that gave length and the effect of hidden knowledge to her liquid, brown eyes. Her face was a charming oval, her nose fine-nostrilled, not yet noticeably large, her lips attractively bowed. Her figure was slender and, Bert was sure, elegant. Age, he estimated, allowing that tropical women mature early, about sixteen.

She had only two packs of Bon Ton cigarettes left, she said, taking them out of the one glass case, where they were displayed as a sign of the quality of the emporium. Bert was the only person thereabouts who would spend the equivalent of twenty-five cents U.S., half a day's pay for a good workman, on a pack of smokes. This was a betrayal of secret wealth, of vast riches concealed behind the simplicity of his overt way of living that, he knew, caused some talk and the raising of prices when he was a buyer. The mules from Sacabil had been delayed, she explained, by a landslide on the road near Uyalá. Her Spanish was more correct, more neatly expressed, than Cayetano's, as good, in fact, as any local Ladino's, although it kept a trace of the Indian lilt. Antón's children had been to school, even, shockingly, to the Protestant mission school at Sacabil, but when the older girl came home and appeared on the street dressed like a Ladina, nay more, with her hair done up on top of her head, city style, the Ladina women had fallen upon her, torn loose her hair, ripped her dress, and set her and her sister once and for all in their place.

The classic definition of a Ladino is a person whose mother tongue is Spanish and who behaves as such. The last, faint echo of a memory of the Caesars, the legions, the builders of arches, was long gone and the memory of Spain had become a dim tradition that called for touchy pride and forbad men to do manual labor, but there was a distinction to be maintained at almost any price. Antón Luch had made it known that to the Ladino who would lawfully marry one of his daughters he would give the fabulous dowry of two thousand *pesos de oro*, a little more than a thousand dollars U.S. Back of that inducement lay the advantages of alliance with his varied trade, his mule trains, his acres of farming land, the many interests of a man with more drive than any two others in the region; yet no one as yet had come forward to ask for either daughter. Only by such a marriage could the women shed the bright, becoming tribal costume for the ill-shaped clothing of a Ladina, only thus could Antón have the pleasure of knowing that his grandchildren would be Ladinos. Under no circumstances would he consider a marriage with an Indian. Often idle, lazy, not too honest, yet a real pride stood up in the Ladinos and the older of Antón's daughters had passed her prime; her hopes, whether they were the same as her father's or what they were, were ended and now the second one was coming ripe and due in time to wither on the vine. Every Ladino buck for leagues around, every passing, enterprising traveller, had had a try at getting one or other to his bed, but their virtue was irrefragable and matrimony was the one thing never offered. There was an irrationality to this refusal, for it was obvious enough that most Ladinos were part Indian and plenty of crossing over had happened, not only when the *conquistadores* married Aztec and Quiché and Raxti princesses, yet now the lines were drawn and Antón's daughters could not cross them.

He said, no, he did not want anything else. She asked if he needed San Lázaro; he said not for now, he had a sufficiency. He would have been inclined to buy out the store, if thereby he could have got her to look him directly in the eye, have broken through to communication, to knowledge of the person, the thoughts, wishes, and all too probably despairs behind that lovely, guarded face.

Cayetano came in. He greeted the house in Spanish, then addressed Bert by name. Bert answered, the girl did not. Cayetano wore a shoddy blue suit, the decorated, native shirt showing under the open jacket, the standard, local, smallish palm-leaf hat, and sandals. He was slim, neat, grey-haired. A straggly beard on his chin, below his hooked nose, did give him a certain goatlike look, and even while the ethnologist spoke to him he remembered that in his dream this man had somehow been connected with Pan.

Cayetano said, "I was looking for you, señor. A little business has come up, so that I cannot come to your house at three today, so if it suits you, I shall come at five."

Like most Indians, he dealt exactly in hours of the day, although he seldom saw a clock of any kind.

It did not really suit, for five was the period Bert liked to have to himself, to enjoy a drink in preparation for the evening meal, but business is business. "Very well, at five, then."

The girl put the cigarette packs on the counter. He laid down the coins, avoiding any chance contact of hands. Her smooth, firm forearms ran into delicate hands the skin of which had not yet been ravaged by the endless grinding, the handling of lime, the biting, homemade soap, that were inseparable from women's work.

He said, *"Con permiso,"* as though she were not Indian, told Cayetano *"Hasta la vista,"* and left.

Antón's Spanish name, Antonio Pérez, was painted large across his store. Antón was rich, Antón was powerful, and apparently, being a man, he could dress as he pleased, even to shoes, but no Ladino would call him *"don,"* none, so far, would marry one of his daughters. Bert imagined the kind of man who might do so, one off the very bottom of the pack, and what the girl's life would be like thereafter, her husband never forgetting that in fact she was Indian, the grudging acceptance and more or less veiled venom of the Ladina women, the many kinds of ready cruelty in a society in which at best a woman was a drudge except, perhaps, for the brief period of her beauty. More likely the younger girl would wither as her sister was already well along in doing, in a land where spinsterhood was almost unthinkable. His bowels were wrung with more than compassion while for a moment he indulged wild fantasy.

Scylla and Charybdis after all, he thought, disgust on one side of the street, pity on the other — pity, and desire. He should have bought a roll of cornhusk cigarettes while he was in the store, to hand out to Indians, but he was not going back there now. He could pick some up at the market. Now he headed for where the house was being built.

From here on, along the *camino real,* Indian houses were distributed haphazard. They did not front on the road, but stood more or less back from it, each in its own yard, some with the definition of a fence or line of cactus, some with no boundary mark. Fruit and alligator-pear trees shaded the grounds, here and there were gardens or small plantings of corn, and there were many flowering bushes. The road was narrow or wide as chance willed, bending to one side or the other, an irregular thoroughfare of earth laced with paths worked by the feet of men, horses, mules, dogs, and pigs.

The building of a house was the work of a convivial group of men, calling to each other, often laughing. The framework was complete and the thatch was going onto the hip roof. They would have the thatching done before the day was over, so tomorrow — the fourth day, the inevitable, Indian four — they would tie on the walls of horizontal rods and plaster them with mud. Then there would be drinks, music, and feasting. There would also be prayer. What prayer? Led by whom? Not by Padre Greiz, that was sure. Cayetano told him only, "They pray, they pray to God, is all," closing him out.

There was nothing here that had not been fully described long since. All he needed to do was to be sure that there was no variation of interest, nothing, for instance, as archeologically significant as a building with rounded ends. Some of the men greeted him in Spanish, not in The Tongue. He sketched the wrapping by which the juncture of a rafter, a plate, and an up-right was bound into a secure joint with *liana*. A couple of men, bundles of thatch on their shoulders, stopped to look, admiring the correct reproduction, pleased, he thought, at this display of interest in their work, then they went on. He had not been totally ignored, yet after a few minutes he began to have once more an odd feeling of uncertainty that in fact he was present.

He went on, to the market, which in this village was not held at the plaza, but where the east-west *camino real* was intersected by the north-south one. It was an informal market, the vendors scattered along the north-south road, sitting in the sun or in shade, as if they were on a picnic, an effect helped by the fact that no houses stood close to the crossroads. To the south, the municipality had put up two long sheds, which were probably essential during the rainy season. Now they were used only when someone had meat to sell, the carcasses being hung in the shade on hooks built in for that purpose. That got the meat away from the rest of the market, a godsend, for even fresh killed meat gives out a slight but oppressive odor in warm weather and the sight of the massed flies is depressing. More important, to Bert's mind, at the crossroads itself, in the northwest quadrant there was a large ceiba, its bole well over six feet in diameter, its wide-sheltering leaves richly greened and neatly patterned, and opposite it a wooden cross twice as tall as a man, set in a square, solid base of roughly squared, large stones. As every Maya scholar knows, the ceiba was to the ancients a tree of many sacred values. On top of the cross's base and on the ground in front of it were miniature stone fireplaces, well smoked, like the ones at Chuultún, and there were always fresh flowers at the foot of the cross itself. The Maya cross — Bert could almost recite a long bibliography about it, from sixteenth century Spanish missionaries on up to within the last decade, some contending that it was pre-Columbian and Christian only by coincidence, some contending the opposite. Perhaps the axis continued to this point. There was something that bound the Indian community together, and until you uncovered that, all you had were observations, pieces, individuals, and never the whole.

The older, permanent, local market women had their places under the ceiba. They formed a sort of club. Along the road were younger vendors of less status and people from other villages, only a few today as it was not Rosario's market day. The woman from whom he usually bought his eggs was there, so he went to her. Far from refrigeration, one bought one's foods in small quantities, to be consumed fresh; in this case, two eggs at a time. They had long ago established a set price, so the transaction was not interesting to either of them, but she brightened and they had a brief, agreeable interlude of haggling when he also purchased one of the packages of a dozen cornhusk cigarettes, tied together with another strip of cornhusk, that she displayed on her napkin. Like most Indian women, she spoke very poor Spanish, but they dealt in that language. He had given up trying to get them to use Raxti; it was part of the refusal, the rebuff. Here at the market, their domain, one felt, the women were pleasant enough. Passing them on the street, unlike the men, they simply did not speak, although they never failed to greet other Indians. The men had to deal with Ladinos and had developed a formula to suit; the women wished only to avoid them and the avoidance extended firmly to visiting foreigners, however kindly intentioned.

He looked over the vendors along the road, to see if there was anything worth noting. His interest really quickened when he saw a little bundle of long, slender, black beeswax candles near one woman's knee. Very seldom had he seen anything to do with the old ritual exposed for sale. He had wondered if that might not be because of the priest's presence. As he turned towards the woman, she quietly drew a striped napkin over the candles and over herself the inevitable, infuriating, perfect armor of incomprehension. In Guatemala, ethnologists such as Chesnes and Van Cleve had bought materials for ceremonial offerings without difficulty, but not

Bert Whittaker in Rosario. Still, he had added a tiny item to his knowledge. He had several times bought honey from that woman, so her household presumably kept bees. This helped confirm, what he thought most likely, that the candles were made locally. To find them on sale in the market meant that some demand existed for them, and since they were never used for light, or in the church, then he was correct in concluding that they were burned in Mayan rituals. Not much had been added to what he already knew, but it was an item, making, you might say, a day not totally lost.

He turned back towards his house, hearing behind him the sound of soft, casual talk and a woman's mild laugh. Isolated, he thought, how isolated can you get? You hear of the loneliness to be experienced in big cities, but it could not be more acute than here in Rosario, a face-to-face community with a total population for the whole *municipio*, the village itself and all outlying settlements, of not over four thousand.

Don Gregorio joined him, on his way to the *cabildo*. It was Don Gregorio's turn that year to be municipal treasurer, a carefully rotated office vital to the Ladino economy. Not as tall nor as fair as Bert, he was, nonetheless, taller and fairer than Latin Americans are popularly supposed to be. Strong genes of the half-Gothic conquerors, Bert had wondered, or a passing traveller of northern stock a few generations back? The former, as like as not. It was his opinion, from his impression of the present-day product, and allowing for the Indian admixture, that these highlands must have been occupied by men from the north of Spain, the fair-skinned, blue-eyed, addicted warriors of Castille, Leon, and Aragon.

They exchanged the inescapable courtesies. "Don Alberto, good morning, at your service." "Good morning, Don Gregorio, at your orders." These they followed with chitchat. In his relations with the Ladinos, who counted him as essentially of their group, Bert had reached their chronic condition. There was simply nothing new to be said. The main difference on that score between himself and these natives was that they had lived all their lives in a state of boredom, relieved from time to time by the most minor incidents, by courtship, adultery when practicable, and by occasional drinking bouts, and they took their condition for granted, accepting it passively, whereas he was painfully aware of the monotony of his routine.

Don Gregorio said, "There's the priest's boy at your door. You will be invited to lunch and then asked for money. Did you know that at the end of the last rains, a leak showed itself in the church roof?"

"No. If there is a leak, I shall be glad to make the little contribution I can."

"We shall appreciate it. With your permission."

"It is yours."

The Ladino left him, and he turned towards his house.

The boy was in his mid-teens, one of the few Indians who attended the little school, primarily for young Ladinos, where Don Tomás presided with more interest than Bert would have expected over the drone of study and the uncertain voices of recitation. He wore the usual palm-leaf hat, a clean blue shirt, tieless and buttoned at the neck, dark trousers, and sandals. He doffed his hat to Bert and they exchanged the Spanish greetings, then, as Don Gregorio had forecast, he gave him the priest's invitation to lunch. Bert accepted and asked the boy to tell Doña Candelaria that he would not be eating at her place.

He decided to honor the occasion by wearing a white shirt and tie, if only as a way of showing that, in the cause of correctness, he could confine his throat just as Padre Greiz did with his collar. The slight difference would be that by noon the priest's collar would not be quite clean. This thought, momentary in his mind, was an expression of a lack of sympathy between the two men. In general, North Americans and North Europeans feel a common unity as against the run of Central Americans. They share the knowledge of a world in which things are done so differently, so exactly, that it would be impossible to convey the way of doing or the concepts behind it to an ordinary Ladino. They expect to find in each other common grounds of education, and they hope for a language to use together other than Spanish. Given two such men, young, of about the same age, the expectation of companionship becomes even stronger.

Padre Greiz, escaped in his late teens from East Germany, spoke his native tongue, competent Spanish with a heavy accent, and knew Latin. Bert could read German as a professional necessity, slowly, dictionary in hand. He was not capable of even a simple conversation in it, and had decided it was wiser to profess no command of the language at all. Their medium of communication, then, was Spanish. The priest, unlike many of his fellow-countrymen, had no interests outside his own work, no curiosity about The Tongue, no sympathy with anthropology, which sought to study in detail and thus preserve what he wished, quite simply, to destroy. He was a plodding, earnest, unhappy young man, theologically trained and yet uneducated. Between the two men there existed the empty form of a relationship, that reminded Bert of when, during his military service, he had for a time been associated with a man who had been in his class for several years in grade school. There was a theoretical bond that in fact did not exist, on account of which they liked each other less than they would have had they come together in the special world of the Army as strangers.

Well, he thought, tying his tie, so the roof leaks and the rains will come in June. He guessed the expedition's funds could be tapped for ten dollars. Yes, a voucher for that much would pass. Ten dollars would buy a lot of work hereabouts. If need be, he could kick in a little of his own money. An instructor's pay is small, but while he was in the field, he had nothing but those extravagant cigarettes, the inexpensive local liquor, and his laundry to spend it on. He took bills from the locked, tin box he kept under some clothing in one of his pack boxes.

The priest's lodging was small. It consisted of little more than a moderate-sized living room, off which at one end there was a mere cell of a bedroom, off the other, a small room or large closet with a window in it not over a foot square, which everyone spoke of as the *oficina*. What business had once been transacted through that wicket Bert had no idea. Padre Greiz stored the grain there.

The establishment was tile roofed and stone floored. It had one good-sized, glass window on the south side, the glass imported by Greiz, its bringing a miracle of transportation on the backs of men chosen in public conclave for their sobriety and sure-footedness. The other windows had only shutters. There was no provision whatever for heat, which was typical. At this altitude, the rooms would be a penance of cold and damp throughout the rainy season. Somehow, in crossing the ocean and fighting their way up from the hot, coastal lowlands, the Spanish had lost the memory of their fine, medieval fireplaces. At all altitudes one built for unbroken hot weather. Then, at the rear one erected an Indian house, dirt-floored, stick-walled, thatch-roofed, where the cooking fire could burn. To this humble and necessary annex the ladies and gentlemen (or his reverence, the priest) retreated during waking hours in cold weather, to extend hands over the coals, or sit squatting on low stools, Indian fashion, and getting in the way of the cook. The alternative was to sit in one's *sala*, correctly (as when receiving a stranger or an enemy), in overcoat and muffler, and take nips of liquor at intervals.

Bert stopped at the front door to be invited in. He and Padre Greiz exchanged the Spanish greetings. As between a North American and a German, the set courtesies sounded more than perfunctory. Speaking Spanish is something of a game; one with a feeling for the language enjoys both its capacity for sharply pointed, direct meaning and the sonorousness that makes trifles sound epic. The formalities are inherent in the language; one cannot stop with the equivalent of "Hello" or "*Grüss Gott*," but must complete the little ritual. In addressing one native to the language this seems natural and proper, and one can, on occasion, enjoy the fine-pointed, Spanish trick of conveying hostility through the very perfection of one's politenesses. With the German, Bert found the exchange almost disagreeable. If they had liked each other better, perhaps they could have amused themselves parodying it, but their relationship was not warm enough, and the German had little humor. He urged his guest to sit and insisted on his taking the comfortable chair with the cowhide seat and back.

Here in his house, the priest wore the robe of his order, in which it was unlawful, in that republic, for him to appear in the street. Had he done so, the Ladinos would have turned him in. They did not admit to being anti-clerical, but they did not relish having a vicar in residence. Don Gregorio, with whom Bert had a more definite friendship than with any of the others, had frankly told him that it was more convenient to have the priest at a little distance. He said that the priest's presence distracted the women from their work and gave them too many ideas. The Ladinos expressed devotion, and left almost all of the worship to women, children, and Indians.

The monastic costume was fitting in that plain room and gave it a slightly romantic quality. The whitewashed walls had become uneven and out of true with the passage of time. Their rugged bareness was broken by a few articles of furniture, mostly heavy. There were the new table, by the glass window, a big, old one in the middle of the room, laid now for the meal with a plaid native cloth that gave a note of brightness, an old chest, one old and one new armoir, the old piece massive and deeply carved in a way that was a primitive reflection, another distant memory, of medieval Spain.

There was a crucifix on one wall, hand carved of wood, elaborated, highly varnished, suggestive of cuckoo clocks. A definitely bad chromo of the Sacred Heart and a good print of a German landscape by a modern painter of whom Bert had never heard were the only outright decorations. What books the priest owned were kept in one of the armoirs; Bert thought he would have displayed them.

Against one wall a shelf hung by ropes from the crude, pole ceiling. On it stood half a dozen bottles, in each of which something different, a fruit, a citrus peel, was steeping in liquor. That, too, seemed appropriate to the monastic life. Experimenting with liquor was about the only hobby the padre had. Bert noticed that he had finally thrown out the bottle that contained his most disastrous failure, an attempt to obtain the effect of Chartreuse by soaking pine needles in San Lázaro.

His host stood by the shelf. "An aperitive? 'A little wine for thy stomach's sake?' " The quotation was so inevitable it was painful. "Here — this is the best, with the lime. It has a freshness that is pleasant in this hot weather. So," (the word was *así*, but it had the true ring of the German *so*) "we make good appetite."

Bert disliked the effect of drinks at noon, he foresaw heavy, hot-weather sleepiness, but he could not refuse the wine glass filled and handed to him. Glass was Padre Greiz's luxury, he thought, tumblers, wine glasses, salt cellers, and the famous window.

The priest said, "*Salud*," raising his glass.

"*Salud*." Their eyes met, blue to blue, and Bert felt a twinge of shame at his lack of sympathy for this man whose life must be so dreary.

A fresh aroma of lime rose from the drink. And on top of the loneliness and monotony, did he scourge himself in the privacy of his cell, as one heard they did? Bert sipped.

The priest looked pleased. "I concocted it as an aperitive; just enough honey to counteract the bitterness of the lime peel. If I can get some vermouth brought in, it might be interesting to mix it, like one of your American cocktails."

Bert thought of a blend, room temperature, with sweet Cinzano, and said nothing.

The priest studied the liquid in his glass. It was clear,

its natural, faintly yellow tinge shaded slightly towards green by the lime. The maid came in to set a water jar on the table. She was an elderly widow, dressed in the tribal costume. She, too, Bert had gathered, was connected in some way which Cayetano, who seemed to be a sort of spider web woven through the community. Was it mere chance that the two aliens, each charged with a potential danger to ancient ways, were visited and served by Cayetano's kin — or the man himself? It was a niece of Cayetano's who swept Bert's house twice a week, assorted relatives or connections who brought firewood and fodder. Cayetano was a web, or had a web, or all the Indian community was united by a web, strong, invisible. The web and the axis. He glanced at the woman. She was a trained servant and had an unusual command of Spanish for a woman.

Greiz turned his glass. "That Cayetano of yours — I have heard a new story about him. It seems that he really is a *brujo*. He had a quarrel with Don Rafael one time, just after Rafael had received a shipment of six bottles of San Lázaro. Cayetano cast a spell on them, and the liquor turned blue. It is one of those stories that one must not believe, yet one can hardly dismiss. Rafael called in witnesses. They tasted the liquor. It was all right, only it was blue."

Bert had become alert. Van Cleve had reported almost the identical incident at Jacaltenango in Guatemala. The point had been that it was a perfectly harmless form of magic, performed, not by a *brujo*, a sorcerer, but by an Indian of priestly status whom the Ladino had mocked.

"Don Rafael told you this?"

"His wife told me first, then he confirmed it. I imagine a number of the others will confirm it. It is a sin to believe such things, but one must make allowance for them." He twirled his glass again. "These men here — they volunteer nothing. I've been here a year, and half of them have not yet been to confession. On Fiesta and Easter they kneel in the back of the church. They might as well be Protestants, like you. As for the women, they confess whenever they have a chance, for lack of occupation, and use piety to pass the time."

The maid had left the room."

"And the Indians?" Bert asked.

"They support the church, and at heart they are heretics. Christians? The situation here calls for an interdict, only the people would not even notice it."

The best thing seemed to be to keep quiet and take another sip of the lime drink.

The priest went on, letting out frustration. "It's the centavos the Indians find, the food they bring, their service, that make it possible for me to be here. I think that, contrary to the Ladinos, they like having a priest in the village. What have you gathered?"

"I think they do." He said it solely to cause pleasure.

"So they drop in to hear mass when they feel like it, on a Sunday or a weekday morning, and they pray at all hours. Have you noticed how they pray outside the church, the way they do?"

"Yes, they face four ways."

"And you know that's heathen. As an ethnologist, you must know."

The maid brought in the soup, self-effacing, not looking at either of them. Bert was conscious of her, and of the boy seated the other side of the doorway, in the kitchen. At that moment he felt honestly sorry for the priest.

"They're just as bad inside," he went on, between mouthfuls of soup and little, slurping noises. "They all but ignore the altar, turn around and firmly pray facing west, *west*, my God, and then over into the corner to adore the 'Old Virgin,' that crude, wooden statue you took such care photographing. As for the *patrona*, she'd might as well not exist."

Bert said, "You must remember that the old one was *la patrona*, and quite famous, until some one brought in the present one about fifty years ago." He refrained from any comment on relative artistic quality. "It is natural that the Indians should continue to revere the original."

Something important about the old image teased at the back of his mind, but he had no chance to call it up now.

The priest said, "*Hmm*. They retain everything old. You visit Chuultún frequently?"

"Not frequently. Any time I go there, a man or two just happens to come strolling along from one of the nearby fields, with a machete in the crook of his elbow. I'd like to map it, but I think better not."

"Yes. There is an account in Schulz of the disappearance of two Ladinos at the end of the last century, probably killed for prying there."

Bert was surprised. Schulz's *Zur Ethnographie des Nördlichen Mittelamerika*, though rather out of date, was still a standard work. He did not know the priest had read anything in that field. "Yes, I remember."

"The Ladinos flatly will not back me up if I try to do anything about those altars out there. They are cowards."

"Also, they remember the uprising at Santa Catalina."

"No doubt. I am not afraid to die, but there is no service to God in dying pointlessly, and all I could achieve would be that perhaps a few of these poor, deluded people would be taken and hanged."

Talk stopped while he devoted himself sturdily to eating. For a time, remarks were occasional and unimportant. When the meal ended, the priest offered another liqueur, which Bert refused. He said a second grace, then accepted with appreciation one of the ethnologist's expensive cigarettes.

"I want to ask you for a little help," he said.

Here comes the bite, Bert thought.

"I can do nothing about Chuultún, but at least I can control my own church. I must get rid of that Old Virgin. She is not really Christian. The carving is crude, the features are Indian, and the face and hands are dark brown. It was not an accident that they were left unpainted. I cannot imagine what the authorities were thinking of when they let her be installed."

The woman servant was standing just beyond the doorway, beside her the youth, still seated, back to them. Bert waited, saying nothing. For a moment or two, in fact, he could not have spoken, for suddenly he realized that the dark goddess of his dream had been a blend of that image and Antón's younger daughter. The girl and the image had the same shape of eyes.

"As an ethnologist," Greiz went on, "you know to what lengths the Indians went — and still go — to get objects of their ancient cult into the Christian temples. Well." His voice became businesslike. "You said that figure was an antiquity. Find me a buyer; you can do it easily, and then I can get a really handsome representation of Our Lady to replace her, or something else. There is a store in Olintlán that offers very fine work, mostly Italian. With your help, this much I can do."

Bert hesitated before answering. He felt really sorry for this priest, he was shocked by the proposal, and he foresaw disagreeableness.

"I regret greatly, Padre," he said, "I fear it cannot be done, and I have to confess that I am in part the cause of that. You have seen my letter of authorization and instruction from *Educación Pública*, and you may remember that I am required to report any antiquity of quality that should be listed in the National Treasure."

The priest did not speak, but his way of looking at Bert changed, hardened, and his lips pressed together.

"You see," Bert said, wanting to explain, wanting to make it clear that he had not acted of his own choice, "that statue is described by Tomás Gage, who passed through Rosario about 1630. It was carved in the late sixteenth century by a famous *santero* in Olintlán, some of whose works are still in the cathedral there. All of his work has that rather stiff, primitive quality. As far back as Gage's time it was an object of special veneration. So I reported it and sent in a photo, and I have an informal letter of acknowledgment. I understand that the *cabildo* has also been notified. You should have received a notice, too, since the church and the image are in your charge. I suppose they'd send it to the archbishop, and so on down, and that might take time."

There was a silence of some seconds, then the priest's expression brightened.

"But then, *amigo*, should the image not be removed to Olintlán and deposited in the National Museum?"

"The policy is to keep objects of the National Treasure *in situ* where possible, and seeing how well this one has been cared for, and knowing the local reverence for it, I'm afraid I recommended that it remain in your church."

"I see." The priest stared at the smoked-down remnant of his cigarette and pressed it out in a small earthenware dish. The silence hung.

Bert rose. "I give you thanks for a very excellent lunch."

"You are welcome."

The ethnologist hesitated, then said awkwardly, "Don Gregorio tells me that you need funds for repairing the church roof before the rains start. May I make a small contribution?"

"That your *idol* may be well covered?" The whole force of it was there, in the voice and the few words.

"Forgive me. By your leave."

"It is yours. *Buen provecho.*"

"*Igualmente. Hasta la vista.*"

He was grateful to be out of the house. He walked towards his own with energetic strides, feeling that he had done an important thing, not only for the charming, archaic figure in the church but for the goddess of his dream, who was once more vivid in memory. She was taller than either the Luch girl or the Old Virgin, and her dress, of bright Oriental material, now he knew was taken from the very smart one that pretty girl — what was her name? — had worn at a dance in the Christmas vacation. The voice, now, it belonged to the actress the University Dramat had had as a guest of honor and with whom he had talked for perhaps two minutes. Of what extraordinary leaps and creations is the mind capable in the freedom of sleep!

He entered his house and sat down. He had carefully not told the priest that the famous *santero* he had mentioned was, also according to Gage, Gonzalo Martínez Choy, descended from Raxti nobility, that he had had trouble with the Inquisition, and that a little before Gage's time there had been talk of destroying all his work because of just what Greiz saw in this example.

The exhilaration died away. The meal had been too heavy for a sultry day, the drink had left him flat, he felt heavy and sticky. Cayetano was not coming until five. What to do now?

You'd might as well face it, what you've done has been to get through a morning, as you've gotten through so many mornings, so many days. Killing time. Now, how do you get through the afternoon? Why not write to the University and say straight out that this expedition is a failure, that the thing may be here but you can't get to it, and you are coming home? And there is no goddess and never has been, make up your mind to that.

Well, this was the siesta hour. He lay down. Before long, lying still became a torment. He sat up, thinking of the long patience and the curious accidents that had opened the way for other ethnologists among the highland Maya. But there was no sign of anything breaking for him, and how long is simple patience supposed to last? Hell, he decided, I'll saddle up and take a dip in the blue pool.

The pool was in the tall forest, about a league up the mountains, a slight widening in the narrow, swift Río Raxjá with a ledge of rock below it forming a natural, partial dam with a small area of quiet water above it. Springing out of limestone a few miles further up the mountain, the stream was strikingly cerulean, its water briskly cool. The people of Rosario did not bathe in it, preferring the broader, slower, tepid Conapjá on the edge of the village. The pool was Bert's own discovery, made through idly following a dim trail. So far as he knew, no one else ever came near there. At this place he had a happy sense of true solitude, of being unreachable, entirely unwatched. His tethered horse sought blades of grass along the bank while he subjected himself to the delightful shock of entering the water, rolled in the stream, clung to a rock and felt the rush of the main current against his body, climbed out, dried himself, and smoked at great leisure. Coming or going, uphill or down, it was a slow, scrambling ride between there and the village, harder on the horse than on himself. By the time he got back, he would have lost this freshness, but he knew how to enjoy the moment while he had it.

He let the horse pick its way back, his mind between thinking and not thinking, vaguely considering new devices that might take him through the wall of secrecy, then meditating fancifully and driftingly on the dark goddess, the Old Virgin, and the axis. They came out of the big trees, passed along steep slopes patched with fields, rounded a shoulder of mountain into the full heat of the afternoon sun. They reached level ground, approaching the cool green of the coffee plantation. The horse stirred itself into a jog trot, knowing that it was near its stable and feed with easy going between.

Rounding a corner of the *cabildo*, they entered the plaza, a rough, rectangular field, with another big ceiba — another possible point on the axis — at the west end opposite the church. There was a commotion on the plaza, many men and boys moving to and fro about a medium-sized, bay horse that maneuvered in a circle, its head high, its heels threatening. About three yards of rope trailed from its hackamore. No one was really trying to get hold of the rope.

Bert recognized Don Rafael's best horse, a fast and rather mean animal. There was no sign of its owner or his son. Then he found himself beside Doña Clara, Don Rafael's wife.

She said, "Don Alberto, can't you catch him? You rode him once; he must know you a little. These people are all afraid. There is not a man among them."

The sensible answer is no, but you can't make it. Why not? A Kiplingesque, silly feeling of a standard to maintain in a foreign land? Or just a private feeling about yourself that is inherent in your culture? Annoyed and feeling a bit silly, he dismounted and asked the first handy Indian to hold his horse.

He moved slowly towards the bay. It inched away and its ears went back on its head. Someone on the other side spread arms wide and the bay hesitated. Bert leaped, grabbed the rope, and tried to brace himself. The horse swirled away, scattering people, and Bert went flat on the ground, knowing with relief that in a few seconds it would be all right for him to let go, his demonstration of whatever he was demonstrating having been made. Then a pair of dark hands seized the rope just above his own and Cayetano said in Spanish, "Hang on, Don Alberto." Bert turned over, got his feet under him. Don Gregorio and Don Tomás suddenly emerged from the crowd and joined them. When the horse lunged again, they were able to hold. After that it was possible for Doña Clara to work her hand up the rope to the hackamore, speak to the horse, touch its nose, be recognized. The *mozo* whose daily chore it was to feed the bay joined her. After a little quieting, the horse could be led off, Doña Clara thanking Bert duly before they went.

There was talk, liveliness, vivacity among the people on the plaza. Something had happened, an incident, almost an event, and that was a boon from God. Don Gregorio congratulated Bert on his seizing of the rope, said frankly that he had always been afraid of the animal, went on to discuss its good qualities, for all Ladino men are horse lovers, then allotted a word of praise to Cayetano. Don Tomás also had his say, then the two of them took their departures with the usual ceremony.

Cayetano said, "It is almost five, señor. Shall we go to your house?"

As they walked together, Bert leading his mount, he said, "I was surprised when you came to help me. I didn't think you would put yourself into an affair of Don Rafael's."

"You are the sort of man who would have hung on until he had been dragged and hurt."

Now, what do you say to that? They put up the horse together. Then they went indoors and sat by the table. The bottle of San Lázaro stood on one of the pack boxes lined up against the back wall. (Bert's furnishings were even more Spartan than Padre Greiz's.) His watch showed ten to five, and he felt ripe for a drink.

After a moment of hesitation he said, "*¿Un trago, Cayetano?*"

"Why not?"

Bert put the bottle on the table and poured Cayetano a shot in an earthenware *copita*, knowing that Indians are not accustomed to mixed or watered drinks. His own he diluted, with cool water from the porous, clay jar, in an enamel cup. The

Indian drank, giving thanks in The Tongue and raising his hat a couple of inches above his head as he took the liquor down. Bert had himself a hearty, comforting swig.

Encouraged by that, feeling somehow nearer to Cayetano than he ever had before, he decided to try a new feeler. Putting the words together slowly in Raxti, he said, "They say that you know how to turn liquor blue. Perhaps there is something you know."

He was pretty sure that "something you know" in this language, as in some related ones, was a euphemism or disguise for having magical or ceremonial knowledge.

Cayetano's eyes half closed, almost sleepily, and he half smiled. There, suddenly, was the benevolent, wise goat, the Pan figure, of the dream. "Perhaps I know a little something. They say that you bathe in Blue River. Have you not heard that that is dangerous, *Cham* Berto?"

Bert started, hearing the Indian title of respect, much stronger than *don*, with a quite new, and, he supposed, Indian version of his name.

Cayetano went on. "That river, it is a seizer. It seizes the souls of people unless they say a prayer when they cross it. No one bathes in it."

It is hopeless, Bert thought, to expect to make a move of any kind without its being known. He took another sip from his cup. "Perhaps there is a little something I know."

Cayetano said, "So says my heart."

Without by your leave, he refilled his jigger and drained it, lifting his hat as before and saying "Through God." Then he produced a cornhusk cigarette and asked for a match. He lit the cigarette, mumbled some words over it, then took a long puff.

Still speaking in The Tongue, he said, "The priest wanted to sell the Lady Mother Virgin, but you stopped him, so I am told. I think you should know about that Lady Virgin, then you can begin to understand our people." For Virgin he used the Spanish word, *virgen*, but the titles he gave her were Indian. "It is all right for you to know this, for I know that there is something you know and that your heart is clear."

He took yet another drink. Bert was experiencing something like goose pimples of excitement. Some degree of drunkenness, he knew, was quite commonly a requirement before a Mayan priest or whatever you would call him could do his stuff.

"I shall tell you this story now. You just listen to it. It is hard to tell you things when I have to keep stopping to let you write, and it troubles my heart to talk to that machine with the ribbon spinning in it. I shall tell you this without stopping, and tomorrow morning I can come here and break it into pieces for your writing, or tell it into that machine — but I am not sure about that, for this is delicate." As he talked, he inserted words or phrases in Spanish occasionally, to clarify his meaning to the white man.

"In the ancient time, before the sun rose, the Lady Our Mother was here then."

Before the sun rose — that was old Mayan, you got it in the Popol Vuh and Annals of the Cakchiquels, and Landa had recorded it for Yuacatán.

"Her heart fought" (that meant that she was frightened) "for her children, that the people with four eyes were coming to steal them. At night they came into the houses like bats and stole them. A safe place to put her village was what she was looking for as she went about, her heart hurting.

"Then the Lord Tsakwinik came to her." Cayetano gestured towards the west, where Tsacuinic's blue triangle cut the sky.

It was getting better and better, and it did not stop. The myth established the lord or spirit of the volcano as protector of a mother goddess. The goddess founded her village at this place and had what was to become the ruin of Chuultún built. In the name of the goddess, gentle and loving, very much the one of his dream, Bert thought, the people paid their tribute of offerings to the protecting god. Back of all this, cloudy, not apparently much of a factor in this particular myth, was Christ, walking about forming the earth and causing the sun to rise. After the sun rose the people could recognize the four directions. The sunlight, also, drove back the people with four eyes, two in the front of their heads and two in the back. They had had the advantage in the long twilight; in the brightness of the sun, they were blinded. The Lady Our Mother Virgin (Bert, listening, was still thinking of her as his goddess) then told her children where the church was to be built. When it was built, she established herself on the altar, after she had planted the two ceiba trees. She left it said how the ritual should move, from the point of sunrise to the point of sunset, and the offerings to the Lord Tsakwinik.

With that, it was clear, the myth proper ended. Cayetano had another drink and Bert fixed one for himself. Cayetano lit a cigarette and talked on, narrating historical facts. Ladino priests had come and set up other images in the church, but not until when Cayetano was an infant did one come who made himself so strong that he could put the Lady Our Mother to one side and set up a Ladina Virgin at the altar.

With soldiers in the village he did this. Putting the Mother aside made no difference. The prayer still ran from the east to her, then to Chuultún, from where one also prayed eastwards to her and westwards to the volcano. On the completion of Thirteen Men — that is, the two hundred and sixty days after the entry of the Year Bearer, when the same lord with the same number occurred again — certain reverend men, *Cham Winikop*, arrived at the crater of Tsacuinic to burn incense and offer turkeys.

After a pause, Cayetano said, "There it is, Cham Berto. What says your heart?"

"My heart says that it is a good story, a strong story." The room was getting dark. Making time to think, he set out and lit a pair of candles. "So here you know the Year Bearer and the count of the days and numbers?"

Truly, Cayetano looked like an amused old goat. "It is getting late, and I must see to the corn my sons are bringing in. I shall be here in the morning. If you are to learn these things correctly, we must not hurry." He stood up. "Thank you for the drinks." He touched the bottle lightly. He passed around the table, and into the blue, deep dusk of the doorway. "We have seen each other."

"We have seen each other, then."

Indeed they had seen each other; for once the words were true. He felt as if he were breathing once more after long stifling. There was the thought of success, the hope that isolation might be ended, the excitement of the information itself. Almost enough to make you start believing in dreams, but when you thought about it, you could see how all you had done was to synthesize innumerable small observations and mix them with the double symbolism, of sexual desire and of his quest, of his composite goddess.

He looked at his watch. Time to start for Doña Candelaria's shortly, but this occasion called for a little extra celebration. He poured a moderate drink into his cup, then he set down bottle and cup and stared. The liquor had turned blue. His scalp crawled, then he laughed aloud. It was, in this case, a gesture of friendship, an assurance. He tasted the stuff. No change. A really nifty trick, he thought, I hope I can get him to show me how he does it. He finished the drink, neat, lit a cigarette, then rose, slightly tipsy and very happy, to go to dinner.